PRAISE FOR MARIANNE DE PIERRES

"Move over stale f/sf themes; enter: *Peacemaker*, a wholly original and thrilling fantasy adventure."
Looking for a Good Book

"*Peacemaker* rollicks along at a cracking pace, and I found myself holding my breath in anticipation at times, which is always a good sign! I got to the end of the book and flipped the last page in disappointment, because while the story ended well (albeit definitely set up for the next volume), I simply didn't want it to stop. Bring on the next instalment!"
Fablecroft

"Tired of the same old thing when it comes to urban fantasy? Look no further than Virgin Jackson."
My Bookish Ways

"The beautiful thing about *Peacemaker* is the mystical. Virgin quickly realizes that her world is not what it seems and de Pierres navigates this storyline well. As a nice parallel to the magic element, de Pierres has a strong political subplot. De Pierres not only shows us the state of the world she writes in but also what the fictional movers and shakers wanted it to be and where they still want it to go."
Literary Escapism

"*Peacemaker* is definitely a cut above the standard for books of this type: intelligent, witty and with a good heart. If you're looking for a fast read that surprises and engages, then look no further."
The Newtown Review of Books

"This is the first novel by Marianne de Pierres I've read, and I hope to read more about Virgin Jackson and (perhaps) Nate Sixkiller. A fun romp that is much more than the parts which comprise it."
Tor.com

MARIANNE DE PIERRES

MYTHMAKER

**ANGRY
ROBOT**

ANGRY ROBOT
An imprint of Watkins Media Ltd

Lace Market House,
54-56 High Pavement,
Nottingham,
NG1 1HW
UK

angryrobotbooks.com
twitter.com/angryrobotbooks
Hiding right outside your world

An Angry Robot paperback original 2015
1

A catalogue record for this book is available from the British Library.

ISBN 978 0 85766 420 4
EBook ISBN 987 0 85766 422 8

Set in Meridien by Epub Services.
Printed and bound in the UK by 4edge Ltd.

ONE

I savoured the sunrise from the eastern butte. Today's was extraordinary: splashes of molten gold as if the sun had dripped burning liquid on the plains. The sand and the silhouette of the distant western ranges gained colour with each moment, turning pale pink like the chest feathers of the cheeky galahs that swept the plains. The mulla-mulla was in flower too after a recent rain – a carpet of deep purple.

Birrimun Park: the last natural habitat in the world.

My father gave his life to this place, and, if it came down to it, so would I. Birrimun was the only place in the world that I felt whole, and sane, which was why I was about to accept a deal with my previously estranged mother and give up my work as park ranger to become her spy.

I sighed loud enough that my horse, Benny's, ears flicked back at me. Perhaps that was an overly dramatic summation of my current situation, but then life had taken some dramatic turns of late.

Not so long ago, Nate Sixkiller of the US Marshal Service had joined Parks Southern as my colleague. I hadn't welcomed the coupling, but I was beginning to tolerate it a little better than at first. I worked better alone, and so, I decided, did he.

Together, he and I were supposed to be assisting the Global Joint Intelligence Commission (GJIC) in their preparation to halt some kind of Other Worldly coup.

You heard me right. *Other World!* I felt ridiculous even thinking the words, but proof of its existence was visible in the fresh scars I had on my shoulder, neck, and back. Nate Sixkiller called the creatures that had attacked me Mythos. According to him, the park was the breakthrough point for them to our world. He also said they came in different forms, but I was yet to witness that.

So what did they want here?

Maybe after my induction into GJIC, I'd know more. At the moment, I could only speculate based on my experiences and some old essays written by my dad. As well as being the ranger in the south east sector before me (and the key figure in the original *Preserve the Land* campaign), he'd loved to keep journals. Some of his essays had even found their way online and, according to my mother, into the hands of the wrong people. GJIC believed that the Mythos had a human faction, called Korax, working to help them. And Korax were using Dad's ideas.

Dad's theory was simple. Dictate the world's mythologies and you control the people. That's what the Mythos was trying to do and that's what we had to stop. But *dictate the world's mythologies* was some kind of concept to get your head around. What did it even mean? And these Mythos... I mean, where did they come from? How did they get here? Were they from another realm? An alternate reality? Or some other equally implausible domain?

I still had some of Dad's journals to read. Maybe they

would offer me more insight – if I could keep them out of the hands of my mother, Commander Oceane Orlean and GJIC.

My phone rang. I pulled it out of my pocket and answered it.

"Look back down the trail," said a familiar voice.

I glanced over my shoulder and saw Marshal Nate Sixkiller at the foot of the butte, astride the rangy, skittish Sombre Vol. He beckoned me.

"What?" I said into the phone.

"Came to escort you in," he replied, in exactly the gallant kind of manner that pissed me off.

"You mean you're watching me?"

"I mean, there's someone waitin' to talk to you on video link."

I sighed again. It'd be dark soon, and putting off this conversation wouldn't change the outcome. It was time to go back to the rest of the world.

Benny nickered as I climbed on her back, and she set off down the trail without even a nudge from me. Part average nag, part racehorse, part endurance and speed-augmented bio-mech, my horse also seemed to be able to read my mind. We'd been in a few tight spots lately and she'd never let me down, but taking on this new job meant less time together in the wide open spaces of Birrimun. And frankly, that sucked.

By the time Benny's hooves hit level ground, Sixkiller had already turned his horse south in the direction of the stables. On impulse, I urged Benny on to catch him. As I drew level, he tipped his ten gallon hat and gave Vol his head. The not-so gelded gelding exploded forwards, legs pumping.

Benny stayed with him for most of the way, but in the final stretch past the public entry in the park wall to the windmill and semi-circle of palms that marked our way back to the stables, Sombre Vol drew right away. Though eating Vol's dust, it was thrilling to see the horse at full stretch. Sixkiller crouched low in the saddle against the sunset, hat somehow magically glued to his head. His body moved in unison with his horse, and, for the first time since we'd met, I felt outright admiration. The man could truly ride. And the horse could truly run.

Vol had been due to go back to the suppliers on account of no one being able to ride him – until now. Sixkiller had requested a stay on that decision, and I was glad. My boss was pretty enamoured with Marshal Sixkiller and had approved the request. That is, my old boss... my new boss was waiting to talk to me on the other side of the Interchange.

Sixkiller dismounted and stood by Sombre Vol's shoulder, waiting for me. The horse heaved, sucking in air, but his ears were forwards and his eyes bright.

"No need to show off now, Marshal," I said, sliding off Benny to join him.

Nate Sixkiller was as tall as me with a ton more muscle, stronger, wider shoulders, and a leaner waist. His hair fell dead straight to his shoulders, and his expression was stamped *stern*. A man who'd seen things that had sucked the spontaneity from his life: a serious man.

I didn't mind that. Guess I was kinda serious too, and in some ways a lot less well socialised than him. Nate Sixkiller knew how to produce manners and a certain charm when required. That charm could be cowboy-folksy or urbane and refined, depending on his mood and the company.

I struggled with time-squandering etiquette. To me it just seemed pointless. In his journal, my dad had put my matter-of-fact and direct nature down to not having a mum around when I was growing up. Having recently met my mother, I didn't think it would've made a whole lot of difference.

It was her that I had to speak to now.

"You just got beat, Ranger." He was using his laconic cowboy drawl on me, and I curled my upper lip at it.

Sixkiller had grown up on the plains somewhere in Oklahoma, been educated in the North East of the United States at a Little Ivy college, and latterly employed by the Marshal Service to work the East Coast. He was a chameleon, switching between personas at will: plainsman, gentleman, lawman.

"I don't call it getting beat when the game is rigged," I retorted. "Out here you only win when the playing field's level. You had a head start."

He tucked his hair behind his ears. "Mebbe you'd best come out West, one day. Find out how real people live."

"You putting me on notice, Marshal?"

He gave a rare grin.

I just began thinking about how it enlivened his face, when the smile dissolved.

"What's wrong?" I asked.

A high-pitched and piercing cry above us sent my skin pimpling as hard as if I was standing naked in a winter gale. Only it was still summer. And there was no wind.

We both turned back to face the park. Most of the colour had bled from the sky. The night had crept up on us like an ink spill, and stars were beginning to pop through.

"Is it Mythos?" I barely breathed.

An image rose unbidden in my mind of the enormous crow that had attacked me out by the Paloma station house. I'd nearly bled to death from its scratches, saved only by an infusion of Marshal Sixkiller's blood.

"Sounds like it," said Sixkiller. He cocked his head to the side, and I felt him looking at me.

We listened, side by side, for a while, but the cry bled away into the dark and wasn't repeated.

"We should go out there and see," I said.

He grabbed my wrist with strong fingers. "No. We should take this meeting. Whatever's coming, it won't be tonight."

"How do you know that?" I said.

"Likely it's an echo," he said.

"What do you mean?"

"Sometimes they leave behind an echo of themselves. Sometimes it's a precursor to them coming." He'd suddenly lost his cowboy drawl and his educated Eastern voice took over.

"How do you tell which it is?"

"You can't. But only a few of us can hear echoes."

I grimaced. "So we're the lucky ones?"

"Well, let's just say that your mom was right about you." Sixkiller spoke quietly, with no malice intended, but I was already primed with fear and ready to displace it, so I bit at him.

"You've been discussing me with her?"

"Yer always so full of it, Ranger?" The drawl returned, and I suddenly realized it was his defence against hard questions and antagonism. "Anyways, I'd be bettin' yer did the same 'bout me," he added.

His reply took some of the steam out of my anger. And I knew I should let it. Sixkiller wasn't my enemy. Neither was he my friend. But he was a colleague. We were in a partnership for the moment, and I had to make it work. He shared my love of the land and that counted for a whole lot.

"Only in the most glowing terms," I said, forcing a smile.

"Yer nose is growin'," he joked in reply. "Truth is, I've seen a full profile on you, and now yer working with GJIC you'll see one on me. In this job, you gotta know yer partner enough to trust 'em." His tone was insistent.

"You got skeletons, Marshal?" I asked softly.

"More 'n' worse than most," he said. "Come on. The boss doesn't like to wait."

TWO

We walked the horses through the Interchange doors into the stables, then both stood adjusting to the bright lights and the hum of air conditioning. I'd worked here for ten years, been coming as my dad's sidekick and offspring for ten before that. Yet the abrupt change from wilderness to city office never failed to disorient me.

The door to Totes – our tech wizard's – office stood open. His collectable dolls decorated the shelf along the edge of his desk, their burnished, brushed hair and stiff little backs presenting like a bunch of school girls giving me the cold shoulder.

"Hurry up, Virgin! My security scan's nearly finished. Your meeting begins in about thirty seconds."

I let go of Benny's reins, doffed my Akubra and ran fingers through my hair. I'd never intended to *freshen up* for this meeting, but now the time was upon me, I wished I had.

"Yer look fine," muttered Sixkiller.

I tucked my hands into my pockets as if I didn't know what he was talking about, and promptly had to take them out when Totes held out a set of headphones. "I'll be in the break room. Call me when you're done."

I went in and took them from him.

"And Virgin," Totes added, "don't touch anything. The girls will tell me if you do."

I slipped into his seat and poked my tongue at their glassy stares.

Sixkiller patted Sombre Vol on the rump as Leecey, our much-pierced stable hand, collected the horses for a rubdown. He pulled a chair over from against the wall and picked up the spare headphones.

The door slid shut, the lights dimmed, and the GJIC emblem flared onto the screens. Just as quickly as it appeared, it was replaced by a head and shoulders view of Commander Oceane Orlean.

"Good evening, Agent Jackson and Marshal Sixkiller."

What? No, "Hello, long-ago-left daughter?"

"Thank you for making yourself available during the working day," she added.

"Actually we've just finished up, ma'am. No trouble at all," said Sixkiller smoothly.

I wanted to shoot him a stop-sucking-up glance, but didn't dare take my eyes off the screen. It was the first time I'd really had a chance to study my mother's face properly. At our last, and first, meeting, shock and exhaustion had clouded my perceptions.

Now, I felt sharper and ready to observe. What had my dad seen in her? Did we share any similarities? The straight nose, brown eyes and high cheekbones, for sure. After that, I couldn't see much else. Her dyed-blonde hair was scraped back from her face and her lips were pursed in a narrow line that suggested permanent preoccupation. She had the sharpest eyes I'd ever seen though. Even from two and a half thousand miles away they bored through me.

I tried hard to detach my mind from the mixture of emotions making my stomach cramp up. How could I possibly take orders from the woman who'd obviously abandoned me and my brother to pursue her career?

"Can we get to it?" I said abruptly. "I've got some questions."

Sixkiller flinched. My manner had him on edge, but that was nothing new, and, right now, I didn't feel like sugar coating myself for him or anyone else.

"Of course, Virgin – if I may call you that. My schedule is also tight. The Marshal has been cleared to share more with you as well. He will take the lead on this next case. Look to him for guidance."

Guidance. If ever there was a word I could choke on when mentioned in the same breath as Nate Sixkiller, it would have been that one.

"What case is that, *ma'am*?" I asked.

"We are investigating a person of interest at Branch Holy University. We'd like you to investigate a Dr Armand Dusan. He's an Associate Professor of the Social Science faculty."

"An academic?" Was it wrong that I sounded so incredulous?

"I gather from your reaction that you didn't have any teachers at university you held in high regard?"

I thought about it. "Maybe one or two."

"Then take a moment to consider how they might have affected your thinking or transformed your perspectives. Young minds are frighteningly absorbent. The case files have been streamed to your encrypted LiFo, along with an overview our analysts have compiled to bring you up to speed. As I mentioned, the Marshal will fill in the gaps."

"A *LiFo*?"

"An encrypted communication device. One is being

couriered to your home address as we speak. It's coded to your DNA. If anyone else tries to access it, the LiFo will lock, and in the case of repeated failed attempts, corrupt. When the courier comes this evening, activate your LiFo immediately and read the case file on the GJIC home page."

"Do those instructions include me, ma'am?" interjected Sixkiller.

"Yours will come separately, Marshal."

"So, you're not really going to tell me anything? You're just sending me a bunch of files to read?" I asked.

"Privacy is a luxury concept in our world, Agent. We now prefer couriers. It keeps the chain intimate and intimacy is the key. Even secure connections like these are not entirely safe. The LiFo will also contain the details of your employment conditions and training. Please endorse the documents as a priority. Again, the Marshal will be your supervisor, and will sign off on your proficiency. Welcome to the only side, Virgin."

The transmission ended and even though my mother's image vanished, the imprint of her grim smile in my mind's eye was slower to fade.

"Well, she's a piece of work," I said, almost to myself.

Sixkiller gave me a vaguely amused look. "Reserve your judgement, Virgin. You might learn to like her. Certainly you will respect her."

I doubted it. "I'm heading home. I'd hate to miss my *LiFi*."

"L-I-F-O," said Sixkiller. "Light Phone. Foldable, three month battery life, IQ-net boosted coverage Wi-Fi, including underwater and underground." He pulled what looked like a wallet from his pocket and opened it up. "Looks like this."

"Oh."

"Next gen technology. Being with GJIC has its perks."

"So you're not a Luddite at all?"

"I'm many things, Virgin, but that ain't one of them." An air of mystery lingered around the phrase, as if he wanted to say more, but the door opened and Totes peered in.

"You two done?"

"And dusted," I said.

A short time later we were being driven home in a sleek, bulletproof sedan by a young woman in uniform.

"You never used this... valet service before," I said to Sixkiller after we settled in the back seat.

"Not when you were around," he said.

"Right." I tapped on the partition between us and the driver. The frosting became translucent and the membrane thinned out so she could hear us. "I'm Virgin Jackson. Nice to meet you."

"I'm Jessie, ma'am." The smile she gave me was more of a grin. And her chin lifted in a lively manner.

"Can I get your number as well, Jessie?"

"My number will be programmed into your LiFo, ma'am. Buzz whenever you need me."

"OK. Thanks."

"You're welcome." The membrane switched opaque again like a windscreen fogging against the cold.

I settled back into the plush fabric seat, which immediately adjusted its temperature to make me more comfortable. Sensitive Polymers – SPs – were into their third generation now for those who could afford them. GJIC clearly had money, and having transport on tap might be handy. Sixkiller and I had reached a level of amicable tension. We could work together. I admired the way he rode, and he could handle himself in most circumstances, despite being a tad trigger-happy. And his moments of surly arrogance, well, I could match surly with the best of them. We'd just agree not to talk then. It would work... So why did I still feel like a flea in a frying pan?

"Say, how d'yer like to have dinner?" he asked.

"Pardon?"

He didn't shift his gaze from watching the city slide by. "Dinner tonight?"

I nearly said yes out of sheer surprise, but caught myself. I needed some time to mull over the last week or so. So much had happened. Nate and I had been through a lot together. I didn't know if that left us in a good space to "have dinner".

For a start, I was still pretty sore about Heart. *Agent* Heart Williams, I should say – an undercover Fed who I'd thought was a dancer working in the Western Quarter. We'd shared a bed for a decent while. Long enough for me to feel betrayed and insulted when I realized he'd been undercover and pretty much spying on me.

Heart and I hadn't spoken or seen each other since the day I found out. The worst thing was that I missed him. Heart had made me feel connected to the world. He and my best friend Caro were the only reason that I hadn't packed up and gone to live in the park alone.

Well... that and the fact that it was illegal to do so and most likely meant I'd end up in gaol.

Sixkiller had never rubbed it in about Heart. Never made me feel foolish or had a laugh at my expense. He was kind in a silent, unspeaking kind of way.

"No," I said to him. "But thanks."

He nodded, and soon after Jessie pulled off the Parkway and into the Cloisters drop-off bay. We got out and waved goodnight, watching as she found her way into the traffic again like a calf being reassimilated into the herd.

Sixkiller hooked his hair behind his ear in a curiously self-conscious gesture and put his finger on the scanner to open the front door. "Another time then," he said.

I stepped in front of him. A young guy wearing a backpack waited in the foyer for the lift. "Anyway, I best be around to receive my *LiFo*. Let's have breakfast tomorrow to compare instructions."

He made a throat-clearing noise.

"What?" I demanded, stopping to look back at him.

"You understand that your appointment to GJIC is only temporary. I expect that you hope to return to being a ranger in due course."

"What are you trying to say, Marshal?"

"I'll be copied in on your instructions, Virgin, but mine are... confidential."

"Is this your way of saying that you're my boss, not my partner?"

He lifted his chin, ready to defend himself against my anger, but I suddenly felt too tired to care.

Behind me, I heard the lift ping open. The young guy disappeared into it.

"You know what... I'll see you tomorrow," I said and jumped in between the closing doors. They faltered for a moment, sensing my movement, then they shut with a clunk, leaving Sixkiller behind.

I nodded at the young guy and leaned against the polished brass handrail, enjoying the pressure of it against the small of my back.

The Cloisters apartments were older than many others in the park vicinity, which lent them character. The ceilings were a bit higher, the trimmings a bit grander, but the paintwork was faded and the air-conditioning system was temperamental. I'd grown fond of its quirks.

The lift shot upwards with a groan and we stood in awkward silence, both apparently going to the same floor. I got out first, and he followed me, walking on past as I entered my apartment. I shut the door and took a deep breath, grateful to be in my own space.

A knock came almost immediately. I stepped back, surprised, and then forwards again to check the sec-cam. It was backpack guy.

I pulled my Smith & Wesson from the holster beneath my coat and took a couple of steps to the left. It'd take serious firepower to penetrate the walls on either side of the door, but a semi-auto would make short work of the door. His backpack could have been harbouring one.

It flashed through my mind that, not so long ago, I didn't wear a pistol to and from work. Not so long ago, people hadn't been trying to kill me.

"What do you want?" I said into the intercom.

"Special delivery for Virgin Jackson."

"Leave it outside the door."

"Sorry, I need a bio-print."

"Who are you?"

"I believe you've been expecting me, ma'am."

"You got some ID?" I felt a little eddy of relief, but if he truly was GJIC he'd have to identify himself before I thought about opening up.

"Just a moment, ma'am," he said and slid his hand into his pocket.

I heard a familiar sound behind me. I didn't need to turn around to know that Aquila – my spirit-guide wedge-tailed eagle – was in the room. She'd taken to appearing lately when I was in danger. If Nate Sixkiller hadn't seen her too, I'd have thought she was just a figment of my imagination – the illusory friend that I'd invented as a teenager suddenly returned to help me as an adult in a time of stress.

And something *was* wrong right now. I saw the courier glancing over his shoulder nervously.

Shit. I yanked the door open. "What's wro–"

The expression on his face caused me to falter. I followed his line of sight to a white figure near the fire stairs at the end of the corridor. The figure glowed in a way that set my teeth on edge – in a way that was terrifyingly unnatural.

"Agent Jackson?" he whispered.

The white apparition began moving towards us in an odd, hopping gait.

"Who else attracts such weird stalkers?" I replied softly.

He pulled out a scanner, pressed my finger onto it. It verified my ID, and he slapped a foam packet in my hands.

"I suggest you get out of here," I said, as Aquila swooped out over my head and down the corridor.

Now it was closer, I could see the white figure was wrapped in some kind of shroud that was tied by a drawstring at the top and the bottom.

Aquila screeched again, and attacked it.

Pieces of material sloughed off the shroud, floating into the air then disappearing.

"Mythos," hissed the courier, who began to back away towards the lift. "I'll get help for you." He raised his phone to his ear, talking rapidly into the mouthpiece as he stepped in and the doors shut.

Now only Aquila stood between the Mythos and me, and I suddenly wished I'd accepted Sixkiller's invitation to dinner. Or gone with the courier. Paralysis had possessed me.

While I stared, the ghostly shroud passed clean through one of the corridor lamp fittings. *Clean through it!*

Right about then I abandoned any notion of shutting my door and hiding under the bed.

Aquila continued to peck and screech at the creature, but every time she shredded some fabric from the shroud, it appeared to replace itself.

I managed to take a few steps backwards.

That got it hopping even faster. Something seemed to be wrestling around inside the shroud. It stretched and undulated as it moved, sending out waves of sulphur dioxide that made my eyes sting.

Aquila became frantic, diving, pecking, and clawing. But her renewed attack had no effect on the creature's advance.

I suddenly panicked and retreated to the lift, stabbing the call button. The thump of my heart seemed to cut off my breathing, and I dropped to one knee as the Mythos passed by the apartment closest to the lift.

Just as it did, the elderly lady who lived there opened her door and walked straight out into it. She was enveloped by the misty shroud, which clung to her.

"Mrs Shelby," I called out hoarsely. "Come here to me quickly, there's someone unsavoury at the other end of the corridor."

She waved her hand in front of her eyes as if she could barely see. "Ranger? Is that you, dear?"

I got up and stepped forwards with my hand out, coaxing her. "Mrs Shelby, come to me."

She gripped her chest. "But-I-don't-feel-well."

I stood a few feet away. A trickle of sweat slid down the side of my face, and I wiped it with the back of my hand. "Please try."

Aquila quit attacking and landed on the floor in front of me, screeching.

"What is it?" I hissed at my disincarnate. "Tell me!"

The eagle danced and fluttered, trying to catch the drawstring floating up from the bottom of the shroud, but the shroud contorted, eluding her efforts.

"Do you want me to touch it?" I asked her.

She doubled her efforts, but her beak snapped on empty air.

Mrs Shelby sagged against the wall and doubled over, gasping. The Mythos contracted with her, writhing as if it was trying to strangle her body.

She began to make choking sounds.

I glanced at the floating string that appeared to tie the top of the shroud. What would happen if I touched it?

Mrs Shelby wheezed and collapsed.

I stepped forwards and grabbed at the top string as the shroud contracted around her again. A freezing sensation paralysed my arm. I grabbed my wrist with my other hand to help pull it away.

The cold sensation began to burn, but I held on, pulling the string taut.

"Mrs Shelby," I yelled. "Get up!"

She didn't move and the cold pain began to spread up through my shoulder to my chest.

"Mrs SHELBY!"

She responded to my bellow by lurching sideways. As she fell, Aquila flew up and latched onto the other string. I jumped backwards as she flapped. The opposing forces made the Mythos spin and thrash, and the string came undone. A wisp of distortion escaped into the air and vanished through the ceiling, and Mrs Shelby and I were left alone in the hallway.

"Everything all right?" called a voice from further down

the hallway. A few doors had opened. Heads poked out. The Cloisters wasn't a close and friendly place, but it also wasn't the kind of community that would ignore a murder happening under their noses. I knew a couple of the people on my floor by name, the rest by nod.

I knelt down. "Can someone call the paramedics? I think she's had a turn."

I lifted Mrs Shelby up and leaned her against the wall, then massaged the blood back into my arm.

Her eyes fluttered open, bloodshot as hell. "Dear?"

"You're OK, Mrs Shelby. Just a bit of a dizzy moment. The paramedics are coming."

She licked her lips and coughed. The colour returned to her face. "I felt so strange. I couldn't breathe, but it seems much better now."

I patted her shoulder.

"I'm sorry to have been such a nuisance," she added.

"Far from it. Just knock on my door if you're ever having problems." I surprised myself by saying that. Maybe it was from relief.

Aquila had flown down and settled on the lamp outside my door and was preening. Preening meant calm. Calm meant no Mythos.

"You are kind, dear. I always feel so safe knowing you're just across the hall from me. And that other man... the policeman with the big hat. I like him too."

"You mean the Marshal? Yeah, well... do you feel able to get up?"

"Not just yet, I think."

"Are there family members I can call to come with you to the hospital?"

"I have a wonderful family, dear. But they live in London."

"Then I'll just wait here until the paramedics arrive."

"Please call me Esther."

"Virgin," I said, tapping my chest.

"That's an old-fashioned name. I haven't heard that since I was a child. There was a man in my street called Virgin. I don't think it's meant to be a girl's name, dear."

I smiled and took her hand in mine. "My father named me. He didn't care much for what people thought."

"Oh, you poor girl. Men can be so thoughtless."

"I'm used to it now."

"Well, it seems you're not one to make a meal out of a snack, are you, dear?"

I wasn't sure quite what she meant by that, but the paramedics arrived then, sparing me anymore of her sympathy.

The people looking out from their doorways disappeared while Esther was settled onto the air-stretcher.

She tapped one of the paramedics on the arm. "Just whizz me past my door before we go, please, dear."

"We're not a valet service, ma'am," he said politely.

"Of course you're not." She winked at me as he shook his head and sent the stretcher into reverse.

When he stopped outside her door she reached out and touched the lock. "Virgin, dear, Trip is inside. He'll need looking after. Take him to your place, and I'll come and collect him when I return. His food is under the sink."

"Trip?"

The paramedic changed the direction again to head to the lift.

"My cat, dear," she said, as she was whisked away. "He likes pickles."

THREE

The tail that curled around the chair leg was the colour of burnt marmalade.

"Trip?"

The tail flapped as if annoyed, but the cat remained firmly out of my reach beneath Esther's sofa.

I got on my haunches and peered underneath. "Cat, come out."

It growled back at me – more like a dog than a feline.

"Ranger?" From the open doorway came a voice that I hadn't hoped to hear again until the morning.

I turned my head to confirm my suspicion: Sixkiller without hat and boots, but with his gun drawn. "I got a message that a ruckus was going on up here. Thought yer might need a hand."

I sighed. "You thought right. You know anything about cats?"

He sized up the situation. "Cat food?"

"Under the sink, I'm told."

As he investigated the contents of Esther's sink cupboard, I

rolled from my knees to my butt and sat thinking about what
had just happened. Then I remembered my door was open
with the LiFo sitting on the floor where I'd dropped it.

"Can you bring the cat to my room?" I said, scrambling to
my feet.

The LiFo was still on the floor. I picked it up, closed the door
and flopped into my chair. When Sixkiller knocked, I was
thumbing through the menu, figuring out the basic functions.

After a quick sec-cam check, I let him in. He had the cat
cradled in one arm, a bunch of cat food sachets in the other,
and a pissed off expression on his face.

He held Trip out to me. "You forgit something?"

I accepted him gingerly, but Trip had other ideas. He took a
swipe at my face with bared claws, and I dropped him.

He scuttled under the sofa, and resumed his tail flicking
posture from there.

"Taken an instant likin' to each other, I see," said Sixkiller
laconically, dumping the sachets on my coffee table.

"I'm only good with native animals," I said.

"Sure." He nodded in a way that suggested he was *actually*
shaking his head, and his eyes held that mocking gleam that
always caused my back to stiffen. "You gonna tell me what
happened to the owner?"

I sat down again and gestured for him to do the same while
I recounted the tale of the Mythos and Esther. "Do you know
what that thing might have been? Will she recover? Will it
come back?" I asked.

"Pass me yer LiFo," he said.

I handed it over and watched as he managed it with a
dexterity that belied his supposed anti-technology tendencies.
Maybe I hadn't sized up this man properly at all.

"This it?" he asked. He handed it back, and I looked at the image on the screen.

"Yes! That's almost exactly like it. It stank like rotten fish, too."

"Not rotten fish, rotten flesh. Call it a Pocong. It's a burial shroud wrapped around a dead 'un."

I took a moment to digest that. Then I said, "Let's have a drink."

"What've yer got?"

"Beer."

"I'll take a glass," he said.

Of course you will!

I grabbed a long neck from the fridge and flipped the cap. Then I opened the dishwasher. I couldn't remember the last time I'd run it, so I took out a glass and swished it under some hot water to be safe.

I took it over to Sixkiller who held it steady, barely raising an eyebrow while I poured. I settled into my armchair opposite him, nursing the rest of the bottle.

"So what's a Pocong doing in my corridor? Was it a Mythos?"

He took a sip and waited for it to go down before he answered. He took up a lot of space on my couch, I noticed. His shoulders were wider than I'd ever realized. His hair was snagged in a loose ponytail.

"Yeah, it was Mythos," he said. "We've only seen Pocong once or twice. I had one turn up when I was trackin' a criminal in Indo."

"What happened?"

He took another long, slow swig and thought about it before he replied. "A shit load o' people died."

"Does that mean that Esther...?"

"From the way yer describin' it, you got to her in time. I'd be bettin' she'll come back good as gold. How did yer know to pull the drawstring?"

"Aquila. She was trying to do it, but couldn't."

"Your eagle's damn clever, Virgin. My advice'd be to never ignore her."

"Sometimes her message gets lost in translation."

"Not this time," he said.

"Not this time." I glanced around. No Aquila. "You said the Pocong had only appeared a few times. I don't get it. The Mythos we saw before were crows. What's the shroud thing?"

"Read the Mythos *Vade Mecum* in yer LiFo. It's a record of all the Mythos we've documented. In the past, yer'd see certain types in certain locations. When they get to moving around like this, it means trouble."

I scrolled back a page on the LiFo and saw the list he was talking about. Some of the generic names I recognised immediately: vampires, spectres, sphinxes, and hellhounds, but it was the subcategories underneath them that caused my eyes to widen. I'd never heard of *saci* or *habrok* or *cat sidhe*. "But these are all imaginary," I said.

He continued sipping beer without answering and stared ahead at my wall as if he was waiting for something.

I scanned through the list again and the implication finally sank in. "Do you mean to say that the imaginary creatures in *all* our cultures are actually Mythos?"

"The ones on that list in yer hands, yeah. Others, like our Bigfoot and yer Bunyip... well... they're just made up to scare kids."

My whole understanding of the world tilted like a bout of vertigo. "So, according to this... this... umm... *Vade Mecum*... the Pocong is part of Indonesian mythology?"

"Yup."

"But you – I mean, GJIC – believe that it's actually part of the Mythos invasion."

"Yup."

"So the Mythos have been with us for years?"

"Yup."

"But occurrences are escalating now?"

He drained his glass and got up. "Yer LiFo has my number programmed into it. Call me if anything else happens tonight. Otherwise, I'll be seeing yer for early breakfast."

I nodded absently, still thinking.

"And Virgin," he said from the door.

"Uh huh?" I glanced around.

"Feed the cat and put some litter out."

I gave him a mock salute. "Yessir."

The door clicked shut and, finally, I was alone.

FOUR

Deciding not to indulge my desire to bang my head against the wall, I took a shower, dove into track pants and a sweater, and made a salami, cheese, and pickle toastie. The food stopped my head from spinning, and settled my nervous gut. Several bites in, though, an unhappy miaow interrupted me.

I set the sandwich down and investigated the pile of sachets Sixkiller had left on my coffee table. My mouth watered some more. Even the cat food looked good.

"Mmm... tuna."

Selecting the tuna deluxe, I squeezed it onto a plate and pulled a pickle out of my toastie to place on top. Then I put the food and a bowl of water on the floor near the end of the couch.

Trip crawled out and we eyed each other over our respective plates.

When I was done, I picked up the LiFo and started to read the *Vade Mecum*. The contents made me nauseous all over again. These... creatures were real. In a way.

Jeez.

After a while, I looked up. The cat tuna and pickle were all gone, except for some bits floating in the water bowl.

"Glad to see you've still got your appetite, Trip," I said.

His tail was curled into a position that suggested he'd gone to sleep, so I returned to my reading.

There were two other files on the GJIC page. I opened the one titled DUSAN. The assignment instructions were concise. I had to assist Nate in finding out as much as we could about an academic named Armand Dusan working as an associate prof at the revered Branch Holy University.

I hadn't attended Branch Holy, but I had done some seminars on campus, and been to a couple of parties in the dorms. Back in my uni days, I'd never been much for the college swim-throughs. Inevitably, someone'd say something about politics that pissed me off, or the environment, and I'd be compelled to argue my point. Drunken debate was about as worthwhile as punching a pillow. I preferred my blows to be felt when I threw them.

Branch was all stone architecture, grand arches, and beetle-harbouring vines – a deliberate attempt to model itself on the Northern Hemisphere's grandest Ivy League institutions. I personally found it pretentious. We weren't that kind of country. We were a red dirt and white sand landscape, baked in sunshine, and swept bare by wind. We suited low ceilings and defiant architecture that hunkered against the elements and didn't overthink its importance.

I reeled my thoughts back in from their fanciful digressions and read on. The file held a detailed background about Branch and a change in the political, social, and academic landscape of the college. There was also a summary of its financial situation. It hadn't received government subsidies in over two decades, so it relied on benefactors – usually alumni

– to keep its floors polished and its digital appetite sated. Universities needed the latest in educational technology to compete, and good educators... which led me on to Professor Dusan's biography. It went on for pages. I started halfway in, glossing over his childhood and teen years. A red marker flagged a section just after he graduated from his first degree. I stopped skimming and read it carefully. Dusan had a penchant for religious conversation, having recently converted to Animism, and was a highly awarded public speaker. He'd presented papers at conferences all over the globe. His picture didn't scream charisma, but that's where photos can let you down.

When I finished the profile, I clicked open the second file, labelled COMTEL.

A short while ago, I'd tracked a guy working with the Korax – the human arm of the Mythos – back to a rigging company called Roscoes. Roscoes contracted to ComTel, the largest telecommunications company in the Southern Hemisphere. If the Korax had infiltrated ComTel, then their sphere of influence was substantial.

Frankly, the ComTel job interested me more than Professor Dusan, but it seemed that Commander Orlean – Mummy dearest – hadn't seen fit to assign me much responsibility. The instructions were clear: provide surveillance support when requested.

The resentment that gripped me felt very real. Like something twisting inside me. I hated being blackmailed into working for GJIC in the first place, but even more, I disagreed with how these jobs had been prioritised. What could possibly make an academic more of an immediate threat than infiltrators inside our leading communications company?

My cell phone rang, and I put the LiFo down to answer it.

"How was it?" asked a sweet but succinct voice.

"Hi Caro? Do you mean my meeting with *Mother*?"

"Don't be dense, Ginny. Of course I meant that. And do I detect some sarcasm in my wholly charitable and mild-mannered friend?"

"Now who's being sarcastic?"

"Spill!" she said, cutting to the chase.

"Can't. Sorry."

"What if I come over?"

I thought about it. "Can you bring food?" The toastie had barely taken the edge off my hunger, and I didn't have anything much in the fridge.

"Spring rolls and red curry sound OK?"

"Hell yeah."

"Champagne?"

"Why? What have you done?"

A sudden knock on my door startled me.

"Hang on." I got up and walked to the door, careful to stay to one side, out of the direct line of fire. After a quick glance at the sec-cam, I flung the door open.

Caro stood there dangling a plastic takeaway bag from her fingers. A bulging satchel hung over her shoulder.

"You moving in?" I asked.

"With you?" she said lightly, and walked on through. "Not likely."

I closed the door and watched as she plonked the food on the coffee table, then promptly got down on her hands and knees.

"Jeez, Virgin, there's a cat under your couch."

"Trip," I said, "meet Caro."

"Hello puss, puss," she crooned. "What catastrophe has befallen you that you should end up here?"

To my amazement, Trip poked his head out and licked Caro's outstretched hand.

"Cats don't lick," I said.

"Of course they do. Poor puss, puss. Come to Caro." My best friend climbed up onto the couch and crooned to the feline to join her.

In a matter of seconds, the ungracious moggy had jumped onto her lap and settled in to be stroked.

I couldn't think of anything sensible to say to that, so I collected cups, plates, and forks and shared the food out. The cork popped in one twist, and I splashed some sparkling wine into the cups. Caro sat contentedly patting Trip while I demolished half the curry and rolls.

"You going to eat?" I asked her.

"In a bit," she said.

I stopped then and looked at her properly: blonde, softly curling hair and a sweet face that belied her insatiably curious and often devious mind. I never failed to be amazed at how charming and affable Caro could be, and how focussed and single-minded, as well. It was as if two people resided in that skin. The fucked-up woman who I'd met having treatment for PTSD was well hidden most of the time. But I knew she was there. Just like I knew, right now, that something was up.

"What is it?" I asked, setting my plate down.

Her smile was almost dreamy. "For someone who doesn't like people much, you seem to be able to read them."

"I know how to read *you*," I retorted. "And you're bothering me. What's going on?"

She took a sip of her bubbles and appeared to savour the cheap, gassy experience. "I need you to promise me something first, Ginny."

I waited, becoming more alarmed by the second.

"What I tell you must not change your behaviour," she said. "If you let it change *anything*, then you and I are done."

It felt like someone was squeezing my windpipe. "I promise," I gasped.

"You know I haven't been overseas for a while–"

"Sure," I said, interrupting her. "PTSD."

"Well, there was that, but it settled. Truth is, I hadn't been feeling right for a long time, even when Hamish pulled me out of that tight spot in Africa."

Hamish. The mention of his name immediately conjured a picture of a densely muscled man, light on his feet, a little smaller than me, and rather unremarkable aside from his disconnected expression. I owed sociopathic and just plain-scary-odd Hamish my life. "You seen him lately?"

She shook her head. "He comes and goes. Count on him to be unpredictable."

"Fortunately."

"Fortunately," she agreed, then hesitated again. "Now, do I have your word, Ginny?"

"You have my word." I nodded with the solemnity that I could see she sought.

"Well, it seems that I have MS. I mean, I've had it for a while. That's why I stopped taking travel assignments."

"You mean... multiple sclerosis?"

"Yes."

I sat rigid in my seat, letting what she had said sink in. I knew a little about multiple sclerosis, not a lot, but enough that I chose my next words with care. "So what do I need to know to help you?"

"I'm having muscle spasms and numbness, which impairs my motor function."

"Anything else?"

"Nothing I want to talk about yet."

I let out a slow breath. "So tell me more when you're ready."

"I'm only telling you this now because you'll notice things. To the rest of the world though, I'm unchanged. Right?"

I frowned. "But wouldn't it be better... easier if some people knew?"

Her eyes blazed and she jerked upright, disrupting Trip's slit-eyed sleep. "If they knew, my work would dry up, and my contacts would abandon me. You don't get to be good at my job by being weak. Do you understand?"

"Being unwell and being weak are two different things," I argued.

"I know what I'm saying, Virgin. I know my profession. No one must know!"

I fell silent.

"And don't let me spot even a pimple of pity on your face, or I swear I'll shoot you."

On any other occasion her ferocity would have made me smile. Not today.

I watched as her sudden anger dissolved and her determination slipped. I saw how pale and exhausted she really was underneath it. "So that's why you haven't been sleeping?"

"I tried sleeping, but it's never enough. I prefer to be awake now and using the time I have while my body still works."

"Should you be drinking?"

She glared at me, and I instantly regretted my words.

I held my hands up to placate her. "Sorry... just give me some time to get used to the idea."

"You have one day," she said, in typical Caro style. "Now tell me about your mother."

FIVE

We talked for a while, finishing the bottle and dipping the spring rolls into the leftover curry sauce. Caro licked the dribbles from her fingers as I told her what I could about the interview with my mother, the chief of spies – leaving out the Mythos bits – making it sound like some kind of babysitting role, with Sixkiller being the baby.

"You know, Ginny, the elephant in this room is in danger of turning into a great hairy fucking mammoth," she said dryly.

I stared at her. "Translate?"

"The strange cuts all over you; the fact that your blood wouldn't clot in hospital until they transfused you with the Marshal's blood; the way you constantly look off into the distance, or above you, like you're expecting something to drop out of the sky. And you can't begin to explain all the chaos in the park away with some smuggling story or whatever. People are trying to kill you, weird shit is happening, and now your overachieving bad-ass mother appears from the dead. To put it plainly, Virgin… what the fuck is going on?"

My jaw dropped open a little.

I knew exactly what she was doing and she'd played me immaculately. I felt a begrudging admiration for her tactics – drop her medical condition bombshell on me, share something deeply personal, then nail me to the wall with the question she really wanted me to answer.

I slow-clapped her. "You're good."

She fluttered her eyelashes. "I don't know what you're talking about."

I burst out laughing. Only Caro could turn an intensely personal and traumatic conversation on its head and use it to get what she wanted.

But how did I answer her?

I took a minute to think about it. The future of our friendship hung on what I said next. Telling her the full story meant I risked her thinking I was completely whacko. Yet she would pick up on a lie in a flash, and probably hold it against me forever.

"First, you need to promise *me* something," I said.

She nodded as if she'd been expecting the proviso. I guess her negotiation skills were better than mine.

"Shoot," she said.

"Don't try to understand this straightaway. Take what I'm going to tell you away and digest it slowly. Lord knows, it's taken me long enough to come to terms with it. Is still taking me… and I can tell you that logic won't work for you."

A flush rose on her cheeks. She nodded.

"OK. Well, here it is. You see, there're these creatures called Mythos and they seem to have…"

The conversation went on long after that. Caro deluged me with questions that I couldn't answer. We finished the champagne and started on a cask of red wine that I'd bought to add to my dried chicken casserole sachets. Somewhere between draining the cask and a second round of toasted cheese, I fell asleep on the floor next to the coffee table.

Caro woke me at daybreak with a toe to the ribs.

My backbone realigned painfully as I rolled over.

Caro was on the couch – Trip stretched alongside her, belly up – her tablet on her lap. She hadn't slept, but she'd made coffee.

"You said you had an early call with the Marshal. Figured you might want to have a shower."

I sat up and scrubbed at my face. *Ugly and monstrous* didn't even begin to describe my hangover. I reached out carefully for the coffee cup and with a trembling hand brought it to my lips. The bitterness made me salivate and dry retch.

"Jeez, Ginny. You sound like a backed-up drain."

I blinked to clear my watery vision, remembering our night-long conversation. "Caro?"

She didn't look up from what she was doing. "I've started my research on the Pocong and the crow Mythos. Do you know how many cultures use the crow in their myths? I've started compiling a list."

I wet my lips before I spoke. While my tongue felt furry, my lips were dry and sore. "I have one," I said, pointing to the LiFo on the arm of my chair. "From GJIC."

She shook her head. "That's their database, and it might be useful for the moment, but we need our own."

"W- we do?"

"Knowledge is queen, baby."

"D- did I tell you everything?"

"I'm guessing so, from the way you were swearing. Now, hit the sprays, friend. You stink of eau de wino."

I felt an explosion of relief. She didn't think I was nuts.

As I got up, she reached out to put her empty cup on the

table. It slipped through her fingers and bounced on the floor. Trip made a growling noise, leapt up, and disappeared under the couch.

I bent to pick it up, but was stayed by her bright, tight stare. "I can do it. Go shower."

I stopped mid-action. "Right."

Pretending not to see the way she was trying to massage sensation back into her fingers, I did as she suggested.

Multiple sclerosis. *Shit.*

I let the hot water drum against my forehead until I could think again. My friend... my dear, dear friend...

I took my health and my body so much for granted. The last few weeks I'd been cut, beaten, weakened, and hurt in a number of ways, but I'd never for a single moment considered that I might not heal or regain my vitality. What Caro was now facing... it turned my insides liquid thinking about it.

Tears came, and I let them flow and be lost in the rivulets of water. By the time I was done and dry, my game face was back in place. I pulled on fresh jeans, a short sleeved button up shirt, and soft-soled shoes – not boots. Branch Holy University had a dress standard.

I smiled, remembering the last time I'd been there – how I'd dealt with a guy who'd been bothering me – but that smile slipped when I walked back into my sitting room and found Sixkiller standing in the kitchenette.

"Morning, Ranger," he said.

"Marshal," I replied. "Make yourself comfortable."

"I have," he said, lifting a mug. "I'll leave the makings here, so I have something to do in future while I'm waiting for you."

I saw the jar labelled Green Tea on the bench, and, from the corner of my eye, Caro chewing the grin from her lips.

"I'm ready," I said.

He raised his eyebrows and drained the drink. "Did you feed the cat?"

"We should go past the hospital and check on Mrs Shelby," I said, ignoring him.

"Still not gettin' along with her furry friend?"

I made a face and looked at Caro. "Stay as long as you like."

She shook her head. "I'm going home."

"We can drop you off then."

"No," she said. "I'll make my own way."

I nodded. "Speak soon then."

Jessie had the car waiting for us downstairs. As we climbed in the back seat, Sixkiller nudged me. I glanced along the street and caught a glimpse of a stocky figure that I knew too well. Detective Chance.

"Seems you made a lifelong friend," said the Marshal.

"Coincidence, I'm sure," I said.

But as Jessie whisked us straight out into the traffic and onto the Park Ringway heading north, a sense of unease lodged under my ribs. Chance had threatened not to give up on the murder charges against me after GJIC had dusted her allegations under their carpet. What did that do to Chance's dogmatic nature? I knew what it would do to mine.

My qualms deepened.

"Did you do your LiFo reading?" Sixkiller asked.

For once, I welcomed his interruption. "Yeah, and I think we should be working on the ComTel connection, not wasting time on this academic."

Sixkiller shook his head. "This *academic* is a leading expert on certain religions. This is your first assignment and you're already questioning your boss? Do you practise that kind of insubordination, or does it come naturally?" There was no cowboy twang in his rebuke.

I glowered at him. "What do you think?"

His expression grew stormy for a moment then, for some reason, he relaxed and chuckled.

Unable to get a rise out of him, I sulked a bit.

"Virgin?"

"All right, I read through the *Vade Mecum*," I said. "I see there're no reported cases of the Pocong appearing in Australia before."

He nodded with a degree more satisfaction now that he could see I was paying attention.

It was an irritating thought. The Green Tea incident was still bothering me too, but I wasn't going to continue the day in a fit of contrariness.

"The file says he's been running salons on Animism for students," I added.

"Makes a change from creationism, I s'pose," observed Sixkiller, in a more casual tone.

"So we're supposed to determine if he's a nut or a threat?"

"Bluntly, yeah."

I thought about that for a bit. "Animists believe that all creatures are created equal," I said.

"More'n that... they don't see a separation between physical and spiritual. They think that animals possess souls. And inanimates too, like rocks, rivers, even the wind."

"This kind of belief is nothing new, though. Animism features in lots of religions. Why are we bothering with this guy?"

Sixkiller shrugged. "Cain't rightly say. I'm not analysin' data and looking for patterns. I go where they tell me. Investigate who they want me to."

"You don't strike me as someone who goes blindly into any situation."

"Not blindly, Virgin. I trust my people. I trust your mo... the Commander. If she says we need to look at this guy, then we do."

He said it like he was mentally folding his arms against any more questions, so I fell silent and stared out the window.

Jessie was driving at a fast clip along the Ringway. It was a long but quick trip from the Cloisters to Branch Holy if you could use the emergency services lanes as, apparently, we could. I glimpsed the miserable expressions on the faces of the commuters stuck in rush hour traffic as we hurtled past.

This section of the Ringway was almost thirty lanes wides and several kilometers from the park wall. Up ahead, I saw the signs for the Branch Holy tunnel. Those thirty lanes dipped and disappeared underground, to re-emerge twenty kilometres away on the other side of the university. One of the most expensive road projects in the Coastal City's history, and all to preserve the land around Branch Holy University. They must have some powerful alumni.

Jessie slid across lanes with expert skill to take the university exit, and suddenly the Ringway, the traffic and the noise vanished. We found ourselves on a moderately busy suburban road leading into the university grounds.

Branch Holy's buildings clustered around and on a gentle hill, giving the students plenty of reason to exercise, and an elevated view of the city sprawl. Not as good as those back up on the dividing ranges to the west, but premium in its location.

At the foot of the hill – above the vanquished Ringway – lay spacious, green sporting fields, several swimming pools, a set of real lawn tennis courts, and a small tavern and café. They ran right down almost to the foot of the park wall, separated by a large ivy-covered mesh fence. It had long been a Branch Holy graduation tradition to climb the fence and graffiti the top section of the wall – so much so that the council no longer demanded the university clean it off every year.

How Branch Holy kept its gardens and fields so green in our arid climate and in spite of city-dictated permanent water restrictions, was difficult to fathom.

We passed student high-rises and some more spacious student cottages. The further we drove up to the top of the hill, the more people were about. It was still a little early for most of the student population, but I glimpsed the beginnings of a market down one street.

Jessie finally pulled into the standing zone at the back of the Chancellor's audacious stone administration building and left the motor running.

Sixkiller lingered inside giving her instructions, but I got out and stretched my legs. The view back down the hillside was something else: a patchwork of glinting garden ponds, olive green groves and terracotta-tiled roofs bookended by the grey majesty of the wall.

The last time I'd felt this refreshed by a vista, outside the park, was during my visit to the Romani mobile park on the seaside marshlands. Hamish, Caro's psycho "fixer" acquaintance, and I had teamed up on surveillance out that way. It seemed like so long ago, and yet it was barely three weeks. Even less, since I'd seen Hamish for the last time; oddly, I missed him.

What did that say about me?

"I'll go talk to a few people in admin. According to our intel, the professor's holdin' a breakfast salon in a place called the Arbour. The map's on your LiFo," said Sixkiller, as he came to stand behind me.

I pulled the device from my pocket and unfolded it. It took a brief caress of the surface with my fingertips to bring up a map of the campus. A pulsing arrow pointed me to a path just ahead between pink oleander bushes.

"Right. You joining me later?" I asked.

"No. You blend in better'n me. The salon runs fer an hour. I'll meet yer back here after thet. Can you handle it?"

Did he mean to be provocative? Or was he concerned for my safety? With Sixkiller, it was always hard to tell. I lifted my shoulders in a disrespectful shrug and sauntered off. He could make of that whatever he liked.

SIX

Once past the oleanders, the path wound upwards between hedges carved into the shapes of human busts. Philosophers probably, though I really didn't know; might just as likely be alumni, or accountants…

As I climbed, following the GPS marker on the LiFo, the manicured hedges turned into a thick unruly hedge of ornamental fig. Waxy leaves, dislodged by my passing, sprang back into place just as quickly, and I felt the sharp stones beneath my canvas shoes. The hedge grew thicker, and the ambient light dimmer, as I reached a fork in the path. A carved signpost pointed to a steep section up to my left. My LiFo arrow agreed with it, so I followed until I reached a clearing.

A group of students sat cross-legged or sprawled about on mould-stained pavers under the interlocked branches of some Poinciana trees, their attention captured by a man leaning against a stone altar.

Armand Dusan was tall and thin with medium colouring. I recognised him from his dossier photo, though the image on my LiFo didn't quite capture the attractive slant of his eyes, the grace of his long limbs, or the languor in his manner.

He had the full attention of his audience, and it was him, not they, who noticed me enter the arbour.

"Welcome, beautiful soul," he said, loud enough for the whole assembly to hear.

Heads turned. Stares were curious but welcoming.

To my dismay, I felt myself blush.

"Did you come for the salon, or just for our famous coffee?" He gestured to a little trestle table set up beside the altar. It was manned by a redheaded woman who was holding a container of plastic spoons in her hand.

"The coffee, of course," I managed to reply. "I've heard it's the best."

"But you realize that there's a price. Er…?"

"Virginia," I proffered. "And what would that be?"

"Conversation, of course." He smiled in a way that seemed to draw us all in.

I sidestepped around the edge of the group towards the trestle. "I'm always good for an opinion," I said.

His smile widened at that and he chuckled. Even though it was early morning, on a hillside in a damp grotto, he managed to pull off a rather seductive sound.

"Sugar? Milk?" He took a clean mug from the table and held it out to the redhead who poured dark liquid from a large flask.

"Neither," I said.

Dusan retrieved it and held it out to me carefully as if it were part of a long-practised ritual.

"Thank you," I said, moving forwards to collect it.

"Please, sit," said Dusan.

"I'm comfortable," I replied. "Don't mind me now."

He tilted his head to one side and regarded me, and his little congregation copied him.

The redhead cleared her throat, and instantly he changed his focus back to the task at hand. "And so it has been shown to be that..."

I lost track of what he said after a while. It was about animistic religions like Jainism and Buddhism. I knew some of what he told them already, from electives I'd taken at university. I'd enrolled in Religions of the World mainly so I could discuss belief systems with Dad. It was his favourite after-dinner topic, along with his vision for the park, and the politics of conservation.

But while Dad's manner had been as dry as a cleanskin merlot, and at times as bombastic, Armand Dusan's manner was smoother than the satin pillow slip Caro had given me for Christmas.

From time to time, Dusan fielded questions from the group. One in particular got my attention.

"What would you wish for our future, Armand?" asked a young woman whose arm lay along the shoulders of her girlfriend.

"I would wish for us to be of one religion. One belief. It is the only way to achieve harmony."

When the smattering of applause had died down, I spoke up. "But what if we don't want harmony?" I asked. "What if war and conflict is our preferred state of being?"

He looked at me with such sadness that I nearly glanced away.

"Why would you wish that, Virginia? What hurt is so great within you that you would damn the human race to eternal misery?"

His students exchanged glances.

"Whoa!" I said, raising a hand. "I thought a salon was a place to discuss ideas, not get personal."

"It's my belief that a healthy soul seeks enlightenment and harmony," he said, in his softest voice.

That was met with murmurs of approval.

He smiled at his audience then glanced back to me. "Unfortunately, I have to give an early lecture, so we must finish now, but perhaps I can share some of our literature with you, Virginia?"

I nodded. "Sure."

I sipped my way slowly through the rest of the bitter-tasting coffee while the congregation stood, and stretched, and said their farewells. When the last had ambled off, I was left with Dusan and the redhead whom he had addressed as Cyndia.

She limped around, collecting cups into a crate and tipping hot water from the flask onto the ground. I looked for the cause of her limp, but saw nothing obvious.

Dusan beckoned me over to the altar.

I approached and stood considerably taller than him, but somehow felt diminished by his languid confidence.

"I apologise, Virginia, if I seemed… judgmental." He sighed. "It isn't often that students challenge my ideas at the salon. I think that they come for the coffee and the bonus credit. You took me by surprise. Are you newly enrolled?"

"Very. Heard about these gatherings from a friend."

"Do you live on campus?"

"Not at the moment. But that may change."

"I'm assuming this is not your first time at university?"

"Did my *mature* looks give me away?"

"Striking and intriguing would seem a more appropriate description."

I felt a flush rising. Twice in a short space of time. Dusan had a way with him.

Even more unsettling was the fact that Aquila had appeared, and was sitting on the altar behind him. My disincarnate – animal guide, imaginary friend or whatever label I wanted to label the wedge-tailed eagle – perched there, eyeing me with a baleful expression. Her yellow eyes blinked slowly, and her posture was alert.

"I apologise if I made you uncomfortable with a compliment," said the professor.

I didn't reply, curious as to how he would handle my silence.

He stared at me for a bit then said, "I host a more… intimate salon for postgraduates and alumni in the evenings. Perhaps you might care to attend one? I'm sure you would find the debate rigorous."

"Here?"

"There's a tavern at the foot of the campus called Beauvoirs. We meet on Fridays, late. In the downstairs bar."

"How late?"

"We have an arrangement with the management. The tavern closes at ten, but they leave a bar attendant for us, and we lock up when we leave." He noted my raised eyebrow and continued, "It's all about atmosphere, Virginia. How many times has the course of world affairs been changed over scones and tea? Big ideas need darkness and the smell of whiskey to birth them."

"That's very poetic of you, professor."

He smiled and it felt like I'd been shot through the heart with graciousness and goodness. It left a warmth inside me.

"Th- thank you for the invitation."

"I hope very much to see you again. Now, sadly, I must rush." He touched me lightly on the arm before heading off down the path.

The gesture was kind and inclusive. Little wonder people were drawn to him. I watched his long, elegant strides until he disappeared then I turned back to Cyndia.

"Could you help me carry this down, Virginia, and I'll take the other?" said Cyndia in a friendly manner, holding out a crate. Her musky-strong perfume enveloped me. It was reminiscent of the spice markets on the edge of the Western Quarter.

Before I could reply though, Aquila left her perch and flew to the ground between us.

What are you trying to tell me?

Aquila flapped her wings and cried so loudly that I stepped backwards instead of forwards.

"Is everything all right?" Cyndia's expression showed genuine concern, and I felt foolish.

"I'm… I'm… sorry… I–" I reached out to take it from her, but Aquila dived at my hand, and I felt a burning spear of heat shoot from my fingers up to my shoulder.

I withdrew abruptly. "I'm sorry, I have… er… a bad back," I said, struggling to find an excuse for my odd behaviour.

Her look of concern grew.

And with it everything shifted. The arbour became very still, as all sounds muted. The tree branches overhead knitted more tightly, like threaded fingers, and a rank smell rose from the soil beneath the pavers.

Cyndia set the crate down on the trestle and opened her arms to me. "You seem distressed. Can I help you?"

I wanted to step right into them, but Aquila swooped straight at my face, and I ducked instinctively. "S- s- so sorry, but I have to go. See you on Friday."

I turned and ran down the path, stumbling and sliding on the stone path until, close to the bottom, I fell over. I got up and looked behind me, but Cyndia hadn't followed. And Aquila had disappeared.

Having just spent an evening convincing Caro that I was sane, I suddenly seriously doubted it. Had I just hallucinated Aquila's presence? Without Nate there to verify it, I felt disbelief seeping in.

Jessie was waiting patiently behind the wheel of the car. I slid into the seat behind her and rested my head back while I calmed down.

The driver's partition slid open. "You OK, Ms Jackson?"

I lifted my head. "Please call me Virgin, Jessie. And yeah, I'm fine."

She handed me a small soft tube. "I find this helps sometimes."

I took it and read the wrapping. It was a caramel-flavoured GU containing caffeine, amino acids and salt. "Thanks."

"I've been in the service for nearly five years. I still need these at least once a week," she added.

I sucked in the gel and felt the welcome flood of energy. "You've been with GJIC that long?"

"No. ASIO. This is a secondment for me. Kind of a promotion. More interesting than driving dignitaries around."

"I'll take that as a compliment."

She smiled into the rear view mirror at me. "Believe me, it is."

"Hey, I'd appreciate it if you didn't mention this to the Marshal."

"Cross my heart," she said with a wide grin. "Marshal's a good man, but he's a machine about this stuff."

Right at that moment, I knew I liked her.

"Where is he anyway?" I had an overwhelming desire to get off campus.

"Here he comes now," she said, nodding towards the admin building.

Sixkiller strode up, opened the car door and folded himself into the seat next to me, moving in a far more muscular, though less elegant, way than Armand Dusan.

"Jessie, drop the ranger at Park Central and then take me on," he said, without preamble. "And give us some privacy in the back, please."

"The hospital first though. We should check in on Esther," I piped in.

Jessie glanced in the rear view mirror back at Sixkiller who must have silently given his consent because she closed the partition and got the car moving without comment.

We sat in silence until we'd left the campus and were back on the Ringway.

"What happened with Dusan?" he asked.

"They were just finishing up, but I have an invitation to another salon, Friday evening late at the tavern down near the foot of the wall."

He frowned. "I won't be able to come with you. I have something else to do."

"Which would be?"

He ignored my question. "What did you make of him?"

I sighed and settled back deeper into the comfort of the plush interior. "He's charismatic, for sure. Kindly. Passionate about his cause. But something strange happened after he left. Aquila appeared."

"Was there anyone else there?"

"A red-haired woman. An assistant, I think. Or an admirer. She'd been making the coffee."

"What happened?"

"Aquila wouldn't let me near her, so I left."

"Red-haired, did you say?"

"Uh huh?"

"Anything else about her?"

"She had a bad limp."

He frowned. "I don't like the sound of it. I'll arrange for you to have backup on Friday night."

"I don't–"

He held up his hand. "My decision. And you will."

"Fine," I said snappily, not liking this arrangement at all. "But what about you? Where's your backup?"

His reply was a powerfully annoying inscrutable stare.

SEVEN

Esther was sitting up eating peaches and jelly when I got to the hospital. Visitors were sitting by the beds of all the other occupants in the ward except hers, and her face brightened when she saw me.

Sixkiller had wandered off to find green tea in the hospital cafeteria – good luck with that, Marshal – and left me to do Esther's interview. At least that's why he'd agreed to come, I realized: a post-Mythos encounter interview.

I'd simply wanted to make sure she was OK.

"Virgin, dear," she said loudly, over the competing murmurs and TV noise. "How's my Trip?"

"He's fine, Esther, though he prefers my best friend's company to mine."

"Don't take it hard, dear. Cats are very particular."

I smiled. Something about this old lady softened that hard, suspicious place I reserved for acquaintances and strangers. "I'll try not to."

"They say I must stay for another day or so. Will you be all right with her?" She reached out and took my hand. "You're very kind, you know. I thought I was on my way to the big moon dance in the sky when you saw me in the corridor. But apparently not yet. Now do tell me... what else was going on there?"

"What do you mean?" I said quickly.

She threw me a shrewd look. "That handsome policeman who came to help as they were wheeling me away... do you have a crush on him?"

My heart jolted back into a regular rhythm. "The Marshal? No, Esther. Strictly work."

She patted my hand again. "So pleased to hear it. Many a good woman has fallen in the name of love. He's not the one for you, dear."

I felt my face fire up with discomfort. Caro was the only person in the world who dared to broach the subject of my love life – or at least the only one who did and lived.

Since Heart Williams, my previous and devious lover, had turned out to be an undercover Fed, the whole topic was even more off limits. I had no time for men in the romantic sense any more, and, so far, I hadn't developed any kind of penchant for women. "So, what are the doctors saying about your health?"

She let go of my hand and picked up the peaches again. "Something about the electrics in my heart being wonky, dear. But I think I'm fine."

"When you collapsed... was it from pain?"

"Not really. I told the delicious young doctor here that I just felt very cold and very weak. That old expression 'somebody walking over your grave' couldn't explain it better... Oh, I get all chilled just thinking about it. Pass me the blanket, Virgin."

I got up, pulled the nylon blanket up from the bottom of

her bed, and spread it over her legs.

She smiled her appreciation and then exclaimed, "Oh, here he is now, Virgin! I've told him all about you..."

An attractive young guy in an open-necked shirt and dark chinos appeared next to me. He touched the wall and activated the privacy screen then held out his hand to shake mine. He had the pallor of someone who worked nights, but, despite that, his smile was frank and his eyes intelligent.

"Rav Namaditje," he said. "Are you the beautiful Esther's daughter?"

Esther giggled: a straight up, embarrassingly girlie sound that made me want to hightail it out of there. I began to back away from his outstretched hand.

"Just a neighbour," I said. "And just leaving."

His smile broadened. "Aaah, so you're Esther's saviour."

I proffered my hand for a handshake. "Virgin Jackson."

His smile faded a little and he frowned as we shook. "Your name sounds... Were you treated here recently?"

"Yes," I said carefully. "Not so long ago."

"I remember. Your case prompted a lot of discussion," he said. "You know that you and your blood might be about to become famous."

The hairs on my body rose up onto their tiptoes. "Really?"

"Yes, they're writing you up to present to a top medical conference."

Shite. "Oh. Look, I'm sorry, I can't chat now, but I'll drop in tomorrow, Esther."

Esther's shrewd old eyes flicked between us, and she waved. "Give Trip a kiss for me."

"Unlikely," I said, and walked straight out through the illusory screen.

Sixkiller was leaning against the wall out in the corridor,

sipping liquid from a cup.

"You found green tea?" I asked.

He blew on the lip of the cup in answer.

The action of him blowing seemed to send some kind of cosmic reverberation through the nurse's station behind us and they began to titter and whisper.

"We should go," I said abruptly, not feeling sympathetic to his admirers.

I strode through the hospital and out to the loading zone where Jessie had the car idling. Instead of getting in though, I waited for Sixkiller to catch up.

"I think I may have a problem," I said, and repeated Dr Namaditje's conversation.

Sixkiller frowned. "We might have to do some damage control there."

"How?" I asked, wondering how GJIC could make this go away.

"Was Namaditje the young doctor that went into the ward just before you came out?"

I nodded.

"You should go on a date with him. Find out what they are saying about you."

I felt my eyes widen. "Beg yours?"

"We need to know how far this might go."

"You go on a date with him then."

He gave me a flat and uncompromising stare. "This is your problem."

"Which makes it yours as well."

We glared at each other for a moment then my cell phone rang. I answered it with half a head of steam. "What!"

"Well, fuck you too, Ranger."

Surprise blew the heat off my anger. "Papa Brise?"

"The one and fuckeen only. You better get down here so we can talk."

"I'm busy," I said.

"Too fuckeen busy to be dead?"

"What's that supposed to mean?"

"Someone's put a fuckeen contract on you. And because I'm such a fuckeen good guy, I thought we should talk about it."

A cold hand gripped my heart and tried to stop it beating. *A hit? On me?*

"Who?" I turned away from Sixkiller so he couldn't see the shock on my face.

"You want to know fuckeen more? I'll be in Juno's tonight."

"I have to do something early on."

"I'm not on my mama's fuckeen tit anymore, Ranger. I can stay out late."

I took his sarcasm as agreement. "I'll see you there around midnight then."

He hung up, and I tucked my phone in my pocket, taking a second to compose my expression before I turned back to the Marshal.

"Turns out, I already have a date tonight anyway," I said.

"The doctor can probably wait a day or two. Set something up for the weekend."

His command thawed my shock a little. In his language, did *no* mean *whatever you fucking say, Marshal*?

I shook my head and got in the car. "Jessie, take us to the park please."

Hospital to park was a quick ride in the EMV lane. Jessie pulled into the parking bays the tourist buses used, and I got out and headed into the station without waiting to see if the Marshal followed.

The smell of hay and horses instantly soothed my fears some. I felt safe here at least. If Papa Brise was right, then this might be the only place I was.

I walked to the tack room to grab a saddle and bridle. Leecey, our much-pierced stable hand, was cleaning bridle bits over a sink of soapy water.

"Thought you were supposed to be using the steriliser for that," I said, glancing at the expensively idle equipment sitting in the corner.

"It's broken again. And I like doing it this way." The water slopped onto the floor as she scrubbed.

I watched her for a moment or two. "What's wrong?"

"Nothing," she said, scrubbing harder.

I only ever scrubbed anything that hard when I needed to think. Something was on her mind for sure. I unhooked Benny's bridle and slid my saddle down off the rail.

"Talk if you need," I offered.

She shook her head.

"OK, well I'm heading out to do my rounds then," I said.

"Is the Marshal going with you?" she asked.

"Don't know. Don't give a shit. See you in a while."

I got as far as the door before she spilled out what was bothering her.

"It's Johnny," she said.

I stopped and turned slowly. Leecey and my junk-addicted little brother Johnny had been an item a while ago. I managed to help pull her back from the brink of self-destruction, but not him. Got her this job. Told myself that helping Leecey might help him. Knew that it was bullshit. Leecey got herself together. But Johnny moved back to DreamWorks – junkie-ville – and I hadn't seen him since.

"What?" I asked.

"He's seeing someone else."

I took a slow, willing-myself-to-be-patient breath. I didn't have time for, nor did I care about, my brother's love life. Not when someone was apparently trying to kill me. But I understood why Leecey did.

I'd also recently learned that feelings don't go away on command at the end of a relationship. I mean, I still couldn't get Heart William's betrayal out of my head. I might not have been in love with Heart (if that was even his real name), but something in me was deeply hurt. I just didn't care to examine it too closely.

"You're better off, Leecey. You know that. Whoever she is, he'll treat her badly."

She dropped the bit she was cleaning in the water, wiped her hands on her dirty apron and turned to me. "It's not that, Virgin. I know that Johnny and I are bad for each other. And I don't want to be in a relationship with him anymore. It's about you."

I frowned at her, mystified.

She continued. "He's seeing that clairvoyant that you used to go to school with."

"Corah?"

"Yeah, I think. You've spoken about her and so has he. I worked out the connection."

I began to sweat a little. Corah didn't do anything without a reason. I'd learned that when we'd been hot-desk buddies at school. I neither trusted her, nor liked her, and it had been bugging me why she had recently bargained with me for an invite to the reopening of Dabrowski's Diner. That night she'd ingratiated herself with a few high profile politicians and business people, which wasn't her style. And now my brother? The parts didn't add up. But when they did, I was sure I wouldn't like it. "Do you know where I can find him?"

"Mystere," she said.

"*Mystere?* With Corah?"

She shrugged. "Just be careful. Don't make him mad."

Johnny liked knives. He had a habit of using them when he wanted things his way. I wasn't afraid of him – had never been. But I was careful. Junkies were unpredictable. "Always. Now put the bits in the steriliser."

She grinned at me, looking happier now she'd unburdened herself. "Nah."

I rode Benny up the steep path to the top of the eastern butte and dismounted. To my relief, Sixkiller hadn't followed me out here. I took some time just to breathe quietly and digest Papa Brise's news. Who would want me dead? Was it the people who'd sent the guy to my apartment? Or someone else? How messy was my life getting?

My only peace at the moment was out here in Birrimun. Since I'd been seconded to GJIC, my boss at Park Southern hadn't retracted my ranger status. He and Sixkiller had agreed it was best that I should come and go, to give the illusion that I still held my regular job. It was the one upside of this whole situation.

Today the plains were an endless iron-red mat of sand and rock; the purple tinge of the mulla-mulla had already begun to blanch in the heat. The sky brimmed with a flawless, burning blue. On days like today, it was impossible to detect the electronic surveillance net that protected it above from intruders.

I wondered how far the investigation on the recent breach to the canopy had gone. ComTel – who had the contract to operate it – was notoriously impenetrable when it came to accountability.

I took my 'scope out of my saddlebag and performed a slow and careful survey of the horizon. It calmed me. The last few times I'd been alone in the park, the Mythos had found me. I should have felt more anxious being here alone, but I refused to let them take my calm place, my true home.

Something about the fingers-shaped outcrop of Los Tribos drew my attention. The illegal immigrants we'd caught had landed there, and, in his journals, my dad identified Los Tribos as a place of concern.

A loud rumble from my stomach reminded me that the coffee I'd had at Branch Holy University was a fair while ago, and I deliberated whether to go back to the stables and grab food, or head over to Los Tribos for a closer look. The thought of having to negotiate questions from Totes, Leecey and possibly Sixkiller helped me make the decision.

I tucked the 'scope away and mounted Benny.

"Los Tribos, girl," I said. "Quick."

She took me at my word, and once we'd descended from the butte, she shifted straight into a gallop that sent the dust kicking up behind us.

The tourist buses had resumed last week, and by this time of the day they'd be hovering out on the northern sector border, having a leisurely lunch while they watched kangaroos drowsing around the Narni waterhole.

Narni billabong pooled in my piece of the park, but the river course that fed it ran north into a ravine and came out again in an identical pond in the adjoining sector. Sometimes the ranger in charge over there, Charlie Billjee, met me for a thermos of tea and a gossip. Billjee had been watching over the northeast of the park for longer than I'd been in the senior ranger's role.

I suppose we could have been gal pals but neither of us were inclined that way. Billjee was maybe six or seven years older than me, and put the backbone in the word stoic. Nothing fazed her and not much moved her, other than visitors damaging her land. *Then* she was capable of almost anything.

One time she'd tracked down a tourist who'd gone missing and found that he'd accidentally pissed on a fragile plains orchid. In her fury, she'd tied him up, ready to drag him behind her horse until he learned his lesson.

Luckily, I was near the border that day and heard him shouting. Found him trussed up like a boneless turkey, covered in dirt, and scared for his life.

He made a lot of noise about pressing charges, but I convinced him that he'd have a huge fine to pay for wandering away from the coach and damaging the flora. It all went away in the end, but she was lucky.

"You can't go maiming the tourists, no matter how much they tick you off," I told her over a thermos some time later.

She doffed her Akubra and sat it on her knee. Then she fixed me with a stare, not unlike the one Sixkiller often used on me. "I can do whatever I like," she said, "long as I'm prepared to take the consequences."

"You'd go to jail over a guy peeing on a park orchid?"

She sipped her coffee out of the thermos lid and looked away into the distance. "If you don't stand by what you believe in, Virgin, then what's the point in anything?"

I thought about that now, as Benny trotted under the long shadows cast by the Los Tribos outcrop. Suddenly, I wanted to talk to her. I had beliefs, and principles. Dad made sure of that – though it hadn't worked so well with Johnny because he'd left home early. I'd stayed and grown in my dad's likeness.

Proximity breeds either sympathy or contempt. With me it was the former.

Though, if I was absolutely honest with myself, the things I believed in... Well, other than Caro, there wasn't a single person in this world who I'd take the fall for, and not a grand notion or ideal I'd die for, outside the preservation of Birrimun Park.

Had knowing about the Mythos changed that in me?

If they were really threatening humanity, as my mother and Sixkiller would have me believe, then where did I actually stand on that notion?

I mean, my personal survival was an obvious motivation to help them out, but did I really care if humanity changed its beliefs? Did I care if the Mythos weeded out the ones they didn't care for?

I hadn't engaged with the wider world since I was a teen. I watched the news and had an opinion, but not one that was any type of call to action. Politics bored me. Celebrities bored me. Everything I wanted was right here.

Yet, as I scoured my conscience and my heart, I touched a hairline crack, a shift in my old values, a widening sense of responsibility and mindfulness.

Or maybe I just needed more sleep.

I reined Benny in and dismounted. The carrion crew had been through and cleaned up the mess left from our encounter with the illegal immigrant drop. In the few weeks since the event, the wind had blown the sand over the mess of tracks and burn marks. The only remaining damage was to one of the Los Tribos' rocky fingers, and to my memory.

I wondered if Charlie Billjee had felt the same painful lump under her breastbone with her missing tourist as I felt now, just remembering the disfiguration to the land.

I dismounted again, took a set of soft foot shells from my saddlebag and slipped them over my boots. They moulded to the sole and heel and protected the rock while still giving me traction.

That made it easier to climb the middle finger of Los Tribos rocks until I got high enough for a decent view. Each vantage point in the park shared a slightly different view. From here, the dunes rose and fell in a dense red sea.

A flock of galahs wheeled overhead and made their way towards Paloma Station House. Their screeching reminded me who this land truly belonged to. I longed to be up there with them, free to glide, and twirl, and dive as their mood demanded.

Benny neighed in response to their chatter and I leaned back against the rock and closed my eyes for just a second.

When I opened them and looked down at Benny, I saw Aquila perched on the pommel of my saddle.

"What are you doing here?" I said, alarmed.

She seemed as oblivious to me as Benny was to her presence and she set about preening her feathers and picking at her claws with much concentration.

I glanced around, but saw nothing threatening.

What was the reason for her sudden appearance? Was there something significant to her about Los Tribos?

The notion seemed fanciful, and yet in Dad's journals he'd said that he felt concerned enough about Los Tribos to put a time lapse camera out here to observe. If only I could find the memory card. Was it lost, or had he hidden it? Had whatever the camera captured got him killed?

The possibility left me felling bleak. My peace had been violated.

I quickly climbed down and headed back.

When I arrived at the stables only Totes was there. He was waiting for me, hands on hips, with Phuti, his favourite companion doll, peeking out of his jacket pocket. His hair looked freshly shaven, showing off his pale, elliptical skull. The blue eyes beneath his eyebrows were unusually intense and angry.

"I got a pile of signoffs that need doing, Virgin. The boss can't expect to lend you out to some government agency and not replace you. The quadrant hasn't been inspected for over a week, and there are damage hotspots showing on my maps that need to be verified. Also, Sombre Vol's supplier says we're in breach of contract and they want the horse back. *And* we got a delivery of consumables yesterday. Who's going to do the inventory? And, *and*, the oat silo has got a bug infestation."

I sighed. "I'll try and catch up this week."

"You *won't*. That's the thing. You can't keep pretending you're working here when you're not."

I took a deep breath and he must have detected the slight flare of my nostrils because he hunched over, ready for me to blow up.

"I'll fix it," I said, more calmly than I felt.

"How?"

I took a moment to think about it. Last thing I wanted was a stranger in my job, but I wasn't sure how long I'd be with GJIC. I mean, they were straight-out blackmailing me, and so far I didn't have a countermeasure. But Totes had a point. I couldn't be in two places at once.

"I'll ask the boss to deputise Leecey."

"What?" Totes blinked. "But she'll make my life hell."

"More than I do?"

He shifted his feet and stroked the side of Princess Phuti's face. "Well, when you put it that way..."

"I'll speak to him now."

"You think Leecey'll be able to handle herself out there?"

"Out where?" said a voice from behind us.

We turned. Leecey was holding a bunch of microfiber saddle cloths watching us. Her eyes were open wide, like she might have heard more than just the tail end of our conversation.

"You're getting a promotion." I draped Benny's reins over her shoulder and headed down the corridor. Sombre Vol snorted at me from his stall as I passed him, and I felt like snorting back.

"What do you mean? What promotion?" Leecey called after me.

"She wants you to be her," I heard Totes say in a squeaky voice. Totes didn't like change. It sent his OCD into crisis.

"No fucking way..." was Leecey's reply.

Or, at least, I think it was; the door into the tunnel under the Ringway clunked shut behind me, and I didn't hear the rest.

I took the Park Lane exit out of the tunnel on the other side because it linked almost directly into the Park Southern office tower. Bull would be at work in his fifty-something floor office and some things are best said in person.

I rode the lift with a bunch of neoprene suits who, recognizing my face, nodded in my direction. When you wear a ranger's uniform, people tend to notice you. Today, I was in civvies on account of the visit to Branch Holy, but clearly they knew me. That made me a little uncomfortable.

Jethro, Superintendent Brian "Bull" Hunt's personal assistant, raised a wary eyebrow at me as I entered the faux-leather, faux-floorboard, and faux-window-boxed office.

I never made appointments, so, unless Bull requested my presence, Jethro never knew when to expect me.

We had an uneasy agreement that I would wait until he found me some spare minutes in Bull's schedule before I started acting impatient, unless it was really important, and then I just walked right on in.

On those days, I saw the glitter of murder in his eyes.

"Virgin?"

"Jethro. I need two mins," I said.

"Virgin! Come in," Bull called through the open door.

I sauntered past Jethro's desk and bestowed him with a nod.

The murder glinted and then vanished as he turned back to his screens.

"Close the door!" Bull barked at me.

He was over by the window, surveying the breathtaking view. From here, you could see the way the sea edged along one side of the park's purple-red expanse.

My boss turned to me. I hadn't seen him in a couple of weeks and he seemed to have put on weight; his torso was becoming one thick chunk of flesh of the same girth from armpit to hip. His neck was flushed red above the collar of his shirt and he was crushing a stress ball in his hand.

"Good day to you too," I said without deference.

"Stick a plug in that attitude of yours, Virgin. What did you come to see me for?"

I steeled myself. Even my fence-sitting, permanently-aggravated boss was normally a mite more pleasant than this.

"You first," I said.

"I've been told I have to put together a park showcase for a bunch of political heavyweights."

"Showcase what?"

"How it's working. How the ecology can successfully be preserved. The lobby who believe the park should be reclaimed for housing and business development are gaining ground. The government's being pressured to cut back our funding and sell off the land."

"Over my corpse," I said.

"Mine too, Virgin." He threw the stress ball at me and folded his arms. "With you on the GJIC assignment, I need to find a replacement who can make sure everything's ready for the meeting."

"Let me do it. It will only take a few hours."

"It'll take a week, finishing up with a presentation from all the rangers. I've spoken to my liaison at GJIC but they won't give you back to me for that long. I've negotiated to have you for the presentation, but that's all."

I crushed the stress ball to show him my feelings.

"I'm looking at bringing in one of the Gulf of Carpentaria rangers–"

"*No!*"

His jaw jutted dangerously. "What do you mean, *no*? It's not your call."

I tried to temper my vehemence. "The gulf rangers don't understand the arid park ecology. They're just as likely to miss a danger sign. Put Leecey in the job."

His eyes widened. Coupled with his raised jaw, it gave him a slightly deranged look. "Piercings, tattoos, stable-hand Leecey?"

"She knows the country and the horses. She loves them."

"She's a stable hand."

"She'll do better than anyone you'll bring in. And Totes knows her. You know how temperamental he can be."

"I won't consider a–"

"Bull, *please*. She's the right person. I know it."

It must have been the *please* that stopped him in his tracks.

His fingers strayed to his chin, which he stroked while his eyes attempted to pierce through skin and bone to see what was going on in my head. "You're sure?"

"I am," I said, refusing to acknowledge a tiny tremor of concern.

He touched his earpiece. "Jethro, make an appointment for me to see Leesa…"

"Gitano," I volunteered.

"Gitano. Yes… that one…" He touched him off and went to sit at his desk. "Make it work, Virgin. You know what's at stake."

I nodded. "More than anyone, Brian." No one called Bull by his real first name. Not even his wife. I saw a little flush of embarrassment seep up his throat and stain his cheeks, but he nodded, understanding that I was making a point.

I saluted goodbye and slipped my hat back on. As I left his office and passed by Jethro, I swear I heard Bull's assistant growl.

EIGHT

I dropped by home to grab a change of clothes and found no Detective Chance hanging around outside, no ghoulish Mythos waiting for me when I got out of the lift, no Aquila, and no one trying to kill me. Maybe today was going to improve. My weather app told me it'd be cool out tonight, so I rolled up my Lillico Driza-Bone and rammed it into my backpack.

I thought about eating in, peeked in the fridge, and changed my mind. Instead, I dropped more cat pellets in a dish for Trip and refreshed the litter tray. At least the damn feline was house-trained.

His tail flicked in annoyance the entire time I was tending to his needs. It was the only part of him I could see, but there was cat fur all over one end of the couch.

"Glad you're making yourself at home in my absence," I told him.

The tail flicked some more, and I left. Clearly Trip and I had one thing in common. We didn't do small talk.

It was late afternoon now, so I figured on an early dinner at

Dabrowski's Diner, before heading back to Branch Holy and then on to Mystere.

I tucked my Smith & Wesson into its holster under my arm. I was licensed to strap it on my hips, but I rarely did that outside the park. Since Papa Brise's phone call it was the closest thing I had to personal security.

I walked to Dabrowski's to give myself some thinking time. I didn't know where Sixkiller had gone with the car, and he hadn't checked in with me. If I called him, he'd want to set up a babysitter for me tonight, and I didn't want that.

The foot traffic on the street was light, but still thick enough that I felt hidden amongst it from snipers or kidnappers. What form was this hit going to take? Surely staying among the public was half safe?

When I was a kid, Dad and I would walk this way to visit Chef Dab and stop outside the arched windows of the Oyster World travel agency. He'd point out the 3D displays of New York and London and say, "Their parks are the size of buttons, Virgin. We can't let that happen here."

It was the only time I ever remember him holding my hand, as though somehow by squeezing my fingers, it would convey his conviction and urgency to me.

I felt his anguish back then. Now even more. Everything about the ever-reaching, never-sleeping, ever-populating city made me nauseous, especially now a killer was out there looking for me.

About a block from the diner, my concerns grew. Someone was watching me. I tried a few obvious tactics to test it out – stopping abruptly, checking reflections, stepping in and out of rotating doors – but either I was imagining it, or my tail was particularly good.

I decided to subject whoever it was, phantom or not, to

some idle time by heading into Chef Dab's and ordering three courses.

Chef Dab's most reliable waitress and current bed partner, Greta, waved me into my favourite booth and set a glass of water in front of me. She was a biggish woman with a smile as wide as her hips and a way of putting misbehaving customers in their place. If I could come back as someone else, it might be Greta. She had things sorted.

Of course, I wouldn't want to be sleeping with Chef Dab. The man did a little too much kink for my taste. That train of thought took me down a track to Heart Williams. I was missing him in a number of ways, sex being around the top of the list.

"You look like you swallowed something squirmy," said Greta.

I hadn't seen her since she helped me into a taxi a few weeks ago, after a rough day. Neither she nor I had realized at the time that the taxi driver was the Korax – the human arm of the Mythos. Seems they'd been keen on the notion of kidnapping me. My guess was that they'd hired the hitman as well.

"I'm right as rain," I said, lying. "And hungry. I'll have the Polish sausage with mash and sauerkraut, a side of beets. And a creaming soda. And some of that cherry jam kiesel."

"You want cream with your kiesel?"

"Sure." This was likely the only meal I'd get today. Maybe my last meal. I might as well claim the calories.

"Back in a flash," she said. "And this one's on the house."

I frowned at her. "What do you mean?"

She tilted her head to one side. "You wanna argue it, go see the boss. But you might as well just give in. You're never gonna have to pay for food here again. Chef says you've had your independence, now it's time you accepted him back as family."

I sighed. Chef Dab and Dad went back so far, I couldn't even really remember how it started. He kind of adopted me when Dad died, which was nice, although Chef's generosity was boundless and could be as smothering as his embrace. But it would be churlish of me to argue the point on this. He was just trying to help.

I took the opportunity to kick back and watch the passing shoppers through the diner's windows. No Sixkiller. No Caro. No hit man. No one but me and my food.

The very idea of it was momentarily euphoric. The last few weeks had been so fraught and so hard to grapple with that I–

"I've ordered," said a voice, interrupting my reverie.

I glanced back and straightened up, almost spilling my glass of water. "Hamish?"

Caro's friend – and I used the term loosely – dropped into the seat opposite me.

"Please tell me *you* were following me," I said.

He shrugged. "I still would be, if you hadn't decided to take a meal break."

Thank heavens! "*Why* are you following?"

"It's my job."

"For who?"

"Those who want you safe."

"You mean GJIC?"

He shrugged.

Greta returned and placed a mound of sausage and mash in front of me and a plate of crispy bacon and something squashy and dark green on Hamish's side.

He saw me staring and picked up his knife and fork. "Spinach."

I nodded and followed his lead with the eating.

Neither of us spoke for a while. But, finally, I had to ask. "Are you my backup for tonight?"

He nodded.

"Hired by the Marshal? Did he contact Caro to find you?"

"Caro isn't part of this," he offered. "But I'm with you for the duration."

"Just the visit to Branch Holy Uni?"

"I plan to see you home tonight in one piece."

"I didn't realize you contracted to the government."

"Like I said, I'll see you home tonight."

I didn't know whether to be amused, grateful, or annoyed. Clearly Sixkiller was truly concerned about me going to Branch Holy Uni alone if he'd hired an outside operator of Hamish's calibre. Or desperate. Or maybe he figured Hamish was the only person I'd work with. Either way, he'd made a bold choice.

"You'd better order dessert then. It's going to be a long one," I said.

He glanced around for Greta, who was hovering close by, trying not to show her curiosity.

Hamish was an ordinary looking guy with a compact build, brown hair, and brown eyes. But if you looked squarely into those his eyes, you felt a little dizzy, and not in any kind of romantic way. It was the highly alert yet slightly disconnected expression that made you spin.

Made *me* spin.

Greta pounced on us. "You want to order something else? Some dessert wine?"

OMG, she thinks I'm on a date!

"Just dessert," said Hamish. "Whatever she's having."

"The kiesel," I grunted.

"You want to share?" Greta suggested.

"No," we said simultaneously.

Greta smiled, tapped the order in with her stylus and sauntered off.

"Thanks," I said.

"For what?" asked Hamish.

"She thinks we're on a date."

I could have sworn he blushed, and so I hastily changed the subject. "Let's just eat and go."

"Not together," he said. "You won't see me again unless you need me."

"Amen to that," I muttered under my breath.

He didn't – or pretended not to – hear me, and the next thing, Greta was back with two plates of kiesel. Each one had a glacé cherry on top.

"Chef sends the cherries with love," she said.

This was getting worse.

I bolted mine down and left.

Without Jessie, the car, or access to the EMV lane, the trip to Branch Holy took longer. I did catch a cab though and charged it to GJIC through my LiFo app. I'd verified the taxi driver's credentials as soon as he pulled up – a habit I'd acquired after the kidnapping attempt – and asked him to drop me outside Beauvoirs tavern.

I had no idea how or if Hamish was following me, but I guessed that was his problem.

We pulled into the parking lot just on dusk. Calling it merely a tavern was a lie. Glittering chandeliers shone out through the arched windows of a Baroque-style building. I immediately saw what kind of ambience this place offered a person like Dusan. A slice of something architecturally historic and beautiful, even by the rest of the campus's standard.

The adjacent tennis courts and the grey and imposing back drop of the park wall seemed totally incongruous in comparison.

I decided to take a look around before I went inside. Dusan had just said that they met *late*, so I was betting most of them wouldn't get here until after dinner.

The large and shutterless windows revealed two separate dining rooms on one side of the building. Upstairs, I saw sparkling glassware and white table cloths, downstairs were laminated wood tables and stiff-backed chairs, and I was betting that the basement bar was just booths and beer.

I walked one full circle around Beauvoirs. Along one side, a mesh fence stood between the building and the tennis courts. The walkway was paved. Halfway down, I saw the side entrance to the basement, but it was padlocked and appeared not to have been used in a while.

At the back, the windows were far less grand. They looked out over a small expanse of garden, another fence, and then beyond that, the chipped-into skyline of the park wall, where years' worth of graduating students had chiselled off little pieces to take with them as a souvenir of their student days. When it had first started happening, Parks Southern had billed the University, but the students hadn't relented. Claiming a fragment of the wall became the Branch Holy Grail, and, over time, everyone turned a blind eye.

Creepers spread from the nearby garden beds, and covered the base section of the wall. Some clever illusionist had threaded LED lights through the vines, and they shivered in the light breeze like hovering fireflies. String music swelled and ebbed from the open windows, and I smelled meat cooking.

The other side ran into well-kept rose gardens whose scents mingled with the kitchens. I strolled past them until I was back at the front again. Other than the overly grand architecture, nothing seemed out of place, yet I couldn't shake an uneasy feeling.

I kept glancing around. If Hamish was here, he was doing a good job of staying out of my sight.

Time to go in.

Ornately carved front doors led into a corridor with the casual dining room on one side, a bar on the other, and a sweeping staircase in the middle. I glanced left and saw patrons devouring plates of steak, chips, and salad. In the bar, they were sipping beer and dipping into small bowls of beer nuts.

While the restaurant side was full, the bar was half-empty. I spied, over near one wall, another set of stairs, much narrower and less imposing, leading downstairs. These were cordoned off, and the people occupying the tables nearby were hunched close, in intimate conversation.

I headed into the bar towards the basement stairs, but a hovering waiter stopped me before I got close.

"The downstairs bar is closed for a private event," he said, in a firm tone.

"Professor Dusan invited me to attend."

"Your name?"

"Virginia."

"Please wait here," he said, and disappeared down the stairs.

While I waited, I tried to identify any video surveillance. It was safe to assume cameras were on somewhere.

The waiter returned and beckoned me through, hooking the cord closed behind me, and watching me descend.

About four steps down the stairs, I reached eye-level with

a pair of shoes protruding from under a tablecloth. They belonged to a guy sitting at a table near the top of the stairs.

Hamish's face was obscured by a beer and a menu, but I recognised his slouch. A sense of relief washed over me. Aquila's reaction to Cyndia was still fresh in my memory. Not that even Hamish was likely to be a help against a Mythos.

I continued downwards into a small reception area with a coat-check counter and cloakroom. To one side was a set of frosted glass doors. I tried opening them, but they were locked.

"Virginia?"

Cyndia emerged from the cloakroom as if she'd unfolded herself from beneath a coat rack.

She wore a black velvet gown that set off the flaming colour of her hair and hugged her figure tight. Her smile tried to be warm, but failed.

"Hi. I guessed the time. Am I too early?"

"Not at all," she said. "Let me open the doors for you."

I stepped aside to avoid contact with her and waited while she put an old-fashioned key into the lock.

Aquila didn't appear. That was a good sign.

"We prefer to keep this door locked before events. Keeps the wrong people out." She pushed one of the doors open. "Please, join us."

I walked through into the small, dark bar. Thick wooden columns carved with gargoyles divided the room, and chunky bench seats were tucked under heavy wood tables. The room smelled of rum and cloves.

Armand Dusan sat on a dais in the middle of the room beneath a candle-laden chandelier, like a mediaeval king on a throne. Only the candles were fine LED-powered copies of the real thing.

I wondered what Papa Brise would make of the pale,

languid philosopher awaiting the arrival of his devotees. The idea of it gave me an urge to laugh.

"Virginia? Welcome. Come sit," he called.

I threaded my way between tables and took a seat near him. He'd changed attire from this morning and wore a tailored suit with an open-necked shirt. I felt underdressed.

"Nice atmosphere," I said.

He tilted his head and looked at me with interest. "As I said before... whiskey, smoke and late nights are the ingredients for the best ideas, and I'm not above a few props. Anything to provoke thought in people who are not accustomed to it."

He had a slightly self-deprecating way that was charming, even to me. But dangerous? No. Not that I could see.

"Well, I'm here to listen," I said.

"Tonight's group are often vociferous. Opinion is king here. You should fit right in."

"You mean queen," I said.

"See! Now what was it that you said you were studying? Perhaps I can introduce you to someone with like interests?" he asked.

I felt a moment of gratitude towards the GJIC file on my LiFo which had given me a basic cover story.

"I'm actually on exchange from TAFE. Just picking up a unit here and there."

He raised an eyebrow. "Aaaah... the Co-Op initiative?"

I nodded. "I expect it's Branch Holy's way of telling the world that their education processes are still relevant. You know... by mixing it with the lowlifes." I watched to see how it he took the direct hit at the institution he worked for.

"Why do I get the feeling you're baiting me?" he said, bestowing a lazy smile on me.

I gave him a wide-eyed innocent stare in return, but we

didn't get to take the conversation any further because people began entering the room.

It seemed like a good time to get a drink, so I went to the bar and sat on a stool. Cyndia appeared through a door that appeared to join with the cloakroom to serve me.

"What will you have?"

"Bundaberg rum," I said. "Straight up."

Her eyes were ringed with eyeliner that tapered into Egyptian-styled lines at her temples, and her red hair was scraped back into a tight ponytail that showed off the lovely angles of her face. I should have been drawn to her beauty, but I just wanted to look away from the glittering green eyes.

Still no sight of Aquila though, so maybe the other day had been an aberration.

My cell rang while she was pouring the shot. It wasn't a number that I recognised, so I let it go to message.

She turned back and placed a coaster and the glass in front of me. "Courtesy of Professor Dusan."

"Really?" I swivelled on the stool and lifted the glass in thanks.

He winked at me from across the room then turned away to speak with someone.

I let the rum relax my stomach while I surveyed the gathering. Possibly thirty people now, and older than this morning's followers: a sprinkle of business suits; a couple from the Western Quarter in matching checked shirts and Levis; a lank-haired, thin giant of a guy in tights and his partner who wore a mauve silk tutu. The one who caught my eye, though, was a middle-aged woman in a forgettable skirt and button-through shirt. She entered and slid into a seat against the wall towards the back of the room as if trying to hide. Curiosity drew me across the room to the table behind her.

My movement through the crowd attracted far too much interest for my liking though. I felt the prickle of their stares, and I wondered how the hell Hamish remained so invisible.

I slumped into the chair and waited for their attention to wander elsewhere.

The light suddenly dimmed and Dusan stood in front of his throne like an elegant lord. The woman in front of me craned to see him.

"Welcome, my friends. Our salon is officially open. I will speak first and then invite you to discuss."

With that he launched into an oration, a beautifully-crafted monologue on how the construct of religion has divided mankind.

"From Christianity, Islam, Hinduism through to Scientology and Realism, we have become a diaspora of belief systems. Naively, we think that this happened at the roll of the dice – that it is simply a case of geography or circumstance – when in fact it is a deliberately divisive act, perpetrated by those who would have us pitted against each other. And why? Well, the gains are many for these *disruption doyens…*"

His silken tone cast a spell on the crowd. The clink of glasses quieted, no one spoke while he did. I found the respect – the reverence – even among this older, less impressionable audience to be fascinating.

Given time, Armand Dusan would be able to fill bigger rooms. He might well be promoting a conspiracy theory, but it was well-wrapped in hope and the promise of a better world.

The woman in front of me typed notes into a tablet while she listened to him. Her eyes never left his face. From my angle it was hard to tell if her expression held devotion or scepticism. Whatever the case, she did not fit in here. And nor did I.

Nor did I.

Right then, the ridiculousness of me being here struck me with force. My expertise was ironstone, dry gulches and desert plants. End of conversation. What was I doing at a pretentious literary salon, on the campus of our most elite university? Especially when there was a contract out on me.

I began to feel annoyed. Professor Dusan was charming and charismatic, but he was hardly some sinister Mythos puppet. It was time to go and see Papa Brise and deal with the real threat to my life.

A few moments later Dusan announced a break, saying they would reconvene for rebuttals after drinks. Lights brightened and someone turned the music up.

I stood and walked quickly towards Cyndia and the exit.

She saw me approaching and stepped in front of the door. Was she annoyed that I was leaving early, or was something else on her mind?

"You leaving, Virginia?" she asked.

"Just going out for some fresh air," I lied.

She nodded and stepped away.

As I stepped out into the coat check area, I pulled up short, feeling like I'd been punched beneath the ribs. Two people were just about to enter: my brother Johnny and his lady of the moment, Madame Corah, psychic and my ex-school mate – the woman I trusted least in the world and most suspected to be capable of anything.

It was awkward and unexpected.

For all of us.

"VJ?" said Johnny.

I hadn't seen him in a while, and I felt a familiar anxious leap in my chest. He was a little taller than me, junkie-thin, with a mess of bleached white hair that framed a sweet, sweet face. But look closely and his lips were inclined to pout, and derision was never absent long from his expression. Johnny wasn't a bad guy – just selfish. I couldn't imagine how he and Corah made it through a day together.

I knew his failings because they were mine as well. Brought up by an obsessive, self-righteous parent could send you two ways – the path to sacrifice and thoughtfulness, or the low road to selfish survivalism. Johnny and I had found the latter. The difference between us was that I believed in something – the park and conservation. I think, hope, it saved me from total self-absorption. Johnny believed in self-gratification – whichever, however, whenever, he could get it. Perhaps Corah and he shared that.

"JJ," I replied, looking straight at Corah. They made a striking couple, but she was the true eye-catcher: a tallish brunette with something faintly exotic and dangerous going on – the intelligence under the sexy package. But there was also a slyness that wasn't so easy to see. "Corah."

"Why, Virgin, my darling. Are you lost?"

"Bothered. Not lost."

She peeled off full length, black gloves and flexed her fingers, admiring her own nail polish. "It's always been easy to bother you."

I switched my gaze to my brother. "Can we speak?"

He shrugged and glanced at Corah, who waved us off.

"Cyndia will buy me a drink, I'm sure. Go play unhappy families. I'll be at the bar." She walked through, slipped her arm into Cyndia's, and the door swung closed behind them. Now the only sound was coming down the stairwell from the bar above.

Johnny's pout surfaced as he watched her go. "What do you want?" He leaned back against the wall, but kept a loose grip on the door handle like he might need to escape.

"Good to see you too, little brother."

"Since when have we ever indulged in pleasantries?"

"Maybe it's time we did?"

"Whatever." He let go of the door handle, felt in his pocket, and pulled out a packet of cigarettes. He lit one then resumed his pose, holding the door.

"Why are you seeing Corah?"

"None of your biz, sis. You've already interfered too much in my life."

"Don't blame me for Leecey seeing you for what you are."

"Leecey would have been fine, if you hadn't dangled that stupid job in front of her nose. She stinks of horseshit now. Just like you and the old man." Johnny tossed insults around like they were gifts.

"She's *living* her life now."

"Y'know, Corah's right about you, Virgin. You've cornered the market on sanctimonious and boring."

A counterattack trembled on my lips, but I swallowed it. "Why are you here?"

He drew deeply on his cig, disappointed that I hadn't risen to the bait. "You first."

"Work," I said.

"Bit far from the red dirt, isn't it?"

"Ain't that the shame of it?" I said and waited.

He took a couple more drags and then dropped the butt, grinding it into the carpet with his boot heel. "Prof Dusan has something to say that's worth listening too. Man's a fucking genius."

"One world, one belief, eh? Remember what Dad used to say about that?"

"Dad was a crazy old coot. Shame you took after him so much."

"He loved you," I said, without thinking.

"Shut the fuck up!"

My tongue burned to tell him about our mother, but that was her call, not mine. Johnny and I had enough drama between us. "Never could handle the truth, could you? Well, that should work perfectly with Corah because she doesn't deal in it much," I said.

It was inflammatory. I knew it, and I didn't much care. I'd go fist to fist with him in a heartbeat if it'd help me get rid of the ache he'd just set off in my chest. But our hostile moment was stalled by some newcomers – two men – staggering down the stairs, drunk. The taller of the two elbowed me out of the way to get past.

Hey!" I protested, not about to let the guy's rudeness pass.

The drunk swayed a bit. "Get out of the way then."

Before I could react, Johnny stepped forwards and headbutted the guy.

The drunk dropped to the floor. His friend turned to defend him, flailing off balance, but Johnny opened the door and shoved him through.

"Next time show some fucking manners," he said, slamming the door. His mate was out cold at our feet.

I stared at the lump already growing on Johnny's forehead and the wild heat in his eyes.

"Why did you do that?"

A long silence stretched between us until, finally, he said, "You're a dogmatic and pious bitch, Virgin. But you're still my sister."

He turned the handle and opened it again. The drunk's mate had already staggered towards the bar. Seeing the way in clear, he went through and shut it after him.

NINE

I swore at the closed door. I didn't need Johnny to protect me, and yet it shocked me that he'd still come to my defence.

"Problem?" Hamish appeared suddenly in the spot Johnny had just vacated. He gestured to the unconscious man on the floor.

"I thought you were upstairs?"

"I was," he replied enigmatically.

"I didn't see you come down."

He shrugged.

I shrugged back. "Let's get out of here."

I headed out of Beauvoirs, not looking back to see if he was following. The ground level bar was full now of diners and drinkers, and I got out as quickly as I could.

As soon as I set foot near the door, Aquila swooped on me from nowhere, beak open. I felt a light pressure on my shoulder and a tug at my hair, but as I turned my head to look at her, she flew down and landed near my feet between me and the building. The scars of her recent battles were white, balding patches in her plumage. Her eyes glinted with agitation, and her feathers were ruffled.

"What is it?" I asked softly.

She opened her beak wider and shrieked, lifting her wings in anger now. It seemed to be directed towards the building, not me. She shrieked again, so loudly that I took a step back. She advanced on me, shrieking again at the same pitch.

This time I took several steps away.

Her wings folded and she turned her head to eye me.

An uncomfortable feeling lodged in my stomach. "Can't you get in there?"

"What is it? Who're you speaking to?" said Hamish, from the doorway.

I lifted my gaze. "Er... you. I said... how did you get in there?"

"No, you didn't."

I stayed silent.

He gave me a measured look and walked off across the street to the bus stop. It was deserted, but headlights advancing towards us along the university road suggested not for long.

I followed, but stood away a little, so it didn't look like we were together.

"Where to?" he asked, staring in the other direction.

"It's personal business. You don't need to come."

He didn't respond.

I thought about insisting that he leave, but if Papa Brise was right about the contract on me, I kind of felt better with Hamish along, and besides, he was getting paid. Who was I to deny him a job?

"A bar in Mystere called Juno's. Just stay at a distance. OK? The guy I'm meeting has a low suspicion threshold."

I think he gave a slight nod, but it was hard to tell because the bus hissed up into the shelter's parking bay, settling on the ground to let people out, and he vanished back into the shadows.

I got off the bus on the Ring Road near the downtown ramp and took a taxi to Lashkar station. It was sometimes hard to get a cab to take you there, but tonight I was lucky. The guy was short of fares and didn't argue. For an extra twenty, he even dropped me off right under the glaring, anti-vandal-protected fluoro, next to the platform steps.

Lashkar was a now-deserted train stop on the coastal rail line; the area around it had become too insalubrious to warrant stopping.

On the other side of the platform lay my shortcut to Mystere. It required climbing through torn chicken wire, crossing the train tracks, and taking a route that crossed an abandoned industrial complex. I only knew it because I'd grown up in the general area, back before Mystere got séance-like weird. I'd never seen anyone else come this way, but I guessed some probably did.

Back then, the industrial complex had been brand-shiny-new, but disputed land ownership meant all the tenants had been told to move out within three months of opening. The claim was still tied up in court all these years later, and the site had fallen into disrepair. Since then Mystere had come into existence. Even if they sorted out the claim now, no one would want to operate this close to the Weird Triangle – not when Gilgul Street, Seer Parade, and Mason Way lay only a few streets away.

If I really did have a contract on my head, I figured my shortcut into Mystere was a better option than the usual bus and bridge that the general public used. However, my "university" attire of jeans, sneakers and sweater, made me feel a little vulnerable, and I missed my customary work boots, collared shirt and ranger's khakis.

To make it worse, Aquila had reappeared. She seemed restless, but not as frantic as when I'd left Beauvoirs and I really didn't know whether to be comforted or alarmed by her presence.

I rang Caro as I crossed the train tracks into the old site. The light from the phone was a small comfort as I left the station and plunged into the darkness.

"Where are you?" she demanded.

"Heading to Mystere. I need to see Papa Brise."

"You alone?"

"Yes. No. Kind of… Sixkiller hired Hamish to shadow me for the evening."

"*My* Hamish?"

"Your Hamish."

"Interesting," she said. "Is he with you now?"

I glanced about. We hadn't shared the taxi, and I hadn't seen him since the bus ride from Branch Holy. "Well… I don't really know."

She laughed. "Not surprising. His expertise was countersurveillance. Until he had an episode and left the service."

"What episode? Which service?

"That's a conversation for another time."

Something to look forward to, I thought grimly. "How are you?"

"What's that mean?"

I paused, realizing I'd made a mistake. I never normally enquired after her health. "Sorry. I just… er…"

"What did you call me for?" she asked more coolly.

"Just checking in."

"Right. Well, don't."

"Right."

The connection died. I gripped my phone tight, feeling foolish and angry at her. Wasn't it natural to feel concern about a sick friend?

Then I chided myself. That's exactly the kind of reaction she'd been worried about from me. In her shoes, I knew I'd feel the same.

A clank in the darkness, and what sounded like a cut-off shout, sent my heart racing. I switched to the torch function on my phone and shone it around. I was in the centre of the complex now. On one side, the remnants of a warehouse roofline ran jaggedly against the starry skyline; on the other lay the skeleton frames of large vehicle hoists.

The sound had come from the hoists. A giant chain hung from one frame, too heavy to be rattled by the light breeze, but maybe rust had got the better of the aging steel? I ran the torch along it and down to the ground.

Nothing.

A stray, perhaps? This place was a haven for rodent marsupials. Once I'd seen a quokka family. I didn't even know they existed on the east coast.

My rationalizations did nothing to stop my scalp prickling relentlessly though, and finally instinct won out. I pulled my Smith & Wesson from my shoulder holster, unclipped the safety, and began to jog.

Somewhere between the crumbling concrete drainage pads and the unsteady remains of the onsite huts, my jog became a sprint.

I crossed the grassless verge at full speed and didn't slow until I saw the dull yellow glow that signalled the homes flanking the outskirts of Mystere. I slowed then, breathing hard, and stepped more carefully, keeping to the centre of the bitumen road to avoid the dogs that were barking and hurling themselves at their fences to get at me. If you lived next door to Mystere, I guess you needed to keep people out of your yard.

In the times I'd used this shortcut over the years, I'd never seen anyone come in and out of these homes. For the most part they were owned by Mystere's more long time vendors, but some were just squats that the owners weren't able to rent or sell on account of their location.

Up ahead a bunch of coloured lights signalled a change in the landscape. In only two streets, I passed from dark and distinctly creepy into bright and bald.

Minutes later, I was standing on the corner of Gilgul and Mason Way, being pummelled by the human rush, wondering where Aquila had gone.

I let the people-tide draw me along until I passed the stall selling bone chimes and human skin masks in front of Corah's Psychic Parlour, and on down Gilgul towards Juno's Cantina. Amongst the press of people, I felt both safe and at risk. Anyone could stab me with a knife or prick me with a poisoned needle, but being shot in such a crowd was less likely. I hoped no one wanted me dead badly enough to take out a bunch of pedestrians at the same time; if, indeed, anyone wanted me dead at all. It crossed my mind – or maybe it was just denial on my part – that Papa Brise might simply be trying to scare me. I hoped so.

I glanced around for Aquila, but she'd gone again. As I began trying to cut a diagonal path through the pedestrians towards Juno's alley, a hand grabbed my elbow, and a voice spoke into my ear. "Keep your head down. Come with me now."

Hamish.

He jerked me hard towards a shop front crowned by neon flashing SURPLUS! SURPLUS! SURPLUS!

Our abrupt change of trajectory sent several people stumbling and knocked a man cloaked by a tasselled shawl to his knees. Hamish wouldn't let me stop to help him up. His fingers just pinched my arm harder, and I didn't have the balance or the strength to prise myself free from them.

He punched our way through, absorbing the worst of the shoves and kicks without flinching. A thickset guy in a singlet tried to punch Hamish in the head, but he ducked and punched him in the groin. The guy fell forwards into someone, but managed to right himself before he got rolled underfoot.

I lost sight of him as Hamish propelled me through the door of the surplus store. He nodded at the shopkeeper standing behind the counter in the way people do when they know each other, and dragged me past a bunch of customers to the very back.

The shop was overstuffed with clothes: shirts, pants, great coats, camping gear, gas masks, and piles and piles of prepacked survival food. Hamish checked out the angle of the surveillance mirrors, then he motioned for me to get down behind a locked, reinforced glass cabinet containing nunchakus. When we were both squatting, he pulled a large circular, overstuffed, mobile rack of army fatigues over the top of us. I pushed a set of khaki pants out of the way so I could see him and noticed he had a lump on one cheekbone and a bloody graze on his forehead.

"What's going on?" I whispered. "What happened to you?"

"Someone tried to shoot you when you took that shortcut."

"What? How? Where?"

He put his fingers to his lips, and used some khakis pants to stem the flow of blood from his scalp.

We stayed nose to nose, in silence, for way longer than I found comfortable. The shop door tinged open and closed a number of times while we waited. Eventually, hurried boot steps sounded on the floor and a conversation which started at the front of the shop grew louder and louder as the people moved closer to us.

I saw three pairs of feet, and a hand disturbed the rack under which we hid.

Hamish's hand stole up to my neck and he pulled me so close that our cheeks touched.

My heart stopped beating as a gun barrel nosed its way in between the clothes and moved about from side to side in the space where my head had just been.

"Hey! You mess, you pay!" the shopkeeper sang out.

The gun stopped moving and withdrew.

My heart restarted, blood began to flow again in my veins, and, after a moment, Hamish slowly let go of my neck. Why was it my breath came in huffs like a broken air conditioner while he seemed serene, almost relaxed?

We listened to a curt interchange with the shopkeeper and finally the boot steps faded.

Hamish held up a finger to signal me to remain still a while longer.

While we waited, I observed a white scar underneath his left cheekbone and the unusual length of his eyelashes. I was physically closer to this man than I'd ever planned to be, and it was not a comfortable feeling. His lips were thin like my father's had been. Not mean lips, but stubborn.

He sensed me studying him and pushed the rack away until we were free from it. Then he settled back against the cabinet and stretched his legs out. I noticed his boots

then. They were softsoled, but appeared to be coated with
something shiny, like the top coat Caro sometimes painted
on her fingernails. I'd seen the same on the Feds in the park.
Foot print camouflage.

"He was waiting for you at that station where the taxi
dropped you and followed you through the old site. I got him
near those old hoists," Hamish said, without being prompted.

"I heard a noise… like something falling… That was you?"

"It wasn't straightforward. He had a partner who got away."

"That was the partner who just came in here?"

He nodded. "I got to you first though."

A whole new level of sweat broke across my body,
drenching me. "Lucky, huh?"

"Call it that if you want. You want to explain why there's a
contract out on you?" asked Hamish.

I shrugged. "I was on my way to find out. I know someone
here – Papa Brise is his name – and he warned me about it
today. Told me to come see him tonight at Juno's Cantina.
That's as much as I've got."

"They were waiting for you. Is it possible this Papa Brise is
setting you up?"

I slid down onto my butt alongside him and stretched my
legs. Mine ran a few inches longer than his. "Possibly, but I
can't think why."

"How far is Juno's Cantina?"

"Three lanes down."

"You still want to meet him?"

I thought about it. My gut told me that Papa Brise wasn't
my problem. "Yes."

"Then I go in first. Be there when you arrive."

"He'll notice you. He knows everyone who goes into that
bar."

Hamish turned his head towards me and gave me his blankest stare.

I held my hands up, palms outward. "Fine. But he's smart. Don't underestimate him. He may remember you from the park."

"He won't."

I shrugged. "Let's go then."

He put a hand on my upper arm. "Give me fifteen minutes then follow me."

"What am I supposed to do while I wait?"

He jerked his head in the direction of the counter. "His name is Ron. Thank him for helping us out, and pay for the clothes I just bled on." He got to his feet in a single movement and disappeared.

I got up more cautiously. The mirrors showed customers in the front of the shop, but no one who looked like they might be waiting to kill me. I hoped.

I sidled up to the counter with the bloody khakis in my hand.

"How much for these?" I asked softly.

Ron eyed the smear, brought a dispenser out from the shelf beneath the register and sprayed the stain. "This'll stop it setting till you can wash them."

Then he pulled disposable gloves from a box and wiggled his fingers into them. He took the pants off me with two fingers and rolled them into a bag. "Hundred dollars."

"What?" I gasped. "That's ridiculous. The tag says twenty!"

He leaned forwards so his customers couldn't hear. "Fifteen for the pants, the rest for the favour. Tell Hugh his order will be in tomorrow."

I hesitated. "My... er... friend Hugh?"

"Don't ask me if he's your friend. Just tell him."

I nodded and pulled out my card to pay.

He completed the transaction. "Thank you, ma'am. Come again."

Unlikely.

I left the store with a tightness in my chest that was mainly caused by the thought that a sniper might be on a rooftop, or lurking in one of the shop fronts nearby, waiting for me, but also in part by the fact that my wallet was a hundred lighter. I took a moment to look around before I joined the throng. Maybe it was my imagination, but the crowds seemed to have eased a little. The neons dazzled even brighter because of it. A party of rowdy, drunken shoppers were buying corked hats and novelty trilbys from the closest stall, so I melded into their wake.

"You want a smaller size, lady?" the stall owner asked me when I tried on an extra-large that covered my ears.

"Fits good, thanks. I'll take the scarf too," I said in answer and waved my card at his reader.

He raised an eyebrow and checked that the sale went through before handing over the goods.

I wrapped the scarf around my neck and pulled the hat low. Today, my brother had punched a stranger unconscious on my account, I was way too many dollars out of pocket, and someone was trying to kill me. His raised eyebrow didn't even figure on my worry scale.

I hung on the edge of the hat-buying group as they drifted back into the main crowd swell, and hoped it was disguise enough. Fortunately, they were heading in the direction of Juno's.

"Hey beautiful, come here!" One of the drunker guys draped his arm over my shoulder and puffed rum breath in my face. "That hat looks so fucking cu-ute on you."

I wanted to shove my pistol into his ribs, but his clumsy advances offered more protection. They also put him at risk.

I wrestled between my conscience and my survival instinct.

Before I could pick a winner, he lurched away from me and vomited onto the high heels of a girl heading in the opposite direction. She and her two male companions didn't take it well.

Suddenly, it was on: punching and swearing, amid a chaotic whirl of corked hats.

I skirted the fight and took the next gap in the foot traffic, hustling across into the Juno's Cantina lane. It was crowded there too, but nobody seemed to be going anywhere, just standing, singing and street drinking.

I tossed the hat and covered my head with the scarf as I pushed on the greasy door handle.

Conversation didn't stop as I walked in, but it quieted, as if the cantina customers thought they might hear something interesting if they lowered their voices.

Papa Brise was in his favourite spot, seated at a roughly-varnished pine table at the back of the room near the bar. It was separated from the diners by a row of cactus plants in large terracotta pots, and a perimeter of strategically placed guards. Behind his table, and the bar, lay a passage to the back exit, and a side door to the kitchen. Either way he had a couple of easy escape routes.

Not that I imagined he'd ever need them. This was his territory, his fiefdom; no one would challenge him here.

I looked for Hamish, but couldn't see him. No slouching sombrero-wearing males sitting alone drinking. My admiration deepened. How did he blend in so well everywhere? I certainly didn't have that talent, so I figured it was time to lose the scarf. If I was going to be safe from a contract killer, it would be here.

Unless, of course, Papa Brise had arranged the hit.

He saw me coming and put down his fork. I saw his pulled pork fajitas and my mouth watered. My meal at the diner seemed like a long time ago.

"Well, fuck me. It's the fuckeen ranger," he said.

I nodded curtly. "Papa Brise."

He pushed a chair out with his foot. "Fajitas or tacos?"

I took the chair but declined the food, despite my stomach's protest. "No, thanks."

He wiped his chin with his sleeve and took a swig of a longneck. "You look fuckeen beat. Someone been keeping you up at night?"

"Just you and your talk of contract killers."

He belly laughed. I could see his gut quivering beneath his shirt. "Always so fuckeen funny, Virgin."

I tried really hard not to purse my lips, but failed. My look of disapproval got him laughing harder.

He stopped, finally, and wiped the tears away with a crumpled silk handkerchief. Papa Brise favoured loud Hawaiian knock off shirts, black Stubbies, and wore double plugger thongs on his feet. The silk hanky was an affectation, which didn't match the rest of the jalapeno-sweat laden package.

"So who's after me, and what do you want for the information?"

His eyes flicked to either side and he lifted his chin. In response, his bodyguards stepped away past the cactus barrier to give us some privacy.

Satisfied that they were far enough removed, his attention returned to me. "You've got a problem. The Crow and fuckeen Circle has put a bounty on your head, Ranger.

You pissed them off."

I tried to keep my expression composed. "And you know this…"

For the first time in any of our conversations he seemed truly pissed with me. "In the way I know any-fuckeen-thing. Because I am Papa Brise." He beat his chest with his fist.

I watched the display of ego and kept the same calm face.

His eyes narrowed at my lack of response. "You winding me up, Ranger? I tell you now, don't fuckeen wind me up. I'm doing you a solid fuckeen favour."

"*Why* are you doing me a solid?"

He leaned back, rested his hands on his belly and steepled his fingers. "I'm told you've had a career change and are working with the government now."

How could he…? "Oh, more than one government," I said lightly, while I gathered my startled thoughts.

"Like I said, Ranger, Papa Brise knows things."

"Only sociopaths talk about themselves in the third person," I snapped.

"Don't play for time, Ranger. You're real fuckeen bad at it."

"Not sure who your sources are, but you need some new ones. I work as a ranger for Park Central."

He let out his breath slowly like he was trying to be patient with a small, irritating child. "Tell you what. This Crow and fuckeen Circle are causing me problems too: taking my trade; preaching shit to the junkies on the street about sharing the same beliefs. You give me information on them from your 'ranger's' job, and I tell you how to find the person trying to kill you."

I stared at him for some long, soul searching moments. I had to be careful here. "If, for argument's sake, I did that, once I'd found the killer and dealt with him, they'd just hire another one to kill me, and my problem would still be the same. You'd have something, and I'd... most likely be dead."

He nodded sanguinely. "It is a fuckeen conundrum. But I'm giving you some time to deal with it. Without my information, you'll not likely be alive, *manana.*"

Hot acid squirted up into my gullet. "Who says?"

"You fuckeen doubt me, Ranger? How was your trip here?"

"Were you following me?" I demanded.

"This is my place. Of course I fuckeen know. You been hiding in a surplus store two blocks away, shitting your panties."

"You did nothing to help."

"We don't have a fuckeen deal yet. How much's your life worth to you, Ranger? Who's gonna watch over your precious park when you go? Not that fuckeen fat bastard boss of yours. Not Mr Fuckeen Stetson. He's got his own country to worry about. Your daddy left you a fuckeen job to do. How you gonna do it if you're fuckeen six feet under?"

I didn't know what rattled me more: his callous approach, or the fact that he knew so much about me. But I've always believed that attack was the best defence, so I took it at him.

"If I tell you anything unsanctioned, they will give me a lethal dose for treason," I said. "Any way you look at it, I'm in trouble. Could be though, if you tell me what's going on, then I can talk to them. They're watching Mystere real closely at the moment. Maybe they won't put you in jail when they come in to clean the place up?"

"You're fuckeen bluffing," he said.

I met his gaze without wavering. "I'm fuckeen not."

He rubbed his chin thoughtfully and squinted as though he was thinking. "Immunity, you say?"

"Maybe. I'd have to have that conversation. Recommend

it. Might be that I can come back to you with an answer real quick. Things are moving at a pace."

He rolled his eyes back in his head as if he was communing with spirits. My guess was that it was just for effect. Papa Brise loved to perform.

"You go back to your governments real quick and ask them what they can do for me. And, as a gesture of good fuckeen faith, I tell you right now that the man you want is waiting for you on the roof above Trick-Mart. He gonna whack you the moment you set foot back on Gilgul."

"How do you know that?"

"We heard they hired local, so we put a fuckeen tail on him."

"Why didn't he shoot me between the surplus stall and here then?"

"We distracted him. Gave you and me some time to speak."

"So you did help me," I said, feeling a little embarrassed about my hat and scarf disguise. "Deals don't get made with dead people, huh?"

"See, Ranger? You are fuckeen smart when you want to be."

"So what now? How do I get home without being shot?"

"I think you send your minder down to Trick-Mart. Do his business. You stay here and eat burritos and drink tequila with Papa Brise."

"What minder?"

"The one who kept you alive out in the junkland."

"What do you mean?"

"We expect you to come on the fuckeen buses. But no, no... you gotta come in through the waste. We only picked you up 'cos we had a tail on the shooters. Your minder kept you from a fuckeen sniper bullet." Papa Brise aimed his pistol at my head and mouthed the words, "Bam, bam!"

I tried to swallow over the dry patch in my throat.

Then I heard a soft grunt and Papa Brise suddenly doubled forwards onto the table. Hamish was squatting by his side, a semiauto pressed into his large belly, a hand on the back of the banger's head.

A dozen of Brise's men leapt to their feet and formed a ring around us. That sent some of the patrons into panic. Some strangled cries, there was the sound of a mini stampede, and the cantina emptied.

"Stand your men down, fat man. I'm just here to join the conversation," said Hamish softly.

Brise looked up at me, and I saw the fury in his face. He lifted his hand, waving his men back. They dropped to a safer distance, but kept their weapons out.

Hamish eased the tip of the semi away from Papa Brise's belly and pulled up a chair.

Papa Brise sat up, his complexion suffused with an unhealthy flush of magenta. He and Hamish glared at each other, and, into the heavy silence, my phone rang.

Hamish kept the semiauto low, aimed at the banger's balls. "Answer that, Ranger. Let the fat man take a moment to consider what comes next."

"No. It's fine–" I began.

"Answer it!" Hamish snapped.

I reached stiffly into my pocket, pulled out my cell phone and stuck it to my ear. "Yeah."

"Ms Jackson? Virgin?"

"Who's this?"

"Rav... I mean, Dr Namaditje."

"From the hospital? Is Mrs Shelby–"

"She's fine. Ready to come home tomorrow. Look, I

apologize for ringing at this hour, but I've just got off my shift and–"

Across from me Papa Brise reached for his napkin and Hamish shoved the semi back in his face. They looked fit to tear each other to bits.

"It's fine," I said, cutting him short. "What do you want?"

"I was wondering if you might be available to have dinner with me. The hospital... well, we have something we'd like to discuss with you. Informally, that is."

I pressed the speaker hard to my ear, hoping that none of the sound leaked out. I wanted to hang up on him, but Sixkiller's voice was in my head, urging me to take a date with the guy. "Fine, yes. When?"

He hesitated. "Are you sure, you don't seem–"

"I said fine. Now when?" I sounded harsh and annoyed, and I couldn't do a damn thing about that. Not with Hamish's finger on the trigger.

"H- How's tomorrow night, around 8pm? I c- can pick you up if you like?" he asked.

"No," I said. "Time is fine. I'll choose the place and let you know."

"OK, I'll see–"

I hung up before he got through.

"You done socializing, Ranger?" asked Papa Brise. "Your friend here's got some fuckeen attitude problems."

"Hamish saved our lives out in the park that day," I said, by way of defusing the situation.

I saw recognition light Papa Brise's eyes. "You had the fuckeen LSAT!"

Hamish nodded. "So we're good then?"

Papa Brise nodded and his chest began to rise and fall more evenly.

Hamish laid his semi down across his lap.

That went a long way to easing the tension. Brise's men slowly holstered their pieces and warily returned to their food. Someone cranked the music up and, within moments, the clientele had found their way back inside as if nothing had ever happened.

"What's your fuckeen problem anyway?" said Papa Brise to Hamish. "You could have just come in with her."

Hamish tilted his head in acknowledgment. "Then I wouldn't have seen where you hide those two guys up near the skylights, and how the bartender has a semi on the third shelf under the tablecloths. Always pays to see a man's firepower when you're in negotiations with him." He looked at me. "And I figure that you are."

Papa Brise's expression became grimmer.

"How much did you hear?" I asked Hamish.

"Enough to know that you got some good advice. You should order the nachos and tequila and get comfortable. I'll be back when it's safe for you to go home."

I stood up and stretched in a deliberate manner. I was tired, and this day had been too long, but I'd be damned if I'd let Hamish fight my battles. "I don't think so. But you're welcome to come with me."

Hamish gave me a look that was hard to read. "You going to let me do my work or not, Ranger?" he asked softly.

"Good fuckeen luck with that," Papa Brise grumbled.

"What you do or don't do is between you and your employer," I said.

Hamish's eyes got shiny with frustration. "I guess it is." He glanced at Papa Brise. "We'll use your roof exit."

It was a statement not a request.

Papa Brise looked at me. "We got a deal, Ranger?"

I nodded.

"Jorge will show you the way." Papa Brise slapped his thighs and stood up, showing surprising agility for a man his size. It didn't pay to underrate him, which is why the semi stayed in Hamish's hands, not pointing anywhere in particular, but still a warning and a precaution.

Jorge materialised next me. His long, wavy hair and pleasant smile belied the aggressive way he moved. All his tattoos were hidden under a denim jacket, except the dugite across the knuckles of his left hand. I tensed as he tugged my arm and beckoned.

Hamish lifted the nozzle of his rifle a fraction in response, and I frowned at him. We were almost out of here without an incident. Almost.

He saw my scowl and lowered the gun again, but his mouth was a thin line of suspicion.

"I'll call you," I said to Papa Brise.

"No," he said. "My boy Jorge will bring you another fuckeen phone tomorrow. It'll have a new number in it."

"Where will he leave it?"

"He will fuckeen find you."

I didn't like that idea at all. I'd been wondering for a while if Papa Brise had eyes on me all the time. This felt like an admission of the fact.

"He'd better not surprise me," I warned.

"Jorge can fuckeen handle himself, Ranger. He's blood, so don' you fuckeen worry."

I didn't push it any further, anxious now to get out of here. I shook my arm free from Jorge's grip and followed him through the swinging doors down the corridor beside the kitchen and up a set of scarred wooden stairs.

Hamish's boots were lighter on the wood behind me, but I

didn't look back at him.

Jorge led us to a small room which appeared to be kept for storage. He shifted a stack of boxes labelled tortillas and nacho chips and made a gap for us to climb through. On the other side of the wall of cartons, a metal ladder hung down from a manhole.

"Look up once you're inside. Another hatch will get you onto the roof."

I nodded. "Right."

He leered at me. "See you soon, Ranger."

"Don't sneak up on me, Jorge."

His smile got wider. I saw Papa Brise in the avaricious curve of his lips. He brushed my thigh as he put his hand on the ladder to steady it.

I climbed up quickly and crawled awkwardly into the ceiling space, taking care to stay on the joist. Hamish was right behind me, and we crouched together on a horizontal beam.

"There," I said, pointing. "You can see the outline. I'll open it."

"Wait," said Hamish. He slipped his knapsack around until it hung in front of him and unzipped it. With lightning quick hand movements he unclipped the cartridge belt from the semi and stripped the weapon back to the bare skeleton, tucking the pieces away in his pack. He then produced a scope and another barrel. He screwed the latter into the semi and clipped the scope atop. He tested it was secure with some quick twisting and shaking, then slipped a much smaller cartridge cupped by an adaptor into the magazine holder.

"What's that?" I whispered.

"Finesse," he said. "Let's go."

TEN

Not so long ago, I'd climbed pegs rammed into the outside wall of an old tenement in Moonee, to visit with a batshit-crazy spiritualist called Kadee Matari. That had been in daylight with a gun pointed at me. Adrenalin had got me through it: I didn't do heights well.

Here, now, though, on top of this rooftop just off Gilgul Street, in the middle of the night, I experienced a different kind of fear. The unknown.

Dark, jagged outlines stretched in either direction. The glow from the neons meant we could see well enough to walk and climb, but there were endless vantage points from which to shoot someone, and no cover for a person crawling in the open. If we approached the hitman from the wrong angle, we'd just be making his job easy. The only advantage we had was that he'd be focussed on me coming out from the cantina arcade.

"Trick-Mart is that way," I said, pointing to what my cell phone told me was north.

"Check it against your LiFo," said Hamish, who was

squinting at the light on his wristwatch.

"How do you know I've got a LiFo?"

He didn't bother to answer. "The map I've got doesn't show that archway."

I got my government issue device out of my pocket and pressed functions until found the sat maps.

"Let me see." Hamish took the LiFo and held it aloft as if comparing the map to the landscape. I caught a whiff of old-fashioned scented lemon soap.

"Trick-Mart is directly behind the arch," he said. "So I figure he's up on there somewhere."

"What are you thinking?" I said.

"One of us needs to flush him out. The other needs to be ready when he runs."

"How do you know he'll run?"

He lifted his shoulders a little. "Snipers don't like proximity. It's too personal."

"Are you speaking from experience?" I asked.

He ignored me. "You flush. I trap."

"You know it's downright rude to never answer a person's questions."

"There's a handrail along the top of the arch. Go carefully. He'll be somewhere where he can wedge himself."

"What should I do when I find him?"

"If he decides not to run, shoot him. Don't miss."

"I'm an officer of the law. I can't do that."

He shrugged again. "Then shoot yourself in the head now. It'll save us all time."

I narrowed my eyes. "I need him to tell me exactly who hired him," I said.

"Yes."

I didn't like the way he said that. As if he was humouring

me. "Alive, Hamish."

He took a slow breath. "Then I flush, you catch."

"Promise me you won't shoot him."

"I won't shoot him... dead."

I gave a little nod. It was the best I'd get. "Where should I go?"

He pointed. "He'll take the fire ladder into that alley. Go down and wait."

I studied the map. "OK. Have you got my phone number?"

Hamish shook his head. "Don't carry one. But your LiFo has a short wave frequency option. Find it and switch it to 65 hertz. I'll give you three short bursts of static, if he's coming your way."

"Primitive," I said.

"Effective."

He zipped his jacket, repositioned his pack, and slipped away over the peak of the roof onto the tiles below.

As soon as he'd gone, Aquila reappeared. She fluttered in from nowhere to perch on the edge of the roof, her silhouette lit by a pulsing pink dance club sign.

"You're back," I said, stating the obvious.

I climbed as quickly as I could over the tiles and corrugated iron sheeting to where she waited near the ladder. It was only two stories down – not like the precarious pegs I'd climbed recently at Moonee – but I had to talk hard to myself to put a foot onto it. I never quite felt in control of my limbs when I had to look down from a height. It did something to my brain that made me dizzy.

The ladder disappeared into the dimness of what looked like a blind alley, but when I reached the bottom, I realized that there was no alley at all, just a small rectangle of grubby pavers locked in by the back doors of a bunch of different premises: a little island of filthy space, littered with butts and used hypo patches. The back door space where folk came for some getting-high privacy.

Once down there, I used my phone torch again. I couldn't see anywhere to hide, which meant choosing a door. I studied them. Which one would offer my would-be assassin the escape route he wanted?

Three of them were badly damaged, graffitied and grimy. The fourth was lacquered red.

I looked for Aquila to give me a sign of some kind, but she was sitting right in the middle of the pavers, watching me.

"Terrific," I muttered, crossing the square and going up the two steps to the red door. Before I even touched the handle though, I heard the low thrum of music and smelled perfume. Three padlocks and an electric sensor eye deterred me from trying the handle.

Brothel.

I turned and went back to inspect the other three doors more closely, listening at each one. I heard voices behind two of them, and doubled back to the one that seemed silent. No padlock on the deadbolt. Just a grubby handle.

Call me fussy, but I pulled my sleeve down to cover my hand before I turned the knob slowly and gently. My other hand rested on my holster.

Behind me, Aquila made a deep clicking noise that I hoped was approval.

Nothing happened as I pushed it open. No one jumped out at me.

I peered in. The smell here said funeral parlour. This time of night, there was a good chance it would be empty except for the night porter. Every business in this part of the city had night security, whether it was human, animal, mechanical, or cyber. You never just locked up your joint in Mystere and went home.

Maybe my assailant had used bribery to pass through here. Or maybe something less savoury.

I hesitated. Once I stepped foot in there, I was breaking the law, and I was bound to report anything illegal that happened. Yet there was no cover anywhere else. If my guy came down here, the simple arc of a flashlight would show me waiting for him.

I weighed the options and their repercussions. If I didn't act, like Papa Brise said, I'd be dead tomorrow. The law wouldn't mean a lot to me then.

The place was chill with air conditioning and reeked of astringents. I was standing in a long corridor lit by a soft downlight. The doors dotted along it had brass plaques with letters engraved on them.

I stood and listened hard. From the other end, I caught the barest strains of music, as thin as if they were emanating from earphones. That meant that the night porter was human, and had probably been paid off by my hitman.

I opened the closest door. The room was full of boxes. Propping the door ajar with my Smith – no way I was getting trapped in this creepy place – I went inside and pulled on one of the cardboard flaps.

Urns. Packed tight like little soldiers. I pulled one free and tested its weight. Heavy enough. I scooped up my pistol, and stepped back out into the corridor.

Now to wait.

I took up a position against the wall behind the back door. It was cool and would have offered a quiet moment if my nose hadn't been full of the smell of burial chemicals, and my head hadn't been buzzing like a saw.

Papa Brise said it was the Korax behind the hit? But why chase me? How did *I* figure in their plans? Unless it was something to do with Dad's journals... I hadn't read every entry yet, but a large part of it so far was his bitterness-tinged philosophies on life.

Other sections were personal, usually about me, or my brother and his concerns for us as a parent. Never once did he mention Oceane Orlean, my mother. And yet, now that I'd met her, it felt like her presence wasn't far from him as he wrote. Maybe I was romancing, but it was as if he'd been writing the journals for her.

Maybe I should just hand them over to GJIC.

Maybe.

Or maybe I would wait a bit longer. Think a bit harder and–

The door handle clunked downwards and the door flung open.

I swung the urn about head height as a person ran through the door. It connected with an ugly thud and the figure collapsed.

The door at the opposite end opened, flooding the corridor with light, and a man with headphones pulled down around his neck and a baton in his hand appeared.

"Oi! Step away and drop the urn!" he shouted at me. He held his phone up to capture a photo of me and the scene.

"I wouldn't do that," said another, calmer, more convincing voice. Hamish stepped over the unconscious body. He aimed his kit rifle with its short butt and long, slender nozzle at the man's head.

The night porter froze.

"You take that photo and you're dead. You don't, and we forget we ever saw each other. No one knows you took a kickback to open the back door, and you keep your job,"

Hamish added in a deceptively mild tone. "Savvy?"

The headphones guy nodded slowly.

"Just slide your phone down the hall towards me, then turn and put your hands on the wall. High as you can reach. Face against the plaster."

As the guard complied, Hamish stooped to my would-be killer. "Lift!" he told me.

We dragged the body up the hallway, past the trembling night porter and out into the front parlour.

"Wait five minutes, lock the back door, and resume whatever you were doing," Hamish said over his shoulder.

I guessed the silence that followed meant that was exactly what he'd do.

The parlour lit every few seconds with a flash of neon. It gave me a glimpse of plastic wreaths and a wall dotted with brass handles.

The guy between us groaned.

Hamish took his full weight. "Check him for weapons."

I frisked him and came up with nothing. "He's clean."

"Try his collar and the hem of his pants."

I did as he told me and felt something. I glanced up at Hamish. The strobe of the neon wasn't flattering to his face. I hardly recognised him.

"Wires?" he asked.

"I guess so."

"There's a knife strapped to my ankle. Cut them out."

I knelt down, lifted his pants leg and removed the knife from its sheath, putting it to work on the hem. Three thin garrotting filaments dropped out on the floor. My stomach clenched. "I thought you said he didn't do close and personal."

"I'm not right about everything. Just most things. Take hold of him," Hamish replied.

He transferred the guy's weight to me, and I struggled to hold the man up now that my adrenalin was waning, while Hamish put his knife back, then rolled them up and tucked the filaments inside his pack.

"We need to get out of here."

"Sure." As we negotiated the front door, I glanced up and down the road trying to think of a place to take him. We were on the coast side of Gilgul, and even though it was after midnight, the crowds hadn't thinned much.

"There's a bunk hire place just across the road," I said, pointing.

Hamish saw the sign and nodded.

We staggered across the road as soon as the traffic got jammed up by the lights and couriers started honking. The bunk hire office was only about as wide as one of its beds. Hamish did the renting while I leaned the unconscious killer against the wall and held him up.

Hamish came out with a token, which got into the foyer. Fortunately, our crib was on the bottom floor.

"Hold him," he said again and went inside first.

I heard shuffling noises, and he emerged a moment later.

We lowered the guy onto the bottom of the bunk bed. With practised hands, Hamish ripped the disposable sheets into strips, plaited them, and tied the guy up.

Relieved of my burden, I shut the crib door and leaned back against it, panting and trembling. Hamish hadn't put the light on. Still, I could feel him looking up at me.

"You should go now," he said quietly.

"Why would I do that? I'm the one he's trying to kill," I said.

"He's not going to give up the name of his employer easily."

"What are you saying?"

"I'm saying you should go home."

Not liking what he was implying, I peered at him. "Is torture in the GJIC brief?"

"Don't be dramatic, Ranger. I'll just detain him here until he's picked up for questioning."

"GJIC want to do that? But this is my personal problem."

He shrugged. "I have to make sure that you're safe. Seems you're more valuable alive."

"How long before they come? You've got no food or water."

"There's a coin snack slot above the basin. I can go out briefly if I need. He's secure."

I couldn't think of anything else to say. I was suddenly desperate for a shower and some sleep. "I should go home then?"

"Yes." He stepped over to the door and tapped in the unlock key. It meant that we were uncomfortably close. When he was done, he just stood there.

"I'll have to squeeze past," I said.

As I did, my chest brushed his.

He grabbed my arm and held me there. His expression stayed stony, and his body felt cool, but rigid. I had my first awareness of him as a man. It brought a rush of butterflies to my stomach. Hamish was dangerous – a sociopath. Being this close to him was like gently sliding a sharp blade against your skin. The temptation to slip and draw blood grew by the second.

"Th- thanks," I said, to break the silence. "For tonight."

He didn't reply, but he let go of me.

I stepped out into the corridor, and took a deep breath, before continuing on. My last glimpse back at Hamish showed him in the same spot staring straight ahead.

•••

I got to bed just before dawn, after sending Sixkiller a message through my LiFo that said I'd see him around mid-afternoon. But dreams kept me tossing and when I finally dozed and woke, it was midmorning.

Uggh!

I rolled over and tried to go back to sleep, but within moments my mind was sharpened into wakefulness by a torrent of questions. How was Hamish? Had GJIC come and taken my hit man from Hamish? Had they found out who was behind it?

I sat up and the questions kept on coming.

Why were Johnny and Corah hanging around Professor Dusan? Where would Dad hide the video data from Los Tribos? And how was Caro?

My LiFo beeped and the display told me that Sixkiller was calling me. I ignored it and climbed out of bed to have a shower. Hot water, fresh clothes and some vegemite and toast later, I was pouring over Dad's journal, trying to get a hint of where he might have hidden the footage. Or if he had! The chances were good that it had been lost or corrupted, or that it still existed, but revealed nothing other than the wind blowing sand around.

I picked back up at the journal thread where he'd mentioned he thought Los Tribos was being used for human trafficking, and reread right through to the end. He'd planned to take leave to run surveillance on the Los Tribos area, but his former colleague and newly appointed boss Bull Hunt hadn't approved it.

Maybe I should talk to Bull? Dad might have mentioned something to him. Before he became Dad's boss, they'd been rangers together. Their friendship went back before I was born.

I exited the journal and opened the index file of his essays. I'd read the one on global mythology that GJIC seemed to think might have become the mantra for the Korax. He'd published that online years ago. Dad's idea had been to use global mythologies as a way of solving the divisions in society. Somehow I didn't think that the Korax had the same agenda. And how exactly were they connected with the Mythos, I wondered? Did the Mythos control them in some way? Or were the humans gifted with being able to see the Mythos like Sixkiller and I, and had chosen to help them?

My LiFo contained only general information about their origins. Either GJIC didn't know a lot, or I was too low on the food chain to be privy to more detail. I didn't like only having selective access to information. I especially didn't like having to clear everything with the Marshal.

But I was stuck with that situation unless I could solve the murder in the park to Detective Chance and Aus-Police's satisfaction. GJIC were the ones who'd quashed the charge against me, but if I didn't continue to help them, it would just be reinstated.

But how do you prove that a creature that doesn't exist murdered a guy in front of you?

More fundamentally though... why were GJIC using me? What did I have that they needed? Was it just Dad's journals? Or my knowledge of the park? I mean, I knew it intimately, the way Dad had. But sending me to Branch Holy to investigate Professor Dusan... that just didn't make sense.

I went back to browsing Dad's essays to avoid the headache that worrying about my predicament was bringing on. An earlier one caught my attention, and I skimmed through it. He had a particularly clipped way of writing, a reflection of his nature. Dad was a man who got to the point, but with a kind of sparse elegance. I could hear his voice in his words, and it set off stinging needles of tears behind my eyelids.

According to this particular essay, he saw the fundamental roadblock to global mythologies lay in the inequality of wealth. I'd never realized – until that moment – that he was a socialist. He'd always been anti-capitalism, but I figured him to have believed in his own brand of free enterprise.

I got up to make a coffee and disturbed Trip whose tail and butt were just visible under the couch. The cat made an ugly rowwwwling sound and disappeared. It reminded me that his kitty litter needed changing. Fortunately, my personal phone rang and gave me an excuse to put it off. "Yes."

"Dear?"

"Esther?"

"I'm so sorry to trouble you, dear, but *could* you help me get home? The ambulance fee is totally ridiculous and, well, you know my family are a long way away and I simply don't trust taxis. So many germs, you know–"

"Of course I will, Esther," I said.

"–and nice Dr Nam won't let me out unaccompanied. You know, dear, that's the trouble when you live too long... all your friends get old, and they can't help you either."

An image of Caro and me as old women together flashed into my head. No guesses as to who the crotchety one would be. "Sit tight. I'll be there soon."

"Oh, you are such a sport, dear."

"Actually, I think Trip needs you," I said.

I hung up, thought for a moment, then rang Jessie.

She answered almost immediately. "Ms Jackson."

"Call me Virgin, please. Are you free?"

"Where would you like to go?"

"The Cloisters to the hospital and back."

"I'll be there shortly. I'll call you when I'm downstairs."

"Thanks. And Jessie? Don't tell the Marshal."

"I... um... of course, Ms Jackson. You got it. Although they do track my GPS."

"Of course they do." I shoved my cell phone and the LiFo into my jeans pockets and raided the fridge. There was some jasmine rice and a dribble of Korma sauce in a plastic container left from Caro's last visit. I mixed them together, microzapped them and grabbed a spare plastic fork from the cutlery mug. Gourmet delight in hand, I headed downstairs to wait for Jessie.

Esther was sitting at the nurse's station when I got there, and thankfully Dr Namaditje was nowhere in sight. She'd already taken care of discharge, so, once they were satisfied they were releasing her into an adult's care, I was able to help her out to the limo.

Jessie was standing, waiting, with the door open.

"Hello, young lady," said Esther, as Jessie helped her inside. "Are you Virgin's chauffeur? I knew she was important."

Jessie bit her cheek, winked at me and said. "Yes indeed, ma'am. I am. Where would you like to go?"

Esther's face glowed with anticipation. "The Cloisters, dearie. I want to see my cat."

"Quick as I can, ma'am," said Jessie, with a respectful salute.

We exchanged glances and grins as she closed the door.

"I really can't abide hospitals," said Esther, as the car picked up speed. "But I'm so glad I went there."

"Why's that?" I asked.

"Because you got to meet that young man. He tells me you're going on a dinner date tonight."

I felt a flush heat my cheeks. "Dinner doesn't always mean

a date, Esther. He said the hospital wished to talk to me about something."

"What about, dear?"

"I'm not really sure," I said vaguely. "I have... unusual blood."

"Well, that doesn't mean you can't wear something nice."

I glanced at her. Her complexion was pale still, but her eyes were bright, and I sensed her excitement to be going home. "I suppose not," I said.

"Good. That's settled. You can come by later on and show me."

"Only if you promise to take Trip home with you."

"Still not on speaking terms?" she asked.

"No," I said. "But he loves the Marshal. And my friend Caro."

"You just need to work a little harder on smiling, dear. Cats do like grinners."

"The Marshal's not a grinner."

"Oh no, dear. He doesn't need to be, he's just charismatic."

I glanced up into Jessie's rear vision mirror, but she wasn't smiling as I expected. She looked troubled.

Her expression filled me with apprehension. Something was wrong. I glanced out of the windows, but I couldn't see any visible threat. And Aquila hadn't appeared. Maybe Sixkiller was in trouble? I suddenly felt guilty that I hadn't returned his call, and that I'd told Jessie not to tell him that I'd requested the car. Or maybe I was imagining Jessie's tension. I turned my attention back to Esther and kept it there until we pulled into the Cloisters drive-through zone.

"Thanks, Jessie," I said, as I helped Esther out.

"You going out again soon?" Jessie asked.

I leaned back in to speak to her. "Yes, probably. Why?"

"I think it would be safer if I waited for you."

"Is something up?"

"No more than usual," she said. "But you're my priority. Better to be safe… I'll be parked around the corner."

"Thanks."

She cleared her throat as though she wanted to say something more.

"Jessie?"

"It's not my place but I… er… just thought you should know… that the Marshal… well, he's got a good reputation in our business," she said quietly. "You can count on him."

"Thanks, Jessie," I said. "I appreciate what you're saying to me. I'm just not the best candidate for being told what to do."

"I understand." She gave a bright smile, relieved that I hadn't taken offence.

"Right. Well, give me time to settle Esther, and I'll be back," I said.

"Don't hurry. I've got these." Her smile widened and she pressed a button on the dashboard which engaged the window shading, and a blinking priority parking sign in a strip along the sides and boot of the car.

"Handy. Now go catch forty winks," I said. "I won't tell a soul."

ELEVEN

I opened the door to my apartment and ushered Esther in.

"Puss puss," Esther crooned.

At the sound of his owner's voice Trip catapulted out from under the couch and rubbed up against Esther's legs. He cast me a haughty look, as if to say he'd well and truly had enough of me, and trotted out of the open door.

I collected the kitty litter and the food and transferred it and Esther back to her flat.

Trip headed straight for his favoured windowsill perch and never looked at me again.

Esther took my hand and patted it. "Never mind, dear. It takes time with some people."

I didn't know whether I was more relieved to be rid of the cat, or annoyed that he hated me. I settled for squeezing Esther's hand. "Do you need anything?"

"I'm fine, dear. I'll get some groceries delivered. But don't be a stranger now. I do want to see you all dressed up for your date."

"It's not a date, so don't get your hopes up," I said

and waved goodbye.

In the lift on the way down, I got my LiFo out to call Sixkiller. As I did, I noticed a new document had been dropped into my file manager. It had a numerical name, which meant nothing to me. I opened and scanned through it quickly. It was a list of Mythos sightings. The graphs showed an increase of seventy percent globally.

I could see why my mother was all bent out of shape about doing something to stop them. What I didn't really understand is what they thought I could do. I'd already proved my complete impotency with the Pocong in my hallway.

I headed out of the building, glancing around out of habit. Sure enough, Detective Chance was leaning against the bus stop half a block to the east. She didn't bother to try to hide. In fact, she began to walk towards me.

I turned west and hurried around the corner looking for the limo. Jessie had pulled up a little way down in a loading zone.

The Mythos activity map on my LiFo made a tiny pinging noise as it updated. I glanced down at the screen as I opened the back door and slid in. The hotspots had updated: one in the park, and another at Branch Holy University.

"Jessie, do you know where the Marshal is?"

She didn't answer me, and I glanced up. Had she dozed off after all?

Then I noticed the stillness of her body.

The partition was shut, so I jumped out of the car, ran around to the driver's side, and reefed the door open. Her head lay back on the headrest in an awkward position and her throat was gashed open, as if someone or something with sharp claws had just torn it out. I could see the pearly colour of her backbone through the gash. Her body and the seat were wet with blood.

"Jessie!" I fell back, gasping. Shocked.

"Virgin Jackson! Step away from the car," called Detective Chance. She was standing at the corner – barely a minute's walk away from the car – with her pistol drawn.

My first thought was to call her over. She was police; she would know what to do.

But a deeper survival instinct kicked in. I saw an alternative scenario unravelling: Chance taking me in on suspicion of murder, bail being denied while she tried to pin it on me, and GJIC cutting their losses.

I made an instant decision and ran with it.

It meant unclipping Jessie's seatbelt and pushing her body across into the next seat.

"Jackson!" bellowed Chance.

She began to run towards me as I fell into the bloodstained driver's seat, hit the starter button, and hauled the door closed.

The windows were dimmed. Chance couldn't see in now, but the car used DNA recognition ignition. It wouldn't start.

Vomit climbed the back of my throat as I grabbed one of Jessie's lifeless hands and held her fingers to the wheel.

I heard the soft click of the locking mechanism, and the car started just as Chance grabbed at the door handle. I rode the accelerator hard, and she jumped back to avoid being hit.

The car fishtailed out into the traffic. Another glance to the rear view mirror told me she was on her phone, calling the licence plate in.

I took three right turns to get back onto the Parkway, but then I had no idea where I was going. The only thing I could think of was that I was sitting in warm blood. And steering the car with a dead woman's hand.

TWELVE

Somewhere along the Ring Road heading west, the in-car phone blared at me. I clicked 'answer' from the steering wheel control.

"Jessie?" said a voice into the silence.

Sixkiller. Relief helped me find my voice. "Nate?"

"Virgin?"

"I need help."

"What's wrong?"

"J- Jessie's dead. Someone's... they... Nate... they slit her throat."

"Where are yer?"

"I'm on the Ring Road. Detective Chance was following me. She saw me at the car. I knew she'd think I'd done it, so I just got in the car and drove."

He didn't answer for a moment. Then he said, "How can yer be driving? It's biosecured to Jessie's..."

"I'm holding her hand on the wheel," I whispered.

He swore almost as softly, then said, "I'm sending yer an address. Just touch it to accept and the GPS will lead yer straight there. Don't stop anywhere."

"What is it?"

"It's a safe house. I'll meet yer and we'll deal with this."

"Just you?"

"Yeah."

"Promise me?"

"Yeah. Now see the tab below the radio transceiver."

"Blue one or black one?"

"The black one. Press it and it'll change the number plate. That will also buy yer some time."

I fumbled with the tab and heard a tiny whirr. "Got it."

"And Virgin…"

"Yes?"

"Jessie… her death… was it a human?"

I couldn't bring myself to look across at her body. Her fingers were still warm and the smell of her blood was making it hard to think.

"Probably not. Please send the address," I said and clicked off.

It flashed up on the dashboard screen a few seconds later. I unclenched the fingers on my right hand from the wheel and reached across to press accept. The GPS rerouted and started giving me instructions. Its flat, measured tones calmed me. I just had to get to Sixkiller before I started to think about Jessie. Before I unravelled.

Concentrate on driving. Steer. Accelerate. Brake. Repeat.

The new route took me into the Downtown Lakes area among embassy buildings and smart bars.

My left hand – the one holding Jessie's to the wheel – began to tire. Her skin was slippery with blood, and her fingers were only thin, making them hard to keep in my grasp. Once or twice I nearly let go.

I knew I couldn't hold her hand up much longer. The weight of her arm was one thing, but the idea of what I was doing was worse. It screamed at me to stop.

An Aus-Pol convoy – four sedans and a Hummer – drove past heading the other way, sending me to new heights of panic. Had they recognised the car?

By the time the GPS directed me to the next offramp, I was shaking uncontrollably. I took a series of right hand turns, until I was in the middle of a street of bright, umbrella-flapping cafés.

My destination was a laneway behind this strip, and a lockup villa with a steep driveway and a roller door at the top.

As I surged up the driveway the door slid open.

I drove straight into the garage and hit the brakes just short of the wall. It wasn't until the door closed behind me and Nate Sixkiller opened the passenger door that I let go of Jessie's hand.

I leaned back so that Sixkiller could see in. His face became still. Only his eyes seemed to have life in them, and they glittered.

"I didn't do it, Nate," I said hoarsely. "I would never... I could never... I'm sorry I ran, but Chance would have... put me straight in jail." I could feel the tears coming. When they started, I wasn't going to be able to stop them. My teeth began to chatter. Whatever else I'd intended to say to him was lost.

He stepped away, rummaged inside a kitbag on a narrow workbench, and pulled out a towel.

"Yer did the right thing. This is not something for Aus-Pol. We handle these things in-house."

I still couldn't answer, but I was glad he wasn't yelling at me.

"Now, Virgin, I'm goin' ta put this towel around yer and

help yer out. Then I'm goin' ta sit yer down and wash the blood off yer face and hands. Yer need to have some glucose for the shock. It's in a tube. Yer just need to suck on it. Do yer understand me?"

I nodded. Why did he sound like he'd fallen down a well?

With surprising gentleness, he draped the towel around my shoulders and helped me from the car. My legs buckled as soon as I tried to stand, but he held me tight and steered me through the garage to a bathroom.

I sat on the edge of the bath and shivered. Without warning, I turned and vomited all over the white porcelain.

He stopped me from overbalancing while I heaved and heaved. When I'd finished, he turned the taps on. Then he took a wash cloth from the rail and, even more gently, sponged me down.

I wanted to thank him, but I really didn't know how to make my tongue and mouth work together anymore. I started to cry in a passive kind of way. The only thing moving was my shoulders. They shook every now and then, as I felt waves of nausea peak and pass.

He left washing my face until last, dabbing and rinsing my arms and neck first.

Dabbing.

Rinsing.

"I'm going to wipe yer face now," he said quietly. "It's OK if yer keep crying."

My shoulders heaved even more at his kindness, and the tears fell faster. The flannel felt cool and rough on my face. I wanted to lean forwards and lay my head against his head for comfort. I needed his arms around me.

"Virgin, yer must take a shower, but in order to do that yer gotta have some of the glucose. The sugar'll help with the shock. I'm goin' to move yer to the chair and give yer a tube to suck on. While yer doing that, I have to make some calls."

I nodded and sucked in a breath.

He helped me across to the chair and pressed the tube into my mouth. "Slowly, mind."

Another nod.

He left me then, and I immediately wished he would come back. I didn't want to be alone. Even if he was in the next room.

What had he said to me? *Suck the glucose. Sit. Wait. Recover.*

I held the tube to my mouth and squeezed. My hands trembled so badly that I missed and squirted the liquid across my cheek. I licked around my lips and tried again. This time I felt the rush of sweetness to my mouth and almost as quickly into my limbs.

My hands steadied, and I reached down to touch my gun.

It was gone.

I squeezed in some more goo and took a couple of deep breaths. Sixkiller was in the garage, speaking to someone. I wanted to know who, and where my pistol had gone. Had I somehow dropped it in the car? I didn't remember unholstering it.

I got to my feet, unsteady but able to walk, and shuffled over to the door.

"...shock. No, I don't think so. Yer should send someone. Aus-Pol will be on alert," I heard him say.

He glanced around and saw me at the door. In the same instant, I saw that he had my pistol in his other hand.

"Give me my piece," I said.

"Excuse me, ma'am. Yeah, soon," he said into his LiFo and hung up. "Yer should be showerin' and restin'," he said to me.

"I can't rest until I have my piece back."

He hesitated. I saw the flash of doubt in his eyes – wondering if maybe I had killed Jessie.

I gave him a moment to decide, knowing somewhere deep inside me that how things went between us from now on was about to be defined. He trusted me. Or he didn't. I wasn't going to try to influence him either way.

His eyes narrowed so much, I could barely see them. His face was as stern as I'd ever seen it.

He held out the gun.

I made it over to him without wobbling, but as I holstered the Smith & Wesson, my knees buckled.

He caught me before I hit the deck and hauled me upright.

"Yer need to rest until your body deals with the shock. There's a downstairs bedroom. The shower c'n come later."

He was right. I needed to lie down.

"W- what about J- Jessie?" I asked.

"I'll look after her," he said. "GJIC is sendin' someone over to take her home. Clean up the car."

"My m- mother?"

He nodded. "Jessie's murder's an escalation."

"Definitely n- not a random killing?"

"No. Her throat was clawed out."

The world receded a little when he said that, slow dots forming across my vision. I shook my head and they settled. It was important I heard what he had to say.

"So the Mythos killed her?" I whispered.

"To be confirmed," he said.

"But you think so?"

"Yeah."

"The graphs I got sent today shows that their presence is increasing," I said.

"At a rate we ain't seen before. 'Specially in this location."

"What does that mean?"

"It means yer need to recover. When yer rested, we'll talk more. Let's go."

I let him help me to the bedroom.

"There's a robe behind the door. It might be more comfortable in thet than yer clothes."

I looked down. My hands and arms were clean, but my shirt was dark with Jessie's blood.

I nodded.

He left me again.

I shut the door, stripped off my jeans and shirt and donned the robe. The bed was single, and not terribly wide. I lay down on my back but nausea welled up, so I rolled over onto my stomach.

Jessie. Poor Jessie...

"Virgin. I've made yer some dinner."

I rolled over, confused and drymouthed. A squint from under my eyelids told me that Marshal Sixkiller was standing over me with a tray.

A tray? Why was he bringing me food?

Then the memory of where I was, and what had brought me there, flooded in. I sat upright and clutched my head as the room spun.

"Easy. Yer've been asleep for a while," he said.

"How long?"

"Twenty-six hours. We had a medic take a look at yer and administer a sedative."

"I don't remember that."

"You were screamin' in your sleep. I figured thet you needed somethin' to settle."

I blinked and looked around. The room was narrow and

the bed was hard. There was nothing on the walls. No other furniture. Yet I had a vague memory of pine drawers.

"Did you take the drawers away?"

"No. You broke 'em."

"How did I...?"

"Look at yer hands."

I did. They were bruised and cut and, now that my mind was beginning to clear, I realized that they were sore. "Why don't I remember?"

"You were kind of dreaming, I think."

I felt the warm flush of embarrassment. "I'm- I'm–"

He held out the tray. "Yer just saw someone yer know with their throat ripped out. Yer entitled to scream."

I took it and balanced it on my knee, proud that my hands were still. "You knew Jessie better than me. How are you dealing with it?"

He looped a stray strand of long dark hair behind his ear. It drew my attention to the slight puffiness under his eyes. For a man who never looked tired, he had me wondering how long it was since he'd last slept.

"I've been huntin' the Mythos a long time," he replied.

"You saying you're immune to this kind of violence?"

"I'm sayin' I'm prepared. Focused. Bad days are comin', Virgin. More people will suffer like Jessie if we don't do our job."

"B- bad days?"

"Eat. Yer clothes are clean. I'll be waitin' for you."

I followed his hand gesture and saw my jeans and shirt laid out on the end of the bed. I glanced down at my chest and saw that I was wearing an oversized tee. Had he taken the robe off me? The idea made me uncomfortable. I wasn't embarrassed about my body, but I was very particular about who saw me naked.

"Nate?"

"Yeah."

"Thanks. I mean, without you…"

"Partners do fer each other, Virgin. Thet's the way of it."

"I'm starting to learn."

He nodded and left, and I chewed slowly through a bagel and some crisp bacon, wetting my mouth frequently with apple juice from a carton. At first my stomach recoiled from the food, but by the time the bacon hit the bread it was beginning to change its mind. When I'd cleaned everything from the plate and drunk the rest of the juice, I got dressed quickly and joined him in the kitchen.

The rest of the apartment was as dark and as sparsely furnished as the bedroom; windows were shuttered with what looked like wood, but I'd lay bets was actually bulletproof plastic. Stools sat snug under the breakfast bar and joined a bench with only a microwave and cook top – no oven. Not the kind of place you baked a Sunday roast for the family.

Sixkiller took my tray and began methodically washing the plates and putting them away.

"GJIC doesn't stretch to a dishwasher?" I asked mildly to break the silence.

"Sometimes yer leave these places in a hurry. The next person mightn't be in for days. Not courteous to leave 'em with the dirty plates. Besides, in our line of work, yer learn to not leave a footprint," he said.

"Right." I approved of that notion. It was like being in the park; only this was more about being invisible, not protecting the ecology.

He finished washing, dried up, and put away. Then he turned to me. He looked perfectly at home leaning against the sink, arms folded, hair loose and wearing jeans and a tee.

The contradictions in his personality really struck me: so urbane and refined – even delicate – at times, and so cowboy and bombastic at others. I'd always put the schism down to the contrast between his upbringing and his education. Maybe it wasn't that simple.

I noticed my LiFo on the bench next to his, charging, and my backpack hanging on the back of one of the stools. "This place comes complete with spare chargers?"

"*This place* comes complete with a bunch of useful things, if yer know where to look for them."

I frowned, wondering what he meant.

"Regard," he said, and reached behind the fridge.

He pulled the cooling coils aside, slid out a whole false back and swung it around. A range of unusual weapons were strapped in there underneath a transparent film.

"The film insulates 'em from the heat of the motor." He selected a short paddle and removed it from its slot. "Keep this. It works as a repellent on the Mythos. Enough to buy yer a few seconds, sometimes minutes, dependin' on their strength."

"What do I do with it?"

"Swing it like a baton."

I took it and examined it. It was light and unremarkable.

"Thanks. What's that?" I pointed to an innocuous looking black box secreted behind vacuum packing.

"Thet's not to be touched. It's an ionic gradient disruptor – works on about a twenty-feet circumference, disruptin' the ionic composition of the air. The Mythos don't do well when that happens. But neither do humans."

"Why is it here if you can't use it yet?"

"Every safe house has one, in case it's compromised. Yer

just turn it on and it'll disperse everything within its reach."

"Disperse?"

"Instant cellular death."

"Can't you set it off remotely?"

"We've tried that, but the thing is…" He hesitated, looking a bit sheepish.

"What?"

"We can't locate the Mythos unless we're with 'em."

"You mean you can't detect them unless you see them?"

"They leave a signature when they enter our world, but by the time we register it, they've usually moved on."

"So the hotspots on the map are signatures?"

"Signatures and sightings combined. Open the latest file on yer LiFo. Go into yer settings, choose *projection* then aim it at the fridge."

I did as he suggested and the data map came alive on the white door of the refrigerator. The hotspots I'd been looking at previously seemed denser.

"Branch Holy," I said, pointing. "Plenty going on."

"Yeah. We've got some people working undercover there. They're seein' lots of activity."

"If you've got people there already, then why did you send me in? I'm hardly experienced."

"Intel comes in all sorts of forms, and in all sorts of ways."

"You're being evasive," I said.

"I don't know the answer to everythin', Virgin."

"Nate, you keep telling me how long you've been doing this."

"I still follow orders."

His obtuseness gave me a sudden headache.

Then I had a flash of insight. "Wait… of course! It's my brother, isn't it? Johnny and Corah? GJIC wanted me to see them. Or more to the point… wanted them to see me."

He inclined his head. "If you mean yer brother and the psychic from Mystere… well, I guess it's possible. But why exactly, I honestly don' know."

"What *do* you know then? And what did you want to tell me?"

"I wanted yer to know that we put some surveillance on Professor Dusan's assistant after yer reaction to her."

"And?"

"We think that she might be an Empusa."

"Is that a Mythos?"

He nodded. "The most dangerous kind."

"I thought they were all dangerous."

"Yeah. But the Empusa have the power to influence the way people think."

"I've seen their name in the *Vade Mecum*, but I can't remember the details," I said, scratching my chin.

"In Greek folklore they're known as *demon vampires*, a damn lethal crossbreed of mythological creature. They're said ter be able to kill men with their beauty. That's *horse-wang*, o' course, but they can influence thought. Yer said yer noticed her limpin'?"

I blinked. "Yes."

"In the incarnation of Empusa, the demon has a bronze leg. It's also said she has a donkey's foot, but we've never been close enough ter one ter confirm that."

"Is the fact that there's an Empusa here significant?"

"Probably. Confirmed demon sightin's are rare. There've only been ten of 'em previous."

"But what does that mean?" I seemed to be stuck on that question.

"Like I said… an escalation o' some kind."

I stared at him. "A bronze leg and a donkey foot. Really?"

He shrugged. "Stories exaggerate. Could just be a club foot."

"You said vampire as well?"

"They inject their victims with a toxin thet causes sleep paralysis. Few years ago, we found a nest o' human bodies – husks, is all – in a cave in Colorado. They'd been put to sleep and fed on by an Empusa, we think. She'd drained 'em dry, but we never caught her. Their skin was like dry leaves. Crumbled with vibration of discovery. I swear I inhaled a good bit of them."

I tried to blank that image from my brain. "How *do* you catch a demon?"

He gave me a funny look. "We don't know because we ain't done it. But we think thet people like you and I – spirit-assisted – have a better resistance to the Empusa's mind influence."

"You mean Aquila stopped her from hypnotizing me at Branch?"

"Not Aquila, but the fact that yer *have* a guide means yer have a similarity to 'other' and are less susceptible."

I thought about it for a moment or two. "Are we – you and I – some kind of hybrid Mythos then?"

"Guess it's possible. I dunno. GJIC don't either. Somehow, we're connected to them. Or they to us."

"So I'm not human? And you aren't human either." I had to say the words out loud. Get them out there, so I could refute them.

"I like to see it as a version of human."

"But are we born like that? Have we been altered? How can such a thing happen? What...? How can...?"

He raised his hand to stop me piling on the questions. "I don't have all the answers yer need and right now we don't have time to spend on speculation. Virgin, yer need to get yer head straight."

I let his last comment hang for a bit before I answered. Then I said, "What do you want me to do?"

"Yer brother and the psychic might know what Dusan's plannin'."

"I'm not exactly on their list of confidantes."

"Investigation takes different forms, Virgin."

"You saying you want me to follow them?"

"Do whatever yer have to, to find out what's goin' on. Just trust yer instincts. Yer also need to reschedule yer dinner date night as well."

"What dinner? Oh shi-it…!" I slapped my forehead lightly. "The doctor. That was supposed to be last night."

"I called the hospital last night and left a message that yer had to go out of town unexpectedly."

"Y- you did? How did you even know that I…" I rolled my eyes. "Never mind. Why is it so important that I go out with him?"

"Knowing who's with us and who's against us is critical at this stage. Might be thet the hospital's just curious or thet they're working with the Korax."

"Fine. I'll make some calls," I said.

"I'll give yer a ride back home. Yer can do it on the way. Just give me a few minutes to pack my gear."

"But the car?"

"It's been detailed overnight."

"OK." I picked at my fingernails before I spoke again, not wanting to go anywhere in the same vehicle. "Nate?"

"Yeah?"

"Will Jessie have a funeral?"

He looped his hair over his ear and gave me a steady look.

"I'll let yer know. It'll depend on her relatives and what they want."

I nodded. "Do you think there'll be a problem with Detective Chance?"

"Yer said she didn't see in the car."

"No."

He took a step towards me and laid his hand on my shoulder. "Yer did the right thing, Virgin. Yer instincts are good. Listen to 'em."

It was the closest thing to a compliment that he'd ever given me. "Is that what you do?" I asked.

My question elicited a proper grin.

"All the time." He winked at me and left the kitchen.

I stood still for a moment, listening to him shifting around in one of the bedrooms, my mind caught between the dull fogginess of the sedatives and the sharp presence of fear. I'd been so close to Cyndia. So close to death. Only Aquila's warning had interrupted whatever she had planned to do to me.

I didn't like having to rely on my disincarnate for warnings. It made me feel vulnerable. And yet I was grateful.

On impulse, I walked over to the fridge and slid the false back out. The heat protection film came off easily, and I peeled open the vacuum pack around the black box. I'd rather go out on my terms with disrupted ions, than be sucked bloodless by a Mythos. My terms.

I closed the back panel, stuffed both weapons into my backpack and shrugged it over my shoulders. GJIC were perfectly comfortable putting me in harm's way, but hadn't seen fit to arm me with much protection. If there was one thing Dad had taught me, it was about self-preservation. I knew how to look after myself.

THIRTEEN

We had a new driver, who introduced himself as Frost. On the drive back, Sixkiller had made polite conversation with him, but I couldn't find anything to say. Every time my glance grazed the steering wheel, I remembered the drive: Jessie bloody and dead on the seat next to me.

Several times, I caught myself wanting to get out of the car at traffic lights, and had to relax my bunched muscles. If Sixkiller noticed my restlessness, he didn't say.

By the time the Cloisters' skyline came into frame, I'd fought my way through the worst of the panic.

It left me with a strange but strengthening resolve.

GJIC might have forced me into this job, but any creature that could inflict such atrocity on another being had to be stopped.

It was that simple.

I settled a little when I'd made that decision. But as the car drew into the Cloisters bay, Detective Chance and a uniformed copper were waiting for me. It almost set me off into a fit of trembling.

Nate put his hand on my arm. "Stay cool. She saw nothing."

I nodded, grateful for his equanimity, and got out.

Chance fronted straight up and didn't waste any time in stating her case. "Ms Jackson, yesterday you refused a direct request from me to stop and be questioned. What were you hiding? Where have you been overnight? We've had people on your building and you did not return."

I stared at her blankly. Why was this woman so determined to see me in prison? Her obsession didn't make sense to me. I'd eluded prosecution on the murder charge, but then I *was* innocent. I reminded myself of that.

"I- I was in a hurry yesterday, and I saw no reason to stop," I said.

Sixkiller got out of the car and stalked around to join our tête-à-tête. "Detective Chance, as yer know, Ms Jackson's workin' for GJIC and is held accountable to international law standards. Her murder case has been dismissed and she's now a free citizen. If yer continue this harassment, *there'll be unpleasant consequences.*"

Chance gripped her holster so tightly that I thought the bullets might just squeeze right on out of the barrel. The dark rings under her eyes grew puffy with indignation. "You saying she's not *accountable* to her own country's law, Marshal?"

He glared harder at her. So hard, *my* eyes watered.

"I'm saying thet vendettas aren't good practice fer any lawman," he said.

To her credit, Indira Chance didn't flinch under his paint-peeling stare, but she did turn her attention back to me. "I know you were hiding something in that car. I'll find out what, and, when your protection is gone, I'll be waiting for you."

She let her hand fall from her holster and swept Sixkiller

and me with a fierce parting glance.

"The detective's got some serious beef with yer," said Sixkiller, when she was out of earshot.

"I don't understand it quite," I said.

"And we don't need the extra problem right now. Maybe I can get her reassigned?"

"No!" I said. "It'll just fuel her."

He shrugged. "Then yer need to be careful. She arrests you a second time on anythin', there might be no coming back from it."

I turned and walked into the foyer, leaving him to follow. Sixkiller had just helped me through something horrible, cared for me even, but I had to spend some time alone.

We rode the lift together, at first in silence, and then I remembered something. "Why did you send Hamish Burns to watch over me?"

He raised his eyebrows. "Hamish Burns?"

"Caro's... friend. The guy who helped me out in the park... when they kidnapped you."

"Why would I do thet? The man's a psychopath. I had him checked out. Discharged from the secret service on medical grounds. Have you seen him?"

The floor beneath me suddenly felt unstable. Hamish had lied to me. "I er... thought I saw him following me when I left Branch Holy last night."

"And?"

"And nothing... I figured maybe you'd hired him as a bodyguard. You know, because you were busy..."

"Well, thet's a lamebrained idea. Where *exactly* did yer see him?"

"Near the bus stop outside the bar. But I could've been wrong."

"What does Caro say?"

"I haven't asked."

He gave me a disbelieving look. "Yer see him again, you call me. Could be he's working with the Korax."

"Korax? No. He helped me against them."

He took his hat off and gripped it between his knees, pulled the band from his pigtail and scooped his hair back to retie it. It was a simple act that humanised his otherwise impenetrable manner. Like when he'd wiped Jessie's blood from my face.

"Men like Hamish Burns change sides quicker'n I can load bullets. They serve who they please, when they please – usually, the people who pay the most," he said.

Curiously, I felt compelled to defend Caro's friend. "Just because he doesn't work for the government doesn't mean he lacks personal integrity."

Sixkiller folded his arms in an uncompromising way. "In my experience, it always does."

I felt my mellowness towards him slipping.

The door pinged open at his floor and he stepped out. "Tell me when yer've come up with a plan about yer brother."

I grunted acknowledgment and held my breath until the doors closed. Then I gave a huge sigh. Compassion, kindness mixed with a healthy pinch of bombastic self-righteousness: Sixkiller's personal brand of seasoning.

I rang Caro as soon as I got inside my front door.

"How did last night go?" she asked.

"Awry," I said. "But it'll take a while to tell. How do you get in contact with Hamish?"

"Why?"

"The Marshal didn't hire him to bodyguard me."

"What? But I thought…"

"*I* want to know what's going on. Why's he following me around?"

Caro coughed. Or was it a laugh?

"What? Sixkiller thinks he might be working for the Korax," I said.

"If he was working for Korax, you'd be a little jar of ashes on my mantelpiece. From what you've said, he's working to make sure that doesn't happen."

"But why?" I said blankly. "Who's paying him?"

"You want my best guess...?"

"Please," I said. "Tell me."

"I think Hamish... likes you."

I felt a welling nausea again. "You really have a sick sense of humour."

"You asked. I do have a way of contacting him, but I can't share it."

"Then please tell him to meet me at 5pm at Dabrowski's Diner today. I'm going to call Johnny, see if he'll meet with me after six."

"You want me there too?"

I wanted to say yes, but then I remembered her health. "No, it's fine. You said you were working on a bible for us. Can you add Empusa to your list and find out how they can be stopped? Seems there's one rampaging about with my name on her lips."

"Mythos?"

"Half-demon, half-vampire with a club foot. Power to influence thoughts and suck a human dry of fluids."

She didn't miss a beat at my description. "Call me when you're done with Johnny."

I love my friend. "Caro?"

"Yeah."

"Thanks again for not thinking I'm crazy."

"You're crazy all right," she said. "Doesn't mean you're not right."

As I hung up, I realized that her response resonated with what I'd said to Sixkiller about Hamish. Different perspectives made the world go round, *and* started a lot of wars. But the trouble that was coming our way at the moment – that was bigger than the way any of us viewed life.

I hadn't had Johnny's phone number for years, but we'd made a deal when Dad died to have a point of contact for each other in an emergency. Mine was Dabrowski's Diner; his was a tattoo parlour on the edge of the Western Quarter. I made the call and left a message with Reg, the tattoo parlour's owner, for Johnny to meet me at Dab's later in the day.

That left me with a few hours to recover. I kicked off my boots and unzipped my jeans while I examined the cupboard and found a small carton of cranberry juice behind the dried noodles. I popped the straw in and sucked the juice down. It gave the little hit of sugar I needed to think about what to do next.

I wanted to go to the park and ride Benny out to Dry Gulch or Los Tribos for the hell of it, but that would be indulgent. I wanted to find Hamish and ask him what was going on and what he'd done with the guy hired to kill me – or maybe I didn't. I wanted to pursue the ComTel lead even though it wasn't in my brief. I wanted to sit and read more of Dad's journals to see if I could work out whether he kept the digital images from Los Tribos. I *should* ring Rav Namaditje and reschedule. I *should* visit Esther and Trip. I *should*–

I was lost in my deliberations when someone knocked at the door. I checked the sec cam and saw Heart Williams standing there in black dress pants and a white T-shirt.

I flung the door open. "What do you want?"

"Hi." His T-shirt was almost translucent and I could see the darker shade of his skin beneath it. I sucked in a deep breath of shock and sudden desire. Then I became acutely aware that my pants were undone. I moved to shut the door, but he blocked me with his foot.

"Virgin. Can I come in?"

I shook my head. "Unlikely."

"It's about Birrimun Park."

I released the pressure on the door. "What about the park?"

He glanced up and down the corridor. "Can we discuss it inside?"

I hesitated. Nothing else he could have said would have made me consider inviting him in. But this I had to know. "You've got five minutes."

I backed away and zipped up my pants. He shut the door, but didn't try to approach me.

"How have you been?" he asked.

I looked him over as coolly as I could manage. He seemed a little thinner than the last time I'd seen him and his normally tanned face was pale as though he'd been indoors a lot. But the angles of his face and the curve of his lips had lost none of their fine architecture, and I felt the familiar tug of attraction.

"What should I call you? Your name is obviously not Heart," I said in answer.

He looked at the floor then back at me. "Samuel Williams. Sam."

"You mean Agent Sam Williams?"

"Special Agent in Charge actually."

"I didn't know SACs worked undercover."

"The promotion is recent."

"Of course." I guessed he was referring to the arrest of

illegal immigrants in the security bust in Birrimun. That's when I'd first learned who he really was – the man who'd been posing as a dancer and my lover for the past year.

It was a particular kind of hurt, the one he'd inflicted on me. I didn't trust people easily, and now, since then, I didn't trust people at all. Except Caro. And maybe Sixkiller, a little. "So what did you want to tell me?"

He flexed the fingers on one of his hands. I noticed the scabs on his knuckles, but didn't ask.

"I heard you've been seconded to work with GJIC," he said. "I can only guess what they've got you working on, but I figure it's something to do with the park."

I stood absolutely still, giving him nothing.

"We've... that is... my agency has tried to connect with GJIC on their presence here, but they're stonewalling us." He rubbed his temple as though it was giving him a headache. "I never did understand the pissing competition that goes on between intelligence bodies."

"It's not a competition," I said finally. "GJIC's brief is... unique."

He frowned at that. "So I hear. Yet no one wants to say what that is."

"If you want information about them, you've come to the wrong person. I'm too low on the food chain to be of use to you."

"I didn't come to ask for information. I came to apologize."

I folded my arms against the tightness in my chest, and looked at the ceiling so he couldn't see my eyes moistening.

"Are you OK?" he asked.

"Get on with it, Sam," I snapped, still staring upwards. "Just say what's on your mind and leave."

"Look Virgin, what I did... with you... was my job. I don't

regret it, and I'd do it again because I believe in what I do. But I do... care for you, Ginny."

"How could I ever believe that?"

He shrugged. "I know you find it hard to trust, so I couldn't leave things between us as they were. Not without trying to..."

"Trying to what? Ease your conscience?"

He shrugged and held his hands up in a helpless gesture. "If I can ever help you out with anything, just remember you can count on me."

"Goodbye, Sam," I said. "Don't come here again."

He took a long, last look around the room as if remembering.

I didn't want to be witness to it, so I walked into the kitchenette and began unstacking the dishwasher. I didn't turn back around until I heard the door close.

The click brought on a backwash of emotion that caught me unawares, and I sobbed out loud. How could anyone have duped me so completely? Was I so desperate for intimacy that I'd missed the obvious signs? I knuckled my stomach and then my eyes to stay the rush. I was not a weeper.

I got my cell phone out of my pocket and rang Rav Namaditje. He answered in two rings.

"Dr... er... Rav, it's Virgin Jackson. I hope you got my message about last night."

"Ms Jackson?"

"Yes."

"Is everything all right? The man who left the message – your colleague – sounded quite terse."

I thought of Jessie. The blood and how heavy her arm had been when I pressed her fingers to the wheel. "Yes, everything's fine. And that's his normal tone."

"I'm relieved," he said.

"Are you free for lunch?" I wasn't one for social phone chats.

"Um... well, this is a little unexpected, but I can take a short lunch break if you want to come by the hospital," he said.

"Sure."

"There's a café across the road called Marty le Muffin. I could meet you there at midday."

"Cute name." I checked the time. Just enough. "See you soon."

I hung up. I'd done it: a date with a doctor who may or may not wish me ill intent. It had to be better than sitting here thinking about my visit from *Sam* Williams.

I went and showered quickly and found some fresh clothes at the bottom of my cupboard. They were the last. Laundry delivery wasn't until tomorrow.

Little choice meant a red T-shirt with a hole under the arm, and jeans that were too tight. As long as I kept my arms down and didn't eat anything, all would be well. I decided to go with boots. I didn't plan on doing any running, and I always felt safer in them.

Lastly, I ran a brush over my hair and pulled it back into a loose ponytail. I wasn't romancing this guy, but a slither of vanity sent me back into the bathroom to apply some blush and a dab of perfume.

Heart... *Sam* had bought the musky scent for me as a birthday gift. The sooner I used it up, the better.

I headed out and caught the Parkway bus to the hospital connection, then switched. The whole trip only took about twenty minutes and I was ensconced with a pitcher of ice water at a Marty le Muffin's table by the time Rav Namaditje arrived.

He saw me, signalled, and threaded his way over.

I forced a smile onto my face, and felt guilty that his looked genuine.

"I only have thirty minutes," he said, as he dropped into the chair. "What can I get you to eat?"

I pushed the menu banner that doubled as a serviette holder towards him. "Nachos. My treat."

He glanced up from underneath long, dark eyelashes. "Would you think it too old-fashioned if I paid for you? I mean, I run an account here anyway that the hospital picks up."

I thawed a little – he did seem like a genuinely nice person. "Let's just split the bill."

He nodded, happier about that, and quickly typed our order into the display. Then he poured himself water and settled his elbows on the table.

I found the gesture curiously calming.

"So, Virgin, tell me about yourself. Forgive me for saying so, but your biochemistry is so unusual. We're curious about your ethnic background."

"Well, I've never had anyone take a fancy to my biochemistry before," I countered lightly.

"I'm sorry. I didn't mean to be offensive to you of all people."

"Oh?" I waited, watching carefully for signs of insincerity or deception.

"You're obviously a decent person. I mean, the way you helped out an old and vulnerable neighbour. It says a lot," he added.

I felt my cheeks and ears heat up. "No more than anyone else would do."

"You'd be surprised. I've worked in Emergency for a few years. I see things that are... frankly... despicable."

I sighed. "I can't imagine doing your job."

"And I can't imagine doing yours. What's it like out in the park? I've never been there. My family don't do well in open spaces." He grinned again. "Crowds and high density living are in my DNA."

I found myself smiling back. He was very easy to be around. "What is your DNA?"

"My mother is Chinese Australian and my father is Kenyan. But I also carry the DNA of an indigenous woman. It's a long and genetics-based explanation, but I pride myself in being a first generation triracial."

"That's pretty cool," I replied. "Much more interesting than my heritage, I'm sure." Not that I knew anything much about it. Dad hadn't been one for keeping in touch with extended family. I think he had a brother somewhere. Jake or John or Joel...

"Well, I'm here to tell you that you're quite special. Your bloodwork is extraordinary. It's teeming with anomalous antibodies. The hospital's leading physician wants to present your case at a world medical conference in London–"

The waiter-cart rolled up, interrupting him, and told us our meals were ready. Its servery hatch opened, arms unfolded, and it placed our plates in front of us. A lot of the uptown restaurants had waiter-bots, but I preferred human service like Greta at Dabrowski's Diner.

My nachos looked crisp, but some of the sauce had slopped over the edge. Rav's was the same.

"Enjoy your meal. Please record any feedback after the tone." The waiter-bot emitted a short high-pitched beep sound.

"I suggest that your levelling sensors need to be recalibrated," said Rav. "You spilled our food."

"Your message will be forwarded to our customer service department. You can expect a reply within five working days." It pumped out a receipt, refolded its arms and trundled off.

We looked at each other and laughed.

"Next time, we'll go human," said Rav.

"Next time?"

He blushed. "I mean, if you'd like to…"

I ate a couple of mouthfuls of the tomatoey-cheesy nachos before putting my fork down and staring at him. "I assume you need my permission to present my case? That's why we're here?"

He stopped chewing and swallowed. "We can present you as an anonymous patient with limited details, but your permission will broaden the reach of our address. So… ideally, yes. Also, the hospital would like you to volunteer for a new study they have about to start. They believe that your blood profile has some implications for curing certain inflammatory diseases. They'll be contacting you officially about that."

"Then this isn't official."

"Friendly official," he said.

"So you're here to persuade me to sign away my confidential medical records?"

"We have a sample of your blood in storage due to the transfusions. You just need to give us permission to use it."

"I'm sorry. The answer is no."

"May I ask why?"

"Not really."

His face fell, and I debated whether to leave right there and then, or to finish my nachos first.

While I toyed with the melted cheese, his smile slowly returned. "Frankly, Virgin, I don't understand your reluctance, but I respect your choice. At least, I can go back to my superiors with a concrete answer. And now that it's done, let's start this again."

I breathed in and out. Well, what the hell! He was nice

enough. "Sure. This food's pretty good. Let's massacre it."

He laughed outright. "Yeah. Let's."

We tucked in, and chatted until our meals were finished. He was surprisingly easy to talk to.

By then the place had filled with young mums and their offspring, and the noise level had risen. I sighed and pushed my plate off to one side. "My dad always used to go nuts at me for doing that," I said.

"Pushing your plate away?"

"Yeah. He was big on table etiquette."

"Not your mum?"

"She wasn't around. Just my brother, my dad, and I."

"What was your dad like?"

"Hard," I said. "Obsessive but fair. Deeply principled. Neurotic."

"Sounds like a tough guy to live with?"

"Like clinging to a pendulum."

His eyebrows lifted.

"One end of the swing, I'd be full of admiration for him. The other, I'd be flying with frustration."

"Your brother feel the same way?"

"Worse," I said. "They never did hit it off."

"Sounds like my sister and my mother. Cats in a barrel."

"I'm not sure whether to find that funny or sexist."

"Scary is what it was," he said. "I learned early how to take the path of least resistance from the combat zone of their relationship. I also learned about how to patch up wounds."

"That bad, huh?"

"My mother was a drug abuser and my sister a cutter. Either way there was always blood."

"That's awful, Rav," I said, meaning it.

"That's life!" he said, still smiling. "I don't let it worry me.

I got out, studied hard and now I get to be whoever I want to be." He glanced at the reflection clock on the wall. "But I have to go. Hey, you want to do this again sometime?"

I hesitated long enough for his smile to fade.

"Sure," I said eventually. "If you're sure you want to. I'm not great company these days."

"Matter of opinion," he said lightly. "I'll call you."

He got up then and negotiated his way back to the door past the strollers and the toddlers. I noticed when he bent to pick up a child's dropped sippy cup, and the material of his scrubs stretched out, that he had a lean, muscled figure.

I think I just liked the man I had lunch with.

Now that was something weird.

FOURTEEN

Caro called me just as I left the Ringway heading back to the Western Quarter and Dabrowski's Diner. I was sprawled along the back seat of the half-empty bus, watching the mid-afternoon traffic flow and scrolling through the Mythos *Vade Mecum* on my LiFo.

The closest passenger was three rows in front – a beautiful young Filipino woman engrossed in refreshing the tattoos on her nails. *Rivera Salons* embroidered in gold sequins rippled on the back of her shirt as she squirmed in her seat.

My inbox chimed with a message from Sixkiller asking for an update on my day. I replied briefly, telling him I'd initiated a meeting with Johnny, and was on my way there. I didn't say where. Johnny wouldn't do well with a lawman breathing down his collar. My ranger's uniform spooked him enough. Of course, I wasn't wearing it today. Hopefully the red T-shirt with the holes would work in my favour.

My cell phone rang and I squinted at the caller ID. "Caro?"

"Come by after your meeting with Johnny. Also, I left word for Hamish that you'd be at the diner by 5pm."

The bus had pulled in to the last of the downtown stops before taking the Ten-Ways roundabout to enter the Western Quarter. Ms Rivera Salon clacked off down the aisle in her heels, leaving. As she put her foot on the steps, someone got up from the seat behind the driver to follow her; someone – or thing – with a long, thin tongue, which unravelled from its mouth. The tongue rolled onto the floor and snaked around Ms Rivera Salon's ankle like a frog sticking a fly.

Mythos. I fumbled in my bag, searching for the flat baton that Sixkiller had given me in the GJIC halfway house.

"Virgin?" said Caro. "Are you still there?"

"I have to go."

"Why, what's–"

I took a quick photo of Ms Rivera then shoved my cell phone in my pocket. "Hey!"

The whole bus turned to look at me. The driver glanced in his rear view.

"Hey, Miss! You... Did you drop this?" I asked.

Ms Rivera Salon stopped and glanced back over her shoulder. "You talkin' to me?"

I advanced down the aisle a few steps. "Yeah. This was under your seat. I thought you'd dropped it."

Now I was closer, I could see the creature more clearly. It looked like an elongated foetus, with a large, unformed mouth and thin limbs.

I lifted the baton higher and pressed the knob on the side. The blunt instrument warmed in my grasp. "See? I just thought it might be important?"

The creature blinked rapidly at the sight of the baton and

retracted its tongue from around her ankle.

Like everyone else on the bus, Ms Rivera seemed oblivious to the threat standing right next to her.

She shrugged. "Not mine, lady." And got off.

"Miss, put the stick away and please sit down, or I will call Aus-Pol," said the driver over his intercom.

The Mythos curled into a ball and rolled under the luggage rack, while I made a show of doing exactly what the driver said, stashing the baton in my backpack, and returning to my seat.

I got out my LiFo, put my hand in front of the mouthpiece, and called Sixkiller.

He answered straight away. "Virgin?"

"I'm on a bus heading into the Western Quarter and there's a Mythos on board."

"What kind?" he asked softly.

"It looks like a foetus with a long tongue that it likes to hang out."

"Aswang," he said. "From Filipino folklore."

"It was about to follow a girl from Rivera Salons, but I scared it. She got off at Senegal Street."

"What's it doin' now?"

"It's curled up under the luggage rack."

"How did yer scare it?"

"I used the baton, and it let go of her."

"Is Aquila there?"

I glanced around. "No."

"Yer in no immediate danger then. Just observe and record. We'll add it to our database."

"But it was after her. Will it try again?"

"Honest, I don't know. Do yer know who she was?"

"No, but I photographed her."

"Send me the image. We'll see what facial rec gives us."

"Is it likely to be random?"

"In the past, I woulda said no, but there've been so many sightin's in the last few weeks. Yers is the thirty-fifth today just in the Mid-City area."

Mid-City was a slice of the megacity that stretched past the Western Quarter to the south, west to downtown and east to the coast: population, probably, a million people. Thirty-five didn't sound like many Mythos, but they were just the recorded ones. What was happening out there that we weren't seeing?

"Has there been an increase in unexplained deaths or injuries?" I asked, as the bus left the Ten-ways roundabout.

"We're runnin' the data on hospital admissions and ambulance call outs, but not everyone goes to public health. The private clinics won't share information."

"Good to see we have some privacy rights left."

"Don't kid yerself. It's just that *we* cain't legally offer bribes."

"Right."

"Where're yer heading?"

I breathed out slowly before I answered. Maybe it was better that he knew where I was. "The diner."

"I've got some things to attend to. I'll come there, soon as I c'n get away."

"Things?"

"Yer Empusa friend's been sighted near the park."

"Cyndia?"

"Yeah. It's a bold move knowin' that we're watchin' the park all the time."

"I should be there with you," I said.

"No. Do what we discussed. I'll join yer shortly."

"You'll scare Johnny. He hates law enforcement."

"I'll wait outside till yer done."

"Promise me, Nate?"

"'Bout time you gave me some credit, Virgin. Doncha think?" He hung up without saying goodbye. People seemed to do that to me a lot.

FIFTEEN

Greta waved at me as I settled into a booth at the front of the diner. The place was half-empty, a lull before the dinner crowd descended. Even the bar only had a few untidy lingerers left over from lunch.

The newly revamped décor was still shiny and a little odd – disco meets dour with chandeliers. But where I sat gave me a great view of the passing street traffic and reminded me of the times Dad and I had spent here arguing politics with Chef Dab and drinking vodka shots.

"I'll have the sauerkraut and sausage," said Hamish, who slid onto the seat opposite me. "And spring water."

"Who said I was buying?" I asked mildly.

"You invited me here." He smiled, which put me off balance. I wasn't sure if it improved his usually blank demeanour because it didn't touch his eyes. They were so... disconnected.

"You lied to me," I said.

He raised both eyebrows.

"You implied GJIC hired you to protect me."

"No," he said. "You decided that. I just didn't dispute it."

I tried to remember our previous conversation. Perhaps I'd assumed it, but he'd certainly allowed me to do that.

"So why *were* you following me?" I lowered my voice to a whisper. "And what did you do with... him?"

Greta walked up to take his order. "Back again? What can I get you two lovebirds?"

My throat constricted, causing me to cough. *Fuck!* "We're colleagues, and we'd like two sauerkrauts and sausage, and two waters on my tab. Thanks, Greta," I said.

She gave me a conspiratorial wink and walked off.

"Hamish, *what happened to the guy*?" I demanded, once she was out of earshot.

His smile vanished. "He won't be coming after you again," he said quietly.

"I don't know what that means," I said.

Silence.

I pursued it. "Did he tell you anything? Who hired him?"

"Perhaps."

I drummed my fingers on the table. "Well?"

"He was employed through a broker who I plan to visit tonight."

"*You* plan to? Hamish, tell me what you know, and I'll deal with it."

"It's not a place you should go to alone."

Before I could respond, Greta came back with the glasses of water and a knowing smile. I grimaced at her, but she wasn't having any of it, and winked at me again as she went back to the counter.

"*Please*, Hamish."

"The broker deals from a downtown apartment near the National Gallery."

"Downtown near the gallery?" That surprised me.

"He's wealthy. He has influence. He's not some lowlife banger from Mystere."

I dialled down my annoyance with him. Hamish was strange, but not stupid. "How dangerous?"

He shrugged. "Let's just say his reputation is founded. I know that for a fact."

"If you're so sure, then you must have some idea who he works for."

He lifted his shoulders slightly. "You heard of Joachim Spears?"

I frowned. "Maybe. Enlighten me?"

He shook his head. "Not yet. When I'm sure, I'll…"

Greta interrupted the conversation again, this time with plates of pickled sauerkraut and fat oily sausage. "The fries are on the house. Chef says you need fattening up. And he likes that you're bringing your boyfriend here," she said, as she plopped them down.

"He's not my boyfriend," I snapped.

She eyerolled.

Hamish said nothing, so I changed the subject.

"Greta, I'm expecting my brother here soon. Could you ask Chef to cook up some eye fillet and mushrooms – medium rare, please?"

"Sure thing, darl."

She left and I turned my attention back to Hamish, who was consuming the chips with quick, efficient movements.

"I'm expecting company," I said, worrying that Johnny would see Hamish and get spooked.

He stopped eating and picked up his plate and glass. "I'll be close by," he said.

It wasn't until I was alone in the booth again that I realized he still hadn't answered my question about why he'd been watching out for me.

I took a mouthful of sausage and contemplated Caro's theory that Hamish was... fond of me. She had to be wrong about that. Psychopaths didn't do *fond*.

I texted her quickly with the name Joachim Spears, and got back to my food.

Halfway through my mound of sauerkraut, a tap on the window drew my attention. Johnny was there, his face pressed up against the glass, nose flat and tongue wiggling.

I recoiled for a moment then scowled at him, which prompted him to give me a sly grin.

"Funny!" I said, when he took the seat that Hamish had recently vacated. "I've ordered you a steak."

"What do you want, VJ?" He leaned forwards, and I swear I could smell Corah's perfume on him.

"Look, Johnny," I said, "you wanted to protect me from a complete stranger out at Branch Holy. I'm returning the favour by warning you off Armand Dusan."

He frowned and I saw the resemblance to Dad in the deep crease between his brows. "You dragged me up here to chastise me about my politics?"

"I'm not chastising you. It's a warning. Dusan's messed up in stuff that's out of your league."

Soon as the words came out, I knew I'd said the wrong thing. Johnny has always fancied himself as a black knight, a criminal entrepreneur. It was his rebellion against the idea that Dad and I worked for the law. He'd also always been in denial that his chemical dependencies precluded him from ever playing in the big leagues. He had the brain for it, but not the restraint nor the discipline.

For that, I was thankful. But I hated how he fucked up

his body and mind with drugs. Deep down inside, I felt like
he was doing it to me as well. Probably the most irrational
notion I'd ever had, but I guess it showed that no matter what
my brother did... he was still part of me.

"Well, fuck you to big old responsibility and sideways, sis.
Anyone ever tell you that you're a bigot and a reactionary?"

I steeled myself against his abuse. "Yeah, you. Quite
regularly."

"You always were slow to learn."

"And you always did like to be part of the cool kids."

We glared at each other.

"Hey, handsome," said Greta, as she placed a medium rare
steak with sauce and fritters in front of my brother. "Good to
see you and your sister getting along."

Johnny half stood to kiss her on the cheek. "Hey, Greta.
Don't tell the big fella I'm here. He'll only hammer me for not
coming in to see him more often."

"Sure, Johnny. But Chef loves you. Don't forget it." She
ground a little black pepper onto his meat without asking and
waved the shaker at him as she left.

"Chef pumping her arse, is he?"

I ignored his crudity and raised him one. "I'd be more
concerned where Corah's putting it about, Johnny. She's
always liked cultured men. She'll be practising politics with
Professor Dusan quicker than you can unzip your fly and say
'Yeah, baby!'"

Heat rose in his cheeks and set his face aglow.

"You're the bitch of all sisters, Virgin. Corah's just
connecting him with people so he can...Wait!" He wagged
his finger at me. "Don't try and play me, girl."

I shrugged, scooped up the last of the hot chips, squashed
them into my mouth and licked the salt off my fingers. Chef

had his own brand of flavoured salts that made his fries totally unique.

Johnny watched me, then picked up his knife and pushed the meat around with his cutlery.

Neither of us said anything for a while. I drank my water and he moved from playing with the meat to nibbling at the chips.

Just when I was thinking about how to kickstart the conversation he spoke again. "What's your problem with Prof Dusan anyway? The guy makes a lot of sense."

"Maybe he does. Maybe his theories about alternate worlds aren't batshit crazy. But I hear that he's got dangerous plans. I'm just saying... don't get sucked along in the vortex."

"You hear? From who?"

I'd been expecting his question and had my answer ready. I let him have my most earnest look. "This might sound ridiculous, but it's the truth. Someone's trying to kill me, Johnny, so I've had to organise some protection. I've hooked up with a guy from Mystere called Papa Brise. Corah gave me his name a while back. He hears and knows things." This would sound right when he spoke to Corah.

He frowned again, but with concentration not anger. "Why would anyone want to kill you? Other than me?"

"Dad might have hidden something that some people want, and others would kill to stop them getting it. Seems they think I know where it is, even though I don't. My apartment's been searched, a guy tried to kill me at my front door, and now Papa Brise says there's a contract out on me. I thought you should know. In case they connect you to me."

"What could the crazy old coot have written that someone would kill for? He was just a paranoid pessimist."

"He was a clever, passionate man, JJ. But Mum's leaving...

well, bitterness screwed him up… h- hardened him."

"Hardened? He was a selfish perfectionist and an antisocial bastard."

"His partner left him to raise two kids on his own. He did his best."

Johnny pressed his fingers to his forehead as though he had a headache. When he looked up again, I saw the glittery anger back in his eyes. "You always defend him, don't you? I say she did well to get away from him. Only you were stupid enough to stay."

"He wasn't so awful, Johnny. You two were just different."

"*Not that bad*? I was so fucked up by him I started see things. I had to get out before I went crazy."

My skin prickled with alarm. "What do you mean, *seeing things*?"

"Insane stuff. Animals and weird shit. I had this fucking fox following me around for years."

A fox? Shit. A heap of questions piled up in my head clamouring to be asked, but one of them won out. "Have you met Cyndia, Dusan's assistant?"

"Why?"

I picked my words carefully. "Be careful of her, JJ. Don't get too close."

He shook his head and fiddled with his cutlery. "You're nuts."

"Have you ever told Corah about the fox?" I asked next.

"Why are you asking me these weird questions? It was just caused by stress – the old man's stress, which he loved to pass on," he said, scowling.

"Has the fox come back again in the last few weeks?"

This time he dropped his fork and it clanged on the plate. He paled and his eyes flew to my face.

I could see the answer in them.

I reached out and touched his hands. "I have an eagle, Johnny. She's come back as well. They're telling us to be careful. You must listen to your fox because–"

He didn't wait to hear me finish. He stood up and stalked out of the restaurant.

"You want me to follow him?" said Hamish in my ear.

I sighed and tried to think. Sixkiller would be here any minute, and I didn't really want him and Hamish running into each other.

"Yes. But I can't afford to pay you," I said.

He nodded as though that was a given. "I'll check in with you later tonight."

"But–" He left swiftly without a backwards glance. "You don't have a phone..." I trailed off.

I stared disconsolately at his disappearing back. What on earth was I doing asking him for help?

Greta reappeared and refilled the jug. "Be careful of that quiet one, Virgin. I see all kinds of strange in him."

I nodded. She was dead right about that. "I'd like the cheesecake with cream."

"Sure thing. And honey..."

"Yeah?" I glanced up as Sixkiller walked through the door.

"*This* one's got my vote."

I grunted. "You know what, Greta?" I said. "He's all yours!"

She grinned and patted me on the shoulder. "My hands are full with Chef. Cheesecake coming right up."

"Mind if I join you?" asked Sixkiller, with the slightest of bows. He had his hat in his hand. The man had manners.

I gestured for him to sit. "He's just left."

He waited, letting me collect my thoughts.

"I think I know why Dusan has recruited him," I said, finally. "And I think I know how it came about. It's Corah."

"The psychic?"

"I think Corah's been making connections for Dusan's cause for a while. Johnny's just inadvertently told me that he's got a disincarnate. It's a fox."

Sixkiller's eyes widened a fraction. "Makes sense. It c'n be hereditary."

"He just thinks he's crazy though. He doesn't know anything else."

"Are yer sure?"

"No. But I need to see the security scans from the night the Diner reopened. Corah was here that night making contacts. I need to see who she spoke to."

He reached for his LiFo. "We c'n subpoena Chef Dabrowski to turn 'em over."

"No one orders Chef to do anything. He'd likely erase them out of spite. He's hard line about his personal freedom. Let me do it my way."

He hesitated. "I'll give yer a chance, but if yer don't get the footage today, we use the law to git it."

"Fine. Wait here and don't eat my cheesecake."

I got up, strolled across to the kitchen doors and pushed them open. Chef was booming at one of the fry cooks, telling him a dirty joke, from the snip of conversation I caught. The rest of the staff were either rolling their eyes or laughing.

Chef saw me almost immediately and welcomed me with a hug that smelled of pickle and cheese. He refused to let me go until I hugged him back.

"Virgin, my sweetheart, where have you been? I am so desolate without you," he declared loudly, as if I'd returned from a long exile.

"I saw you two weeks ago, Chef," I said, feeling the warm signs of embarrassment creeping up my neck.

The staff went back to work, grinning at my discomfort.

He hugged me harder.

"Chef, can we speak? Do you have a moment?" I said quietly into his ear.

He let go of me and swept low, waving his hands with a flourish. "To my office."

I walked on through and up the stairs, feeling slightly abashed for no good reason. I sat on the stool near the bar he'd had installed across from his desk and waited for him to position himself behind it. He poured us both a shot of vodka and toasted.

"*Na zdrowie!*"

"*Na zdrowie!*" I echoed.

We clinked and knocked back our drinks. As the white spirit hit my stomach, I felt grateful that I hadn't yet eaten my cheesecake.

"*Jak leci?*" he asked.

I thought for a moment that I should tell him about working for my mother then decided against it. "Personal favour, Chef. I'm worried about Johnny. He's hooked up with Corah the Psychic."

"Aaah, the boy has always had bad judgement," said Chef sadly. "And that woman is not one to trust."

"I was wondering, do you have security vision of the new opening of the diner? Corah was here, and I want to see who she was talking to."

He frowned. "You must not overinvolve yourself in your brother's life, Virgin. He is his own man."

"I'm not planning on interfering, Chef. But I believe she's dragging him into something serious. I need to be able to help him when the time comes. Dad would have wanted me to."

Chef moved his head from side to side, thinking. "You are right."

He knelt down behind the bar and fished around on the floor under the rubber matting. I knew he kept his main safe there. He said that a concrete floor was a lot harder to crack than a wall. His safe wasn't going anywhere.

When he straightened up, he was holding a slick, black data bug in his hands. "The invitation list for the opening. I will mark in red those who came. It says, too, how to find them."

"Their contact details?"

"Yes."

"Marked in red for loyalty, eh?"

"Red for Poland." He pounded his fist to his chest.

"Is the video on there as well?"

He shook his head. "I do not like spying on my patrons."

"But you've got surveillance cameras up everywhere."

He shrugged. "It is good enough just to look that way."

I reached for the bug, but he closed his fist on it. "This is the goodwill that makes my business what it is, Virgin. Make no copies. Show no one else."

I knew he was deadly serious because his breathing came heavy.

"I understand. Your client list's been built up over many years. I'd never compromise it."

He nodded. "These people... I protect their privacy and they give me loyalty. You understand? Some of them invest in my place."

"You have shareholders?"

He waved his hands, not prepared to answer.

A weight descended on me. Sixkiller and GJIC would want this list, and now I couldn't let them have it. Chef was the closest family I had other than Johnny.

"OK," I said.

He opened his fist.

I took the bug and stuffed it in the zippered part of my wallet alongside my One Card. Then I leaned across the bar and kissed him on both cheeks. "Thank you, Chef."

He smiled broadly and lined up two more vodka shots. "Now, once more! Zubrowka!"

I toasted his favourite vodka, and before I could escape, once more again. When I finally made it back to my booth and Sixkiller, I felt numb from the vodka rush.

"Virgin?" He gave me a quizzical look as I wobbled in and sat down to my cheesecake. "Are you drunk?"

I licked my lips. "It's tradition. Chef gets his Zubrowka from up near the Lithuanian border. It tastes like bison."

His eyes narrowed and he leaned forwards. "The vodka is flavoured with bison?"

Through the buzz, I remembered Sixkiller's disincarnate, Ohitika, was a bison, and hastened to correct his misunderstanding. "No, I mean it's flavoured with something called bison weed, or bison grass."

He relaxed and leaned back. "And did you get what you need?"

I shook my head. "Not exactly. The cameras aren't connected, and he had no exact recollection of who was there that night, but he's going to send me a list of names of people that he can remember."

"When?"

"He said I'd have it by tomorrow night."

Sixkiller scowled with impatience. "Too long!"

"Why? What did you find out about Cyndia?"

"She took the tourist bus trip to La Paloma."

I thought back to a few weeks ago when Sixkiller and I had

been trapped inside the Paloma station house by a huge crow Mythos. I'd nearly died when it'd attacked me and left me bleeding to death. Only an infusion of Sixkiller's blood had saved me. I wondered if having his blood had changed me in any fundamental way. Would I even know if it had?

"Why can everyone see certain Mythos like Cyndia, but not others like the Pocong?"

"I can give yer an explanation. It ain't necessarily accurate, but it's the one we're workin' with."

"I'm listening."

"We think it depends on the strength of the individual creature. Jus' remember I'm usin' the word 'creature' in a loose kinda way, Virgin. We actually don't know what the real form of the Mythos is. But we think they've been crossing over here for as long as we've been recordin' history. We've known they're here a long while, but not why. Now the appearances are more frequent, and we're seeing other changes."

"Like?"

"Commander Orlean believes there's a shift towards a more centralised belief system amongst religions. Last week, the Christian churches announced a symposium to discuss the creatin' of a common text."

"Like a common Bible?"

"Yeah. We've also been chartin' the world's mythologies. Vampires, fer instance, are present in the mythology of most cultures, but belief in their existence has become so strong in recent times, thet we're seein' an increase in blood cults. And you know thet vampire stories *pervade* entertainment."

"The Mythos attempting to unify world beliefs so they can do what...?"

He shrugged. "All I can think of is that it's what they need to do to take our world for their own. Commander's inclined to agree with me."

What he was saying was so pervasive and encompassing and nothing like Dad's vision for a better world.

"The Mythos thet you saw on the bus was definitely an Aswang – vampiric, but sometimes half-dog," Sixkiller added.

"Why did it follow that particular girl?"

"We're just lookin' into her background now."

I made a mental note to read the *Vade Mecum* entry on Aswang. "If the Korax are the human arm of the Mythos, then are they being controlled by them somehow?"

"We haven't been able to get people on the inside of the Korax."

"Best guess then?"

He spread his hands wide like he was making an apology. "I think the Korax're bein' manipulated by the Mythos."

"To do what?"

"Cause trouble. Back, sixty or seventy years ago, when the Middle East blew up, everyone blamed the CIA. GJIC believe that was the Korax. And not just then either. I got sent here 'cause of the concentration of sightin's. Mystere and Birrimun Park seem to be a focal point."

That fitted with what Papa Brise had told me about the trouble brewing on his turf. "But I still don't understand how human conflict helps the Mythos? Aren't they supposed to be trying to unify us with their one mythology?"

"We think conflict has a thinnin' effect on the fabric of our world. Makes it easier for them to cross. Once here, they try'n influence our myths, and the way we think. Start leadin' us down the path they want us to go."

"So, what about major conflicts like the World Wars?"

"Lots of them… many crossed over then."

I shook my head. It felt like it was stuffed with raw dough.

We sat in silence for a moment or two.

"Papa Brise contacted me a few days ago. He wants me to use my government influence to give him information. He says a gang called the Korax – he calls them the Crow and Circle – are moving in on his turf. He thinks I can help him with them."

"He knows yer workin' for us?"

I shrugged. "World's worst kept secret."

"What did yer tell him?"

"That you'd shoot me for treason if I shared any secrets."

He nodded. "And when were you going to tell me?"

"Now seems about right. Little thing about our driver having her throat torn out got in the way earlier..."

His frown grew deeper. "I'll let the Commander know. He might be useful."

"I said you might give him immunity if he shares intel. But watch him, he's tricky," I said.

"Indeed. And Virgin... yer should know that she... Commander Orlean... disagrees with me. She thinks thet the Mythos're in direct contact with the Korax. That it's *collaboration*, not manipulation," said Sixkiller.

"Which makes them even more dangerous?"

"Yeah."

I scraped up the last of the cheesecake crumbs and spooned them into my mouth. My therapist had told me to enjoy the little things in life. Right now, this cheesecake was the best thing I had going on.

"The Commander thinks thet the Korax are people who c'n see 'other'. Like you and me."

Jeez! "Johnny then?"

"It's probably why they're recruitin' him." Sixkiller pinched the skin between his eyebrows like he was in pain and closed his eyes.

I didn't like seeing him so upset. "We really need that list from the diner's opening night," I said. "See who Corah was targeting."

Sixkiller opened his eyes. "I took my own surveillance footage thet evenin', but it wasn't thorough. Yer might remember thet things got messy."

I wasn't likely to forget the night Detective Chance had tried to arrest me, and I'd later been kidnapped by the Korax. "*You* were filming. Doesn't GJIC have like... global surveillance? You know, drones disguised as raindrops and spy-eyes in the sugar granules?"

"Not since the new privacy acts. Officers and agents c'n use personal surveillance equipment, but nothing unmanned. It's an accountability issue. Though we can subpoena footage owned by someone else."

"Who knew personal freedom could be so inconvenient?"

He scowled at me and I scowled back. At least the worry had gone out of his face.

"I have to go see Caro soon and then get some sleep," I said, by way of winding up our conflab. "There's a park versus developers meeting tomorrow. Hunt wants me to be at it."

"*Us*," said Sixkiller. "Then we should go to Mystere and talk to yer Papa Brise."

"He's not *my* Papa Brise."

Greta arrived with two coffees.

Sixkiller fixed her with his most charming style. "Could yer be puttin' thet on the ranger's tab, please?" he said.

I sighed in agreement.

She chuckled as she set the coffee down and moved on.

"Anything else?" I asked him.

"Jessie's funeral service is scheduled for day after tomorrow. You've been given clearance to attend."

Something twisted painfully in my chest. "Whereabouts?"

"Soldiers Cemetery. I think it's near the water."

I sipped my coffee and pictured steep calcite cliffs and clipped green lawns. Dad had been buried at Soldiers. At least he had a plot and a plaque. I'd spread most of his ashes in Birrimun. "It looks out on the Palisade reefs. Not far from the place I did surveillance on the Romani."

He nodded, remembering. "The new driver'll take us out there. It'll be private."

"How long had she been working for GJIC?"

"I cain't talk about it."

The twist of pain intensified. "Of course you can't. Well, I didn't want many people at my funeral either. With the way you guys keep me in the dark, I expect I'll be getting my wish sometime soon." I got up and nodded formally at him.

"Virgin!" he called after me.

But I didn't stop to hear what he wanted to say.

SIXTEEN

Caro was in her nightie sipping green tea. The shadows under her eyes were deeper and darker, but she smiled when she opened the door for me.

"Did you catch up with Hamish?" she asked.

I tossed my head and my hands. "Kind of. He's off shadowing Johnny."

She squeezed my arm. "Sit down. I'll make you one of these."

I nodded gratefully, stepped over the box of burner phones, and flopped onto her chintz divan that was set into a reclining position. I caught a whiff of stain repellent on the fabric. "Is this new?"

"I'm not sleeping so well. It doubles as a bed and desk."

I wanted to ask her more about how she was feeling, but let it go. Today had been difficult enough without Caro having a meltdown.

She came back carrying a mug of tea for me, watching it with great concentration so it didn't spill.

"Shove over," she said.

We wiggled around until we were both side by side on the divan.

I sipped in silence for a bit until I felt my eyelids beginning to close.

"Oh, no, uh uh!" she said, snatching my empty cup away. "Now you talk. What's been happening?"

I sat up straighter. "I saw a Mythos on the bus going to the Quarter. It was going to follow a girl, but I got to it first."

"How did you get to it?"

I reached for my backpack, pulled the zipper and showed her the short baton. "I don't know what it is, but it worked a bit like an electric prodder."

"Did the passengers think you were crazy?"

"Certifiable," I said.

She crawled to the end of the divan, retrieved two devices and handed one to me. "Ginny, that name you gave me… Joachim Spears… I thought it rang bells. One of my colleagues interviewed him last year. He's a billionaire recluse. Nobody's seen him in person for a long time. Her interview was a video hookup."

"Is he Australian?"

"Yes. His primary company was a tech startup twenty years ago. They've got some of the brightest and best engineering and applied physicists in the world working for them."

"What's the company called?"

"Ready to be grossed out? It's Sparagmos."

"Strange name, but hardly gross. Why, what does it mean?"

"Sparagmos is the act of dismembering an animal or a human being."

"Why would you call a company by that name?"

"Because you're weird," she replied.

I pulled Chef's memory bug from my wallet and lodged it in the tablet's port. His list was in a neat table with clear headings. "Get your fingers ready," I told her.

She limbered them dramatically and licked her lips in anticipation.

"Right, let's check these names and see if we can build connections."

"What kind?" she said.

"Anything that links Corah, Johnny, and Professor Armand Dusan. Or Joachim Spears."

"Let me set up a flow chart." Her fingers flew over the screen, pinching and prodding until she had a skeleton graph ready.

We got down to it: me reading names from the list, scouting their online profiles, and Caro entering items into her graph.

After an hour, we took a break. She broke out the red wine and some crystal glasses.

"Fancy," I said.

"Vital."

We got back to it, and a little after midnight, Caro gave a low grunt of satisfaction.

"So Sparagmos – the Spears-owned group – is a parent company of one of ComTel's instrumentation contractors."

"ComTel? Really?"

"The link to the company tree was buried pretty deep behind a chain of shelf-Corporations, but I found it. And... the installation of the park's security canopy was overseen by a ComTel project manager named Radric Bowen. According to a dark net genealogy site that I subscribe to, he's Joachin Spears son-in-law."

I felt a flutter in my belly. One strong connection made.

"Where *did* you get the name Joachim Spears?" asked Caro.

"Hamish mentioned him. Seems someone has put out a contract on me."

"Spears?"

"Maybe."

She looked like she might cry, so I diverted her with something else.

"Heart... I mean, *Sam* Williams came to see me today," I said, managing to suppress a sigh.

"At home?"

I put the tablet down on my lap and picked up my glass of red wine. "Yeah. Just like that. He visited."

"Oh, Ginny," she said, her brow furrowed with concern. "How did you do?"

"Asked him to leave and not come back again." I gulped the contents of the glass, set it down again, and pushed the armrest out of the way. "He knows I'm working with GJIC."

"Small town. But more importantly, why would Joachim Spears want you dead, Ginny?" she said, not letting me distract her for too long.

"I'm not sure. Maybe he's got something to hide, which he thinks I might know about... like maybe his nephew disabled the canopy for the illegals to get in? But surely the Feds would have worked out that connection?"

"Feds can't access the real dark net. Their IP addresses are like flashing lights."

"Haven't they got ways around that?"

Caro's mouth twisted in amusement. "You'd be surprised how little they know about the real online criminal activity."

"You still surprise me, Caro."

She ruffled my hair like I was a child and pinched my cheek. "So mistrustful but still so naïve, Ginny. It's such an endearing mix."

I poked my tongue at her. "What do I know about anything? I muck out water troughs for a living, remember?"

She took a sip of wine and looked me straight in the eyes. "What you are doing," she said calmly – seriously, "is preserving from extinction the only *real* part of our world left. Without you, and your dad, our country would've long ago disappeared under a puddle of concrete, sunscreen lotion, lattes, and don't-give-a-fucks – like the rest of the world. Your work is not just important; it's our lifeline."

I appreciated her sentiment. "Not just Dad and me, Caro. Many people fought for Birrimun."

"And you'll keep on fighting. But I don't like the sound of this guy Spears. He's got resources."

"We still haven't found anything to connect Corah with Armand Dusan other than her attending his discussion salons."

She sighed. "Let's have a break, and talk about the Empusa."

I crossed my legs and wiggled around on the divan to face her. "Shoot!"

"Greek mythology says that the Empusa's the daughter of the goddess Hecate. Historically the Empusa's potency as a monster ebbed and flowed depending on the period and the person telling the story. But uniformly, she's seen as a vampiric demon with a donkey foot and a brass leg."

"Why so blessed?" I asked sarcastically.

"It's not clear, really. But according to some of the folklore, she's also supposedly a shapeshifter."

"Maybe that's why we can see her?"

Caro's eyebrows lifted. "What do you mean?"

"I asked Nate why only some of the Mythos can be seen by everyone. He said something about their strength. I'm beginning to think it's because of their shapeshifting ability."

"I don't like how blind they have you working on this, Ginny. Even black ops would afford you more details."

"And what do you know about black ops?"

She waved her fingers. "Hellooo... Hamish."

"Aaah, yes."

"Don't stress about him. He doesn't create problems. He cleans them up."

I thought about the hit man that had disappeared. "He does, at that."

We sat quietly thinking our own thoughts for a bit.

"What happened on the bus today?" she asked.

"I saw a Mythos following a woman."

"And...?"

"Nate called it an Aswang. It's vampiric, like the Empusa." I drummed my fingers on the divan, and an idea came to me. "Hey, let's add the name Rivera, or Rivera Salons, to our search parameters." I spelled it out loud for Caro as she typed it in.

"Well, what do you know?" she said. "Joe Rivera owns a very large chain of hair salons. He's also a major shareholder in a bioware supplies company owned by Joachim Spears. And he's on Chef's list. He was there the night of the opening."

My hands trembled. "You got an image?"

She lifted the tablet so I could see her screen. I recognised the short, stout man with large studded earrings.

"Yeah," I said. "I remember him."

"OK, let me search his business profile a little more," said Caro. "Go and make some coffee."

I did as she asked, grateful to stretch my legs and straighten my back. I was already losing muscle tone from not riding every day.

A pang of regret hit me. I missed Benny, my horse,

and I hadn't checked in with Leecey at all. But it was too late tonight, and I needed some sleep before the meeting tomorrow.

I poured the coffee into matching cups and tipped sugar cubes in. After dragging the spoon around a couple of times, I dropped it in the sink and carried the mugs out.

"Can't stop the signal, Ginny," she said. It was a quote from some old movie she loved. She said it whenever she found something she was searching for. Her cheeks usually turned a complementary pink.

"What've you got?"

"I'm no hacker, but I know places that take me other places. Have a look."

I browsed six images of a couple catching a taxi: Corah and Joe Rivera. "When was this?"

"Night of the opening."

"How did you…"

"Taxis keep their surveillance data on a metacloud."

"You hacked the cloud. That's totally illegal," I said automatically.

"Not really. I'm a beta tester for the company who owns the cloud."

I shook my head in wonder. "How did you…" My hand rose. "No, don't tell me."

"Don't look so freaked. I answered an advertisement. My credentials are good, Ginny, and they gave me the job. I've been accessing data from all over the world for years. Who could be more perfect as a tester than an investigative journalist?"

"How did you know the taxi data was there?"

"I didn't answer just any ad," she said, slightly indignantly. "I knew they were aiming for government clients."

I leaned forwards and ruffled her hair. "Thank you."

She smiled in a lukewarm way. "I need sleep," she said suddenly.

"Me too. We'll talk tomorrow."

"Stay if you like?"

"Nah."

I let myself out and hailed a taxi from the closest rank. It was too late at night to be messing with buses. I checked the number on my SAFE TRAVEL app before I got in though. As I settled back on the sticky vinyl, I promised myself that tomorrow I'd find out what Joe Rivera was worth to Armand Dusan and the Mythos.

Tomorrow.

I nodded off almost straightaway but was jerked awake a while later by the taxi driver stepping hard on the brakes.

"What?" I snapped out of a dream, totally disorientated.

We were less than two blocks from the Cloisters, where the Southway ramp peeled off the Ringway.

"A girl flagged me down," said the cabby through his intercom. "She's in trouble."

We were parked on the shoulder of the ramp with still enough room to reverse onto the Ringway. The light tower array above us cast harsh illumination downwards. Just us here. I couldn't see any girl.

"What girl?" I demanded.

The cabby was peering out the front passenger window. "I don't understand. I just saw her. She should be right here. Maybe she went down the ladder over there." He pointed to some steel piping that disappeared over the edge of the ramp: a maintenance ladder down onto the next level.

Aquila swooped down to land on it, and every nerve in my body twitched into alertness.

The cabby put his hand to his door and flipped open his lock. "I'll just go and take a look, in case she's fallen down–"

Quicker than I knew I could, I drew my pistol and pressed it up against the partition. "I'm an intelligence agent working for the government," I said calmly. "This particular pistol can crack your bullet proofing as easy as slicing tofu. Now, I'm telling you to take your hand off the door, and get-us-the-fuck-back on the Ringway."

He stiffened. "Hey lady. No drama. Go easy with that hardware, and we'll hit the road. Just trying to do the right thing by some poor kid."

"Admirable," I said. "But stupid. It's the middle of the night, and we're on the edge of the freeway. How long have you been driving cabs?"

"Since before you were born. But we got a call tonight – a cabby's daughter's been abducted. He's asking us to BOLO for her. Just relax now, and we'll be on our way."

Part of me admired his composure in the face of a gunwielding stranger. "Believe me, whoever you saw here, is not your friend's daughter."

"Got it. So let's just get you home. I'm just gonna lock the door now, OK?" he said.

"Sure thing." I let the intensity seep out of my voice. It was a hard thing to do with Aquila flapping her wings just a few meters away.

But as he moved his hand something flung itself against the door. The car rocked with the force. Then it hit the windscreen, followed by a thumping on the roof and behind me on the boot.

"What the–" the cabby began, but never finished his thought.

Something appeared at my window, eyes fierce and jaw snapping. The cab rocked again from the impact. Suddenly we were inundated on all sides by growling and hurtling missiles of fury.

"W- wild d- dogs," I stuttered. "G- go."

How many, I couldn't tell, but enough to totally obscure our view.

The cabby slammed his hand down on the door lock and began to accelerate. "Can't fucking see," he said. "Can't fucking *see*—"

I couldn't either, but something told me that his trajectory was wrong. We were heading off the shoulder of the ramp. The drop would kill us. But if he pulled too far the other way, we'd veer into traffic on the Ringway.

A series of shotgun-like clicks alerted us to the windscreen cracking under the onslaught.

"Right. Steer *right*!" I shouted, fumbling in my bag for the box I'd taken from the safe house. What had Sixkiller said? I couldn't remember. Something about ionic disruption. Could I risk using it with the cabby? What if I killed him? Did he have a family?

He did as I said, spinning the steering wheel, shouting back at me, "Red fucking eyes! See them?"

I did and I knew what they were. "Weave but keep right!"

He wrenched the steering wheel from side to side, and the wild dogs began to slide off. I felt the clunk as he ran over a couple. The tyres left the rough bitumen of the shoulder and we scraped the safety concrete wall, fishtailing in between a semitrailer and a bus. They honked us, but the cabby held his line.

Only one dog was left, its jaw locked onto the windscreen wipers, spittle stringing from its mouth. It stared back at us from the bonnet with a rabid maliciousness that turned my insides liquid.

I dropped the box and grabbed my LiFo to photograph it. But the cabby swerved violently again and sent it yowling under the wheels.

Neither of us spoke until he pulled up in the Cloisters dropoff bay. Then he opened the partition.

I saw his face properly for the first time: close-cropped and dark hair, deep set eyes, and a heavily lined face. He'd been a heavy smoker once. I'd lay bets he was thinking about lighting up right now.

"Done this job for fifteen years. Never seen nothin' like that before. Wild fucking dogs in the middle of the city. Wild fucking dogs with red eyes," he said, shaking his head.

"You did good," I said. "Kept your cool and listened to me."

"You really a spy?"

"No. And yes," I said. "But don't spread it around."

"I'll leave it out of my report."

"Yeah, you should. Hey, one more thing…"

He raised his eyebrows. "Well, I guess we're bonded now, so shoot…"

"What's the name of your driver friend whose daughter is supposed to be missing?"

"Pascal Cabria. Not a friend, but I know him. Been working the same beats as me for the last few. He's got a tribe of kids. Girls though. One of them's always in trouble. Wife self-medicates." He delivered the synopsis in a thoughtful tone, tinged with concern.

"You drivers all look out for each other?"

He shrugged. "Course. That's the way the world works."

I thought of Sixkiller. And Hamish. "You wanna give me your cab code?" I asked.

He hesitated, then reached for his cab ID.

I aimed my One Card at it until they synced. "OK if I call you again?"

"Long as there're no dogs." He held out his hand. "Vic Manslo."

"Virgin Jackson," I replied.

"Virgin? Bet you got hell for that growing up."

"Learned how to give hell, more like," I said with a grin.

He nodded. "What doesn't kill ya... call me anytime. I'll send my shift driver if I'm not on. His name's Davey. Lives on protein powder and chorizo. Decent kid."

"Thanks, Vic." I paid him with my LiFo's credit app, and got out.

He waved as he pulled back into the flow.

I dragged myself over to the front door, but, before I could open the foyer door, a figure stepped out of the shadows.

I grabbed for my Smith, but came up short as a knife pressed into my ribs.

"Easy now, Ranger."

His face was hidden by a cap and a bandana. "Special delivery." He thrust an object into my free hand and I glanced down at it. A burner phone.

"Jorge?"

"Papa says you call him soon, or the deal's off."

"Hey, I said it might take–"

But I was talking to the sweet night air.

Clutching the burner, I got inside the building as soon as I could. I thought about calling Sixkiller as I rode the lift to my floor, but it was almost 2am. Yesterday had bled badly into today, and I was totally over it.

Aquila was still with me, hopping down the corridor, flying up to sit on the lamp above my door. I couldn't relax until I was inside with the door locked.

Thankfully, she didn't follow me in.

I shucked off my boots and backpack, peeled my clothes in a single movement, and lay down.

I think I reached for the bed covers...

SEVENTEEN

...But I woke up naked and shivering under the air conditioning, the alarm clarping. I slapped it off and rolled onto my back. Both my arms had gone to sleep and my head was pounding like a tenderiser on meat.

Without opening my eyes, I felt for my water tube and glugged enough down to unstick my tongue. A couple of throat clears and some Advil later, I was sitting up contemplating that I hadn't recovered my clean clothes from the laundry.

Worse than that, someone was knocking at my door.

I pulled on yesterday's shirt and some tracky pants and staggered over to the sec cam. It was Esther.

"Virgin, can you open the door?"

I did as she asked with an excuse about running late on my lips.

She held a large plastic bag in her hands and was trembling with the weight. "Oh thank goodness you're home, dear. It was rather heavier than I expected."

"Hello, Esther. What is?"

"Your washing. I just happened to be down in the laundry

picking up some things, and I noticed that yours was ready. We're alphabetical, you know, according to floor. That nice young girl down there carried them to the lift for me. She's new, I think, but couldn't have been more helpful. Well, other than to have come up here with me and brought them to your door. But I couldn't let her do that. She had so much to do–"

I took the bag from her. "Esther, you carried this by yourself? You should have called me. But thank you! You're kind for doing that."

"Well, dear, you're the kind one. I was really just looking for an excuse to hear how your date went."

I drew a blank for an instant and then recalled my coffee with Rav. "Come in and let me make you tea. I don't have long. I have a big meeting to get to," I said.

She smiled with undisguised delight. "I'd love to come in. It's been so dreary taking it quietly, if you know what I mean. Dr Rav said no bowling or shopping for another fortnight."

I cleared the couch of dirty plates, and patted it. "I'll put the jug on and be back in a jiffy. Just need to shower. Thanks again, Esther."

"You're welcome, my dear. I'll just sit here."

When I got back though, she'd found clean cups in the dishwasher and made coffee for us both and toast for me. She sipped hers happily while I hunted for the vegemite, which I found behind the salt and pepper shakers on the drainer, instead of in the pantry.

I joined her then and began to munch into the salty deliciousness.

"Did you go somewhere nice, dear?" she asked.

Clearly I wasn't getting out of telling her.

"We met across the road from the hospital in the café. It

was to make up for our evening... er... date being postponed."

"Daytime is always good the first time. No pressure to get involved in any shenanigans!" She gave me a conspiratorial wink.

I took a sip of my coffee and considered how Caro would pay money to hear her say this to me. "It was strictly work, Esther. Though he talked about his family and he said he'd call me again. That's all there is to tell," I told her.

"Slow and steady wins the race," she said, nodding her approval. "You want a keeper, Virgin. Not like that other one."

"You mean... er... Heart?"

"Oh, I never knew his name, dear. Just saw him coming and going. He was the most divine young man, but I knew that meant trouble."

"Well, not so much trouble, Esther. He turned out to be a federal policeman."

"A snitch?"

I smiled. "No, that's something else. He was an undercover agent."

She sipped some more, her eyes twinkling with interest at the news. "Not that I'm interfering in your business or anything, dear, but you wouldn't want to keep seeing him and scare off that nice Dr Rav. Would you?"

Something about her manner made it impossible for me to be irritated with her. And yet, usually, I hated anyone knowing my business. "I'm not seeing him anymore, Esther. He dropped by the other day, just to... er... collect some clothes."

"Not that I was looking, but I did notice him in the corridor. Well, it's a very good thing that you gave him his marching orders. You deserve better."

I lifted my cup in a toast. "Here's to that."

My phone rang then, saving me from round two of the inquisition.

"Virgin," demanded Bull Hunt. "Are you in transit?"

"On my way," I told Bull, and motioned to Esther that I had to go.

I hung up, grabbed my boots and ushered her to her door. "Thanks again, Esther."

"Standards, Virgin. Remember that!"

"Standards it is, Esther."

Twenty minutes later I walked up the underpass stairs and entered through the stable's front doors. Totes was standing in the corridor tugging at his hair. When he saw me his face lit up. "Virgin!"

I gave him a wave and detoured into the tack room. Leecey was in there changing the bit on her bridle.

"Hey," she said, showing relief to see me.

Hers and Totes' warm welcome smelled of the park hierarchy visiting.

"OK for me to ride Benny?" I said.

"You're still the boss, Virgin," she said, grinning.

"You're doing the job, Leecey. Not me."

She tossed me a bridle from the hook beside her. "Your horse has missed you. The meeting's at La Paloma. Superintendent Hunt thought it would be good to have it there. Get the government people out of their offices; make 'em come face to face with the land they're trying to destroy."

I nodded my approval of his plan. "He already gone?"

"Yeah. He took the small hova. But the Marshal's waiting for you."

"You coming?" I asked.

She grinned. "Not now you're here. I've got supply

inventory and coach routes to complete."

I felt a pang of guilt. "You catching up on my backlog?"

"Slowly. But mainly we're working on a re-eval of the eastern butte topography. Too much degradation of the ascension trails. Totes's helping me chart a new one. We've got a gnamma hole to skirt around. " Her tone charged with interest and her cheeks tinged with colour as she spoke.

"Bull gave you permission to reroute past a gnamma hole?" I asked with surprise. The naturally occurring granite cavities were among the most precious, most protected elements of park landscape. They had a deep connection to the indigenous land owners.

She shook her head. "We're going to present it to him with all the environmental protocols in place. Hope he'll go for it." A worried look flitted across her face. "Is that OK with you?"

"Not only OK. I'm impressed. And I'm glad to see you and Totes getting along."

She breathed out with relief. "He's flaky, Virgin. But he's OK."

"Definitely flaky. Don't let him bug your apartment," I said. "Hey... I saw Johnny last night."

Her expression altered. She glanced at the floor, not wanting me to see the emotion in her eyes.

"He's with Corah and they're caught up in something ugly. Keep clear of him," I warned.

She pursed her lips, and I knew she was holding back. It wasn't my place to tell her what to do, but I couldn't help it. Leecey had found her way out. I wanted her to stay there.

"Say it," I said.

"Nothing to say." She unhooked my saddle from its rest and dropped it into my arms. "Go save our world, Virgin."

"If it kills me," I said.

And I meant it.

I carried my tack to Benny's stall. She nickered and walked straight up to me, pushing her nose into my shoulder. I dropped the tack and put my arms around her neck. She smelled of sweet oats and sweet freedom. I ran my hand over her coat and felt the ripples of the augmentation nodes under her skin. Scratching around them always made her whinny, and she rewarded me by lipping my forearm.

"Time for some sunshine," I whispered in her ear.

Though the stables had natural light windows, they were bullet and bomb proof. The light always seemed so remote through the protection layers.

I led her out of the stall and down the corridor past Totes' office. He pounced on me before I reached the foyer, waving his control panel remote in my face to get my attention.

Benny wasn't impressed with the delay and promptly lifted her tail to evacuate her bowels.

Totes scowled at her and pressed a button to activate the stables' cleaners. They whirred up to the steaming pile and got to work, scooping, converting, and spraying disinfectant around.

"What is it, Totes?" I said.

"You've been ignoring my messages," he said, with a slightly hysterical inflection in his voice. His scalp shone from a recent exfoliation and his thin nose and half-closed eyes seemed thinner and more closed than usual. This time his favourite doll, Princess Phuti, was strapped to his back like a baby in a backpack.

"No more or less than usual," I said. "The only difference is that you don't have recording devices in my apartment anymore. You feeling a bit out of touch?" I delivered the last with fake sympathy. Truth is, I was still mightily pissed that the little brainiac had been spying on me.

"It was only audio. You're so unforgiving, Virgin."

"And you so overstepped," I said.

"Can we *please* put this to rest?" he whinged.

I took a slow, deep breath. "Fine. But you owe me. Now tell me what's been going on in two sentences or less. I've got to get out to La Paloma."

"Bull's got the AD and the Conservation Prime with him. They're scared, Virgin. I could hear it in their voices. This new lobby group who wants to sell off the park is gaining traction."

"So I'm told."

"And Leecey's working out real well. Either way you might be out of a job."

"You too."

He grunted in annoyance and disappeared back into his cubbyhole.

I turned my attention to Sixkiller, who was frowning up a storm over by the Interface doors. He tightened Sombre Vol's girth strap as I approached.

"Marshal," I said.

"Ranger," he replied. "Let's talk outside."

I had no argument with that, so we mounted and rode on through.

EIGHTEEN

The sun always bit into your skin harder out in Birrimun. Shade was scarce, and the park retained its desert climate: cold at night, hot during the day. I checked the thermostat on my cell phone and saw it was already approaching thirty-eight degrees Celsius.

"A hunn'ed degrees and no shade," sang Sixkiller, going by his Fahrenheit measure. He slid his water bladder around his waist and sucked on the tube.

I copied him and nudged Benny over to the trough. The ride to Paloma would be dusty and hot. Even augmented horses got thirsty on days like this.

She drank some and flicked Sombre Vol with her tail as the not-so-gelded gelding pushed in.

I didn't wait for Vol to finish guzzling. Benny and I trotted on out past the ring of palm trees into the open.

I thought of the murder I'd witnessed in this spot just a few weeks ago. It had triggered a bunch of events that had led me to view the world entirely differently. I also now knew what I'd seen that night was a Mythos killing a human, and that it was somehow connected with the illegals we'd caught entering the country through the park. That event had added ammunition to the anti-park lobby.

"Pascal Cabria," I said to Sixkiller, when he caught up with me.

"Excuse me?"

"Last night I caught a taxi home. The taxi driver pulled onto the shoulder of an offramp. Thought he'd seen a colleague's daughter standing there."

"Who? What's yer point, Virgin?"

Sombre Vol's gait was longer and more fluid than Benny's, which meant that I jiggled in the saddle while Sixkiller looked as graceful as a dancer. "My point is that a taxi driver called Pascal Cabria put out an alert on the taxi grapevine that his daughter was missing. Every driver from here to the Territories is on the lookout for her."

"So?"

"When we pulled up to rescue this girl my cabby saw, she wasn't there. We got attacked by wolves instead. And not the regular kind."

Sixkiller's head swivelled in my direction. "Why didn't yer call me right away?"

"Well, first, I was busy surviving the whole thing. When I got home, it was late and I was tired. I wanted to sleep on it. Make sure I hadn't imagined the whole thing. I mean, it's getting harder and harder to do that, you know – pick what's real and what isn't, I mean." My tone was thoroughly conversational, as though we were discussing the weather, or what we'd eaten for dinner. It was strange to hear it.

"What about this morning? Yer could've called me first thing."

"Esther woke me up. Soon as she'd gone, I came here. So

I'm telling you now... maybe you should check out this Pascal Cabria. Could be a coincidence, or could be he's Korax."

"Yer sure the wolves were Mythos?"

"Their eyes glowed red."

"Right." Grim definitely described the set of his mouth.

"Taxi driver saw them too. And we felt them buffeting the car."

"They're gaining strength," he said.

"So it seems."

"No injuries?"

"Unscathed. But the cabby was a little freaked. I tried to make light of it, y'know. Suggested they were feral dogs."

Sixkiller got his LiFo out and started speaking quickly to someone, somewhere.

I didn't really listen, my thoughts racing ahead to the meeting.

"Who's going to be at La Paloma?" I asked him when he finished his call.

He shrugged. "Not sure, but we're there to *watch* negotiations only. Got it?"

"Clearly," I said.

We pressed the horses on, and, as was usual, for a time Benny stayed shoulder to shoulder with Sombre Vol, until, eventually, the bigger horse gained distance and we were eating his dust. Even with augmentations and enhanced endurance Benny couldn't match Vol.

By the time we passed Los Tribos, both horses were beginning to slow, their sides heaving from the run.

I felt the pull of the place, as we skirted the perimeter. The heat shimmered and twisted inside the cupped, rocky fingers, and the burn scars from the firefight had almost all dusted over. Somewhere in there was an answer I was looking for. If only I could locate the data from Dad's camera.

I should tell Sixkiller how I'd learned that Jo Rivera was linked to the diner and possibly Corah, but he'd ask more questions, and I didn't want Caro dragged into it yet. After the meeting was done, I'd snoop around Rivera's Salons and see what I could dig up. Then I'd share with the Marshal.

Sombre Vol had dropped back to a walk, so I trotted up alongside.

"How come I get the feeling that yer keepin' things from me, Ranger? Yer supposed to be my partner."

His directness threw me for a moment. The man had an uncanny talent for reading my mind. "*Partners* suggest we're on an equal footing, Marshal. Last I heard I was working for you."

He made an impatient sound. "Only 'cause my experience with the Mythos is extensive. But I thought we shared the same goal."

I twisted in my saddle, letting him see my expression. "I've been blackmailed into this job, Nate. *My* goal is to keep Birrimun safe. If that means ridding the world of the Mythos, then you and I have the same purpose. But don't think that I'm a convert to your service or to my mother."

He stiffened in his saddle. "Never a chance of yer not being direct?"

"I learned it young. Same as you." I didn't have a clue what he learned when he was young, but he didn't prevaricate or dissemble, so someone taught him to shoot straight. "It's an attractive quality."

His eyes narrowed so much that I thought he'd closed them.

"Thet meant to be a compliment?" he asked.

I shrugged. "It's the truth. Take it how you like."

Suddenly his face relaxed, the tightness drained, and he laughed. "Come on!"

He loosened his reins and Vol set off again, kicking a spray of red sand over Benny and me.

I didn't bother chasing hard this time. Instead, I took the chance to enjoy the expansive sky and the screeds of cockatoos wheeling, diving, and screeching across it. The hot wind set my body into a sweat that felt cleansing. I'd been spending too much time in the city.

Vol's trail of dust led me past a defiant spatter of Mulla Mulla and the Paloma station yards where I'd see the giant Mythos. But the unusual sight there today was an inflatable habi-cube rippling in the light breeze, several hova-coaches, and a camo-outfitted security escort.

When I finally caught up with Sixkiller, he'd already tied Vol up to the tethering post.

I joined him on the porch, and waited while a guard in a black suit wanded me over and took my pistol. His suit said secret service, but the 3D insignia flickering on his suit pocket suggested private security.

I felt immediately resentful. This was my park! Why did private security get to say who came and went here?

Sixkiller remained passive alongside my seething disapproval, and gestured to me to remove my hat when we were allowed through into the station house.

Someone with the same insignia ushered us through the public area main living room and along the corridor into the kitchen at the back of the house.

Part of the meeting contingent sat around the original hardwood table. I was pleased to see that the home-fashioned chairs had been carefully moved to one side and each person was seated on an inflatable stool.

The only other change to the room was a mobile air conditioner puffing at the end of the table. I shivered as the cooler air chilled the sweat on my body.

Ranger Solly White and Ranger Jenna Wong from the southwest and northwest quadrants were standing abreast behind the cooler, arms folded. I hadn't seen either in over a month, but it felt much longer than that.

We nodded at each other. Solly and Jenna were good people. Right now they looked as uncomfortable as I felt.

Bull was seated at the table with *his* boss, Jools Abe, and *her* boss, Michael Day. I knew them both, though with Chief Director Day it was more by reputation. While Assistant Chief Director Jools Abe was energetic, young and always in a hurry, the boss of Park Southern, Day, was an older, gnarlier version of Bull Hunt: big bellied with a florid complexion and an inclination to bad temper.

Dad had always said that Day was a good man to have on your side and a formidable enemy. He'd been a ranger before Dad, and had deep connections in the coastal city's old business community. That had made him the ideal candidate for the top job.

The three of them turned their eyes to us as we entered the room. Bull looked as relieved to see me as Totes and Leecey had.

"Jackson," grunted Chief Day. "American government hasn't seduced you away yet?"

"Not likely, sir," I said.

He grunted again. But this one sounded like approval. "Marshal Sixkiller," he added. "Trust you're being ably assisted?"

I held my breath.

It seemed like a too-lengthy pause before Sixkiller said,

"Yer people are good at what they do, Chief Director. I got no complaints."

C-Director Day nodded. "I assume that means that you'll be wrapping up your business here soon, and I'll get one of my best rangers back."

"Soon as possible, sir," said Sixkiller.

Best rangers? His praise inflated a warm bubble inside me.

"When you're done, Marshal, come and see me about a job," the C-Director added.

The warm bubble popped and left me with heartburn. *Gawd, no.*

"Thank you, sir," said the Marshal.

Day waved us both back to stand directly behind them. I leaned against the resin-coated weatherboard wall in order to touch something solid. Today felt very uncertain.

Bull rubbed the back of his neck and threw me a quick, meaningful glance over his shoulder, but I couldn't decipher what it was he was trying to say.

"Something's up," I whispered to Sixkiller.

Any reply he was going to make was forestalled by four people shuffling in from the corridor. They wore masks, boot covers, and protection films over their clothes. As they ditched the layers, I realized one of them was Billjee. She must have been showing the other three through the closed-to-the-public sections of the station house.

Billjee collected the discarded items into a bag while her guests patted their civvies into order and sat down on the opposite side to the Park Southern bosses.

I nodded a silent greeting at her and she winked as she took up position behind her charges. Rangers were stationed at three points of the compass around the room, leaving one spot empty.

I studied each new face carefully: one woman around my age and two older men. The woman was the only familiar one, but I couldn't place her exactly. Her hair was smooth, dark and short, and her cheek bones high enough to hang Christmas mistletoe on. She had an arresting, intelligent face. Both the men were unremarkable, aside from being fair-haired with heavy builds.

The woman cleared her throat, and tapped her fingers on the table.

"You can see what a precious commodity we have here, minister," said Day, in a gruff, formidable voice before she could speak.

Minister. Of course! The recently appointed Environment and Land Heritage Minister, Joelle Anders. She'd replaced the previous minister just over two months ago when he'd become ill with pancreatic cancer. I'd been so concerned with Sixkiller and my own affairs that I hadn't taken a lot of notice of her press appearances.

She glanced around before answering. "Agent Williams," she called out.

Two men in suits appeared from the corridor. One took up a position on the vacant wall and the other handed a tablet to the minister. She quickly thumbed through her ID protocol.

Sam?

He scanned the room automatically, and his eyes slid over me without acknowledgment.

What were the Feds doing here? Didn't the minister have her own secret service bodyguard?

Next to me, Sixkiller stirred, recognizing him as well.

"I had no idea," I whispered.

Sixkiller didn't answer, but he inched closer to me so that our elbows were touching. It wasn't for my comfort, but something told me not to move away.

His thigh pressed closer to mine, and in that body contact he pushed something into my hand.

I took it and slipped my hand behind my back. Whatever it was felt soft and round.

Sixkiller inched away, back into his previous pose.

Sam gave us a sharp glance.

I carefully wedged the object in between my belt and skin. If I stayed very still, it would remain in place. If I moved, it would either drop onto the floor, or into my pants. Neither was a good option, considering my concern that it was a weapon.

I slowly folded my arms in front to show Sam that my hands were empty, and fixed him with an icy stare.

He looked away and delved into the satchel he carried, bringing out a small device which he set on the table.

The minister reached out and touched his wrist in thanks. Her fingers lingered on his cuff for a moment in a gesture that was intimate. She smiled at him and depressed a button on the back of the device. It made a low whirring noise, barely discernible over the portable air conditioner, as it lifted into the air.

"Good morning," said Minister Anders. "The Prime Minister has asked me to chair this moderation meeting between the Park Southern working directors and the Urban Lifestyle lobby group. This meeting will be recorded and streamed to the Offices of the Interior for quality assurance, an integrity audit, and general record. Could you please state your name and agreement for the recording?"

Everyone dutifully gave their name and permission to the whirring device.

"Thank you all for being here today. I will state the nature of the debate and then open the floor for discussion. I'd like to remind you all that your conduct will be on public record. The Prime Minister has been a longtime supporter of the Park Project; however, the cost of operations is now far outstripping the revenue earned. Less people, according to our surveys, want this kind of outdoors experience. In the meantime, we are desperate for more housing and infrastructure to support our population. I'd like to hear proposals from both sides. The Prime Minister is looking for creative solutions to this dilemma that will satisfy both parties..."

I stopped listening after a while, partly because my anger threatened to become something I couldn't control. The Urban Lifestyle anti-park lobby group's proposal amounted to a reduction of over seventy-five percent of the park area, and urban landscaping of the remaining twenty-five percent, turning it into Japanese-style gardens with waterfalls. Their only concession to the natural habitat was to retain Los Tribos and the La Paloma station house. That meant all of Billjee's, Jenna's and Solly's quadrants would be subsumed.

During the discussion Billjee's expression changed from amicable to stony, her hands clasped tight in front of her. I wondered whether her thoughts were ranging towards murder in the way mine were.

"Breathe," Sixkiller whispered. "It's just rhetoric."

I took his advice: slow, deep breaths that steadied the growing vortex inside. Everything Dad had worked and died for was being weighed up and priced in front of me. Everything I stood for.

When would Bull and Day and Jools become impassioned? When would they call bullshit?

But other than the flush rising up Bull's neck, I could see no sign of emotion; the argument stayed polarised but civil.

They broke for refreshments around midmorning. I watched them file out, making sure I was the last of the rangers to leave the room, so I could avoid Sam, and extract the object wedged in my pants.

I had a quick look at it – w*hat the hell?* – before transferring it carefully to my pocket. That question remained on my lips as I caught up with Sixkiller on the porch.

The lobbyists, the minister, and the directors had retired into the habi-cube to eat. Food waste was carefully controlled in the park, since it had been proved that additives degraded the fragile food chain. On my longer rides, I was only permitted tube food. Every time I returned, Totes inventoried my refuse. He was meticulous, and so was I.

Sixkiller was standing, reading his LiFo. Everyone else – including Sam – looked to be inside the cube except a circle of security guards stationed around it.

"What was that... thing you gave me?"

"I'll explain in a moment," he said quietly, nodding his head at the guards.

"Why so much private security and no secret service?" I asked instead.

"Must have been part of the meeting terms – using Federals and contractors instead of the service. Your... friend. He's a Fed, isn't he?"

"Apparently," I said.

The whole thing was really bothering me, and not just because Sam was here. As Sixkiller walked over to the guards, I took a surreptitious photo of the closest guy on my cell phone then turned my back while I enlarged and cropped it, until I got a reasonable image of the insignia on their jackets. I sent it to Caro, asking her to find out who owned the company.

Sixkiller's hand clamped down on my shoulder as I was tucking my cell away.

"Let's do a perimeter sweep," he said and walked on.

I followed him towards the back of the house, where I caught up.

"What's up?" I asked.

"I want to check the water tank at the back."

"Why? And tell me what this is?" Now we were out of sight, I pulled the soft ball he'd given me out of my pocket.

He took it out of my hand. "Fast-acting Midazolam bomb."

"What?"

"Airborne amnesiac. I thought we might haveta use it. If we had a problem with the Mythos."

"You expecting a problem?"

"We've gotta hotspot of activity registerin' here."

"Here? Meaning La Paloma?"

"Yeah." He kept walking quickly.

I followed less enthusiastically. Last time I'd encountered Mythos in the park, I'd spent a week in hospital.

The water tank was a late addition to the station house, built about the same time as the adjacent stone meathouse in the vain hope of collecting what little rainfall was around when the climate began to change. The sixty thousand gallon iron shell showed remnants of green paint around the base, and pinpricks of light shone through rust holes.

I put my nose to the now unusable tap, and sniffed. Though dry, the inside of the pipe carried a sweet straw scent. Dad always said it smelled like the old hessian water bags the prospectors had carried with them. He'd shown me pictures of the bags, but no one had made them in fifty or sixty years: dirty white, misshapen and unhygienic. He'd carried one on rides until they'd forced him to take a tube bladder.

"Virgin," whispered Sixkiller.

He was a few meters away, over by the corner of the sand-brick meathouse that the original station people had hung their newly killed carcasses in to bleed.

I joined him. "What is it?"

"Nothing good." He nodded to indicate that I should look around the corner.

I crept forwards, brushing past him.

On the red sand a few body lengths away, a bison shimmered. Saliva streamed from its nostrils. Its eyes gazed at me impassively, watching. Disturbingly, Aquila was perched on his rump.

Ohitika and Aquila.

I stepped back and leaned against the meathouse wall, trembling all over. Both our spirit guides. Together. What the hell was coming?

"Be calm. It might just be a warning."

"You said Ohitika only ever appears when someone's likely to kill you. *Really likely*," I whispered.

He kept his voice low. "Yeah. But this's different. They're together. It's a message."

I shook my head. "Chrissakes, Nate. Tell me something useful."

He held up his hand to silence me; I could see he was thinking.

Taking a deep breath, I stepped forwards to look again. The air around them seemed quite distorted. Suddenly, Aquila lifted off Ohitika's back and the bison reared on his hind legs. Then both of them disappeared.

I blinked a couple of times to make sure my eyes weren't playing tricks. The only evidence that they'd been there was a slight disturbance in the sand.

I left Sixkiller and walked over to the spot, resisting the urge to run my fingers through the air they'd inhabited. What was going on? And then I saw it... similar to the strange air distortion, but in the sand at my feet.

"Nate," I called out low and urgent.

The tiny little downwards spin of the sound was widening into a swirl of movement.

"Nate!" Louder.

I glanced over my shoulder. He was coming towards me.

Then the ground gave way and I began to slip. I threw myself sideways, using my hands like scoops, digging wildly into the sand to get purchase. "S- sink h- hole!"

He began to run. "Don't struggle, Virgin. Stop!"

I was already up to my waist. Even though I knew he was right, telling me to keep still went against every survival instinct. I stopped kicking, but kept slipping anyway. Suddenly, I was up to my armpits.

Sixkiller threw his belt to me. I floundered around until I grabbed it, then he began hauling me hard. As I slid free of the sinkhole, the sand seemed to settle for a moment then vented upwards like a geyser.

We both fell back staring upwards.

A creature materialised on top of the vent: a huge bird with scales on its body. It gave a screech that sent me shrinking instinctively against Sixkiller.

He put one hand up to ward it off; the other stayed clamped around my shoulders. But the Mythos didn't seem interested in us, and flapped hard and fast away to the north.

"What the fuck was that?" said an incredulous voice from behind us.

Sam Williams stood there, mouth open in disbelief.

Sixkiller sprang to his feet, pulling me along with him.

"Use the bomb," he told me.

"How?"

He didn't wait to answer, shoving his fingers deep into my pocket to retrieve the soft-coated gas ball.

Seeing Sixkiller's movement, Sam reached for his piece. "Hey, put your hands where I can–"

The Marshal let go of it and pressed it into my palm. Then he lifted his hands in the air.

"Now, Virgin!" he urged under his breath.

I took two large strides towards Sam and threw the ball right in his face. On impact the soft ball stuck and burst right over his nose.

Sam stepped away, grabbing at his face and coughing. Then his legs folded. Sixkiller ran forwards and caught him, lowering him to the ground.

"Come and wait here with him until he comes around. I have to make some calls and get this meeting adjourned," said Sixkiller.

"No way. I mean… what will I say to him? He'll know we drugged him."

"He'll be confused. Think of something."

"But what about the Mythos… and the sinkhole? What's it mean? Are more coming out of there?" I pointed to the sand well.

"Take care of this agent, Virgin. *Please*." He pulled his LiFo out of his shirt pocket and strode off.

Shite. I approached my former lover with caution, hoping he didn't come out of his amnesia swinging punches.

I squatted down and shook his shoulder gingerly. "Sam? Sam? Are you OK?"

He stirred and his eyes flickered open. When he recognised me, he grabbed my shoulder and hugged me close. Too close.

His familiar scent was painful to me.

"Sam. It's OK. I just found you out here. You must have passed out," I said.

"Ginny?" He let go of me and sat up, rubbing his forehead. Sand had stuck to his clothes and his skin.

I resisted the urge to brush it off, and offered him a hand.

We pulled each other up, and stood facing each other, awkwardly.

"I don't know what happened. I came out here to look for… something…" He glanced around, bewildered. "I thought I saw…"

"Saw what?" I pretended to look around with concern as well. How would I explain the sand disturbance from the sink well…?

But it had vanished and all we could see was the stunted line of bushes in the distance that marked the beginnings of dry gulch.

He shook his head a couple of times and pressed the bridge of his nose. "I feel… odd."

"You eaten today?" I asked.

"Some. I had an early start. What were you doing out the back here?"

I tried to look nonchalant. "This meeting is in my park. I was just checking around while you all had a break."

He didn't seem convinced, but he clearly had no other explanation. "Come back with me?"

"Yeah, sure. I need to catch up with the Marshal anyway."

"How are things with you two?" he asked, as we walked towards the front of the station house together.

I shrugged, not wanting to be drawn on any aspect of my life.

He stopped and said, "Look, I apologize if today is uncomfortable for you."

"Good of you to consider my feelings, Sam," I replied, with undisguised sarcasm. Sixkiller hadn't instructed me to be nice to him. "But you're just doing your job."

He pursed his lips and kept on walking.

We didn't speak again, and when we entered the habi-cube he headed straight for the minister.

I grabbed a bagel and a coffee from the food table, and watched Sam take his seat next to his boss. She'd organised a plate of food for him: a salad the same as hers and some bread rolls.

The hurt feelings in my chest found their way to my stomach, making me queasy, and the cream cheese bagel tasted like soap.

Sam took the plate and forked his way through the salad, listening attentively to what was being said around him. Our eyes met once, and he looked away first.

I drank the coffee and forced the rest of the bagel down. He was an officer of the law, I reminded myself. Perhaps I should just get over it and forgive him.

Thankfully, Sixkiller came in and my attention turned to more important, more dangerous issues.

"Oceane has been in touch with the Feds. We'll be ordered out any minute," he said quietly to me.

"What reason did she use?" I asked.

He shrugged, helped himself to some celery sticks and began crunching.

Within seconds of him biting into the first one, buzzers went off everywhere. Sam was the first to react, whispering in the minister's ear.

She nodded and he stood up.

"Excuse me everyone, can I have your attention? We've been instructed to leave and return to the city immediately.

Please proceed directly to your transport."

"What's this?" boomed back Director Day.

"I believe there's been some kind of malfunction in the canopy and the filters are concentrating rather than reducing harmful amounts of UV rays. If you can all line up by the entrance to the tent, we'll provide shade for you to get into your coaches."

Director Day glared at Jools Abe. She was on the phone already, and she nodded at him that Sam was correct. Day swore openly, knowing that this did not help our position. It was the second time in a few weeks that there'd been a problem with the canopy.

"That excuse makes us look bad," I said, turning to Sixkiller with a furious whisper.

"We *have* to close the park down," he said. "The canopy is the most acceptable excuse."

We were face to face, breathing hotly on each other.

"The lack of revenue will play right into their hands. You heard their economic projections. You're just giving them ammunition."

"We have to investigate this, Virgin. It's not safe here. Now help me get these people out. You escort the Park contingent to their hova. I'll take the others."

I scowled and we both headed to the tent flap.

Sam was already standing outside, directing traffic and security guards. The guards had formed two lines to the hova-coaches and were holding the emergency space blankets over their heads providing shade protection.

Billjee led the lobbyists and the minister to their coach, while I led the park directors to theirs.

Solly and Jenna trailed and then split to ride shotgun alongside the hova-drivers. Director Day's complexion had turned an unhealthy shade of purple with annoyance, while Jools Abe had her phone stuck to her ear managing the damage control.

"Virgin, you'd better ride back with us," said Bull, who was the last to get in.

"I'll see things tidied up out here first, sir." I *never* called Bull sir, but it seemed like an occasion for it. "The stables can send the retrieval car out for me later."

"I'll call you when we have more information on this situation," he said.

"I'll also get Leecey to cancel today's tours."

He grunted in exasperation and nodded. Then he slid the door shut.

The security guards piled into their own bus, and the Feds in theirs as well. I retreated to stand under the shade of the habi-cube canopy, which is where Sam found me.

"It's dangerous to stay, Virgin."

"We need to do some tidy up. We'll use our haz-suits. They're good to filter the full spectrum EM wavelengths. The Marshal's getting them from our saddle packs now."

I pointed to Sixkiller, who was standing near Sombre Vol, shrouded in a space blanket.

"What about the horses?"

"Their coats are already treated. But we'll move them into the station stables until the problem is fixed." The charade felt ridiculous, and I was no actor, so I tried to cut it short. "We'll be picked up later. Get your minister to safety."

He gave me a look. "She's not… it's just work, Ginny."

"Sure, agent." I couldn't help but enjoy the way he smelled up close. "I understand."

He hesitated and bit his lip like he wanted to say something more. Then he seemed to change his mind. "See you later."

"Unlikely," I said.

He touched my shoulder. "Virgin. I'm sorry. Truly. *Please.*"

I sighed, relenting. "It'll be OK. Just give me some time."

Light crept into his expression and he gave a quick nod. "Better go."

He turned up his collar to protect his neck, and sprinted across to the minister's car. The blowers engaged in unison and all the ACVs lifted and swung around. Within minutes, all I could see of the entire party was the billowing dust in their wake.

Sixkiller joined me. He folded the space blanket away and dropped it in the entry of the habi-cube.

"One of our people is coming out to test the area of the sink hole," he said.

"How are they going to get here? We're in lockdown."

"By the time the others make it back to the city, there'll be another call to say it was a malfunction in one of the sensors, but that we should keep the park vacant until it's been fixed."

"Fine. I'll tell Leecey to bring your analyst, and some of the retrieval staff. They can take this down, and dispose of the food inside," I said, kicking the side of the habi-cube.

"I'll wait here."

"I'll stay too then."

"No. You go to Papa Brise and tell him GJIC will give him full immunity against conviction, if he'll share all his information about the Korax."

"Won't a phone call do?" I wanted to go to the Rivera Salons, not to Mystere.

"No, nothing that can be tapped," he said. "Besides, we've just had intel that the Korax have taken one of Papa Brise's men. It will be a good time to speak to him. Get a gauge of things."

"Taken? How do you know?"

"Anonymous tip."

"You believe it?"

"They sent images of the body."

"Images can be forged."

"Not these. If the Korax are active in Mystere, it's for a reason. We have to know what it is," he said.

"Just like we have to know how a Mythos just burst out of a sand geyser out of the desert."

"Depending on what our analysis shows, GJIC presence is likely to increase significantly in your city."

"More of you," I said, with a lighter tone. "I can't wait."

He almost smiled. "About the other rangers…" he said.

"Yes?"

"If you had to pick one that would understand, would accept the situation quickly, who would it be?"

"Billjee," I said, without hesitation. "She's spiritual by nature and she loves this land like I do. The others are good people, but Billjee sees beyond the obvious."

"We may need to bring her on board."

"I'd welcome that," I said.

"Good to know."

On impulse I put my hand out.

He eyed me with curiosity, but clasped it.

I held his hand firmly as we shook, conveying my sincerity. "Thanks for having my back, partner."

He seemed lost for words.

NINETEEN

Sixkiller had told me to use the work car to get to Mystere, but I couldn't face being in it, so I called Vic Manslo on the way up to my apartment.

"You got strange tastes in locations," he said.

"You taking me or not?"

"Close as I can. I'll be outside in fifteen minutes."

That gave me enough time to tiptoe past Esther's, change my dress shirt and my workboots, wash up, and grab some extra ammunition for the Smith. I got to the standing bay with a few minutes to spare and rang Caro.

"How did it go?" she asked.

I told her.

"Shi-it," she said with feeling. "Up out of the sand, you say?"

"Like an erupting volcano. Then it just up and flew north."

"And now?"

"I'm going to Mystere. Papa Brise is about to become an official source for GJIC."

"You obviously haven't heard the news."

"What news?"

"Someone set a bomb off down there today. Army's stopped the public going in."

"That explains it," I said.

"What?"

"Why the taxi driver wasn't keen."

"And nor should you be. You can't go in there now. I've been hearing from my sources that it's a gang war... MY3s versus Moonees."

"That's exactly why I have to go."

"Then take Hamish."

"I don't know where he is."

"I'll find him."

"Caro–"

But she'd already hung up.

I suddenly wished that I had more than my park-issue Smith & Wesson for protection. A bulletproof vest would be nice. My main concern, though, was how I would get past the army.

"Take me to the Lashkar station. I'll walk the rest," I said to Manslo, as I got in the back.

"You do know there's a war going on down there."

I made a dismissive noise. "Media exaggeration. How've you been since the other night?"

"All right, I guess. Been thinking about those dogs that attacked us though. We felt them pounding the doors and the bonnet, right?"

"Sure," I said, wondering what he was getting out. "Scary."

"Then why aren't there any marks on the car?"

Crap, I thought. "I dunno what you mean."

"I mean, there should be scratches and dents where those things hit the car and there's nothing."

"Maybe it felt worse than it was. We were out of there

pretty damn quick."

He shook his head. "Something's off."

"Sure is off where I'm going," I said, hoping to change the subject. "You heard much about it?"

Either my diversion worked, or he chose to let it go. "It's the MY3s fighting over territory. Funny though," he said.

"Funny?"

"Place is full of psychics and not one of them predicted it was coming. They say the bomb took out a whole section of Gilgul."

Manslo's news sent a whole new batch of adrenalin squirting into my gut. Where was Johnny? I had to get there quickly.

"Can you hurry, Vic? Please."

He must have picked the tone in my voice because he dropped the small talk and hit the pedal. When we pulled up at Lashkar station, he turned off the readout, and opened the partition. "You want me to wait for you off the clock?"

"I appreciate the offer, Vic. But it could be a while. You have to make a living."

"Yeah." He scratched his head and looked ahead, fidgeting. "But I'll try and get work in the area. Call me if you need transport home."

"I will." Then I added, "Something on your mind?"

He tilted his head from side to side. "I talked to the others about the girl. Some of them thought they saw her too, and pulled over. Instead, they got attacked. Felix, over in the Scarp, had crows beating down on him. And we lost a guy on the Salt Way offramp. Same night. He drove right off the edge. His black box recorded him saying stuff about wild dogs."

"I'm sorry," I said. "I didn't know."

"That's another strange thing. None of it made the news.

Least not in a way anyone would notice."

"I have to go, Vic," I said.

"Just so you know… I got a feeling about you, and I got your back."

I stared into the rear view mirror and we locked glances. "Cheers."

He reached over his shoulder without turning and held out a canvas case. "Take this."

I saw the butt of a Taser.

"I got a spare. It's charged, and I want it back," he said.

I was touched, but I pulled out the Smith and held it up. "I'm good."

Walking from Lashkar to Mystere in the daylight was almost creepier than at night; the daytime heat had me in a sweat and the sunshine stripped away any illusion of cover. This time, at least, there was no sniper waiting. I glanced skywards, relieved to see clouds building up in the north. Rain coming.

Now how to get past the army cordon? They'd have set up their watch perimeter around the strip of homes between here and the triangle.

I ran most of the way past the warehouses and rusting cranes, slowing down when I reached the old wool presses. The army were there all right, a command post set up in a habi-cube like the one in the park. It was surrounded by half a dozen A-T jeeps and at least twenty or thirty soldiers patrolling on Segways. The chance of slipping past seemed unlikely.

I sat down with my back against the base of a wool press and tried to think of a plan. I could call Sixkiller, explain the situation and hope that GJIC could use their influence. No doubt my mother had clout enough to get inside an army operation. Or, I could walk on out there now and try to negotiate my way in, using my GJIC status.

Both options meant time. But maybe Johnny was in there, and didn't have time?

I remembered suddenly that Hamish had followed him after he left the diner. Where had they gone? Maybe he wasn't even in Mystere.

I hugged my knees. My forehead pounded. My brain was approaching overload – seeing the minister romancing Sam, being scared witless by the Mythos exploding out of the sand, and now this; today had been full of all kinds of shite. The fact that I was sitting here, trying to figure out how to get past an armed perimeter, suggested it wasn't going to improve.

"You maybe want to take some painkillers for that?" said a quiet voice in my ear.

Fright made me release a tiny, hot trickle of urine in my pants. "Fuck you, Hamish!" I said with feeling, when I looked up. "You made me pee my pants."

He blinked in his disconnected way.

"And what the hell are you wearing? They're army fatigues." I was suddenly wildly furious with him.

"If you want to get into Mystere, then calm down." His tone turned abrupt, almost nasty.

I lifted my chin and sucked in my anger. Hamish didn't respond well to threats.

"How?" I asked.

"See that jeep at the end?" He pointed to an army habi-cube surrounded by vehicles.

I glanced around and nodded.

"I've left the back hatch open. Ten minutes' time, I'll be doing a surveillance run past here. I'll stop and do a three-point turn to change direction. You'll have about six seconds to get in the back before I start moving again. Can you do that?"

"Yes," I said, without hesitation.

He nodded and crawled away.

"Hamish?"

He paused.

"How did you know where to find me?"

He tilted his head as if I'd said something truly dumb. "You brother's in there. This is the way you come."

"Is he?"

"I followed him back to the psychic's parlour." He started crawling again, keeping below the line of the wool presses until, eventually, I lost track of him threading his way through the skeletons of old cranes.

I got back up onto my knees, wiped my hands off, and then got into a crouch.

I had to be ready.

Nine minutes later, the jeep reversed away from the habi-cube and headed in my direction. The plating on the side rippled with camo shades, as it assumed the colour of whatever object it passed. At a slow speed, it became hard to see. The wheels bled into the bitumen and the body of the vehicle took on the mottled hues of the homes in front of it. It appeared to meander in and out of streets and a few times I lost track of it altogether.

I began to sweat. Where had Hamish gone? Only the low whistle of the hybrid engine convinced me that it hadn't disappeared altogether. It grew louder and louder until, suddenly, the back end of the jeep slung around in front of my hiding spot.

I rushed at it, wrenching the hatch open and threw myself

in. My knee caught on the lip of the door and I heard it crack, but I kept on rolling.

"Shut the back," Hamish growled at me from the front seat.

I scrambled forwards and pulled it closed, just as he accelerated away.

"Now get into the gun case."

Clutching my knee, I tried to focus outside the pain. What gun case?

"You've got thirty seconds before we pass through the infrared scanners," he added. "Wrap yourself in the Mylar."

I knelt on my good knee and looked around. A long black case with heavy duty latches lay flush with the driver's seat.

"Black?"

"Yeah."

"I better not die in here, Hamish," I said, as I opened it and looked inside the hollowed out death trap.

"The Mylar sheet's strapped to the wall. The case is airtight, so you'll have to hold your breath as we go through."

Angry and scared, I grabbed the sheet from its strapping. When had we discussed this bit?

"Don't stop to chat, will you? If I don't suffocate to death in a minute, I'll be suffering from heat exhaustion inside two."

"Just keep still in there," he said, without a hint of concern in his voice.

I rolled in the space blanket then flopped over into the case. "Count me in," I said, lowering the lid.

"Five, four, three, two, one... close it!" he said.

I pulled the case closed.

The first minute or two went OK, until the oxygen depleted.

After that, panic took over. It was the heat. Sweat leached out of my pores. I felt wet at the root of every hair follicle. Moisture trickled into my ears, pooled between my buttocks, and rivulets ran from my forehead. My pulse went into hammer mode. I took a last breath and held.

Count. Calm. Count.

The jeep had stopped.

Thirty, thirty-one…

Still stopped.

Forty-eight, forty-nine…

Stopped.

Pressure built in my head and chest.

I can't make it… fifty, fifty-one…

Movement? Maybe?

Sixty-three… where is he?

Seventy-five, seventy-six…

I flung the case open, pulled the Mylar away from my face and gulped in air in huge, shuddering gasps.

When the dots cleared from my eyes, I saw Hamish sitting on the bench seat in the back just near me, arms folded, watching.

"You… you…" I couldn't even think what to call him other than *fucking psycho*, but those words got lost in my incoherent fury. "You… fucker! How? Long?"

His gaze never wavered, and he showed no emotion. "It took fifty-four seconds to get past the checkpoint."

"That's twenty seconds longer than I needed to be in there. Why did you do that?"

"Good to know a person's limits. World record is twenty-two minutes. You need to practise."

I so badly wanted to smack him that my sweaty palms itched. "How do you even know that?"

"I hold it. Unofficially, of course."

I didn't know if he was kidding, being an arse, or telling the truth. "Now what?"

He crawled past me, over the box, and back into the driver's seat. "I'll get us as close to the action as I can, but the last bit we'll have to do on foot."

I copied him and climbed into the passenger seat. He stank of stale sweat. Mine was fresh at least. "What do you mean, as far as you can go?"

"This is no lightweight driveby shooting," he said. "MY3s have got a bunch of RPGs, and an unhealthy supply of SAWs and UZIs."

"And Kadee Matari?"

"The Moonees packed C-4 into a car and aimed it straight at the Mexican Cantina where the MY3s eat their salsa. Lucky for the fat man, its bumper caught on a parked van. It blew up at the opening to the alley."

Jeez. "Juno's Cantina? Why did they do that? How many hurt? And how do you know this?"

"I'm guessing maybe a hundred or more dead. The army locked the place down within an hour. The ones that panicked got out ahead of it. The ones who figured it was no big deal... well, they're stuck now. No one in or out, so there're bound to be more dead by now."

"You mean they didn't send EMVs in for the injured?"

"It's Mystere. A shithole. Probably hoping they'll all kill each other off and then they can burn the place."

"But it's always full of tourists. That's outrageous. They can't just leave them there to die."

He pressed the ignition button and steered left. The jeep responded. "Not making the rules, Virgin."

"What *are* you doing then?"

"Well, I was watching your brother and his woman. But after what they did, it got busy with people trampling each other."

I gripped his arm. "Johnny? What did he do?"

"He sold a lethal speedball to a MY3."

"One of Papa Brise's men?"

He nodded. "He stayed and watched the guy OD."

"You saying it was intentional? M- murder?"

"Can't think of another name for it."

"Johnny's no killer."

"Believe what you like."

"What about Corah?"

"She played her part. Left Moonee feathers on the guy's chest. It's what sparked this little shebang. The fat man shot a Moonee in retaliation, and the Moonees packed the car with C-4."

I trembled, struggling to take in what he was telling me. It meant that Johnny and Corah were definitely Korax. And they'd made it look like the Moonees had murdered a MY3.

Something dawned on me... "You made the anonymous tip and sent the photos to Sixkiller!"

Nothing.

"But you didn't say who they were – Johnny and Corah. Y- you protected them? Why?"

"Once the place was in lockdown, I knew you'd try and get in to find him. Knew where you'd come to."

"You mean Caro rang you."

He shrugged with annoying disinterest. "Hung around for the fun. Borrowed some camo and blended in."

I didn't want to know what *borrowing some camo* meant.

"Your specialty," I said.

His face in profile was composed. His lips slightly parted. He wasn't smiling, but he seemed happy. "Who the hell are you, Hamish?"

He didn't reply.

I sagged back in my seat, sickened by what he'd told me. "So where's Johnny now?" I had to find Papa Brise and explain that the Korax had started this.

He shrugged again.

"Is Juno's still standing?"

"Didn't get to take a tour, but I guess. That where we're going then?"

I nodded. "And drive as close to it as you can. My knee is killing me."

TWENTY

Death hung moistly in the air. Fresh. Blood.

Gilgul was deserted. Tyres burned on overturned cars, bodies lay among strewn Mexican hats and dream catchers. Windows were shuttered and barricaded with brick and wood and plastic. People who were left here alive had hunkered down.

We got halfway down Gilgul before a pileup of cars blocked the road.

"We should go past Corah's place first," I said, "in case they went back there. It's on the next lane."

Hamish reached into the back of the jeep and retrieved two semiauto rifles out of a case. "Here."

"No." I shook my head. "I can't... they're military issue."

"Suit yourself." He frowned and reached into the bag again. This time he pulled out two Kevlar vests and two hoods. He threw me a set.

I hesitated, then put the vest on. "What's this?" I asked, fingering the hood.

"Memory foam combat helmets. This is a war zone. Be

smart to put it on."

I should have been impressed by his resourcefulness, and concerned about the consequences of stealing an army jeep. It scarcely seemed to matter though, now I knew that my brother had murdered someone and sparked a gang war.

I pulled the hood on.

The memory foam fitted snugly around the contours of my head and as soon as it contacted my ear, I heard static followed by sharp commands as the military channel came online.

I waved my hands at Hamish. "Can they hear me?" I mouthed at him.

"Just don't press over your ear. That will give you talkback with them," he said. "Listen to their status reports," he added.

He shrugged his vest and hood on, and slung both rifles over his shoulder. Before we got out of the jeep, he got something out of his jeans pocket and leaned close. "We get separated, or things go sideways, I'll meet you in the storage locker we rented." He pressed a magnetic chip into my hand. "This will get you in."

I stared at it. "You took out a longterm rental on it?"

"Sentimental reasons."

Was he joking?

A burst of gunfire started up before I could ask him what that meant.

Hamish leaned further over me and pushed my door open. "Go. Stay low."

I fell out and, with my pulse racing, crawled towards the shops, using a damaged vendor's cart and an upended motorbike for cover. The bulletproof vest I was wearing didn't make me feel any safer in the crossfire.

I propped behind the door of the twisted falafel cart, and waited for Hamish to join me. While I peered around and down the street, he helped himself to falafels from the bain-marie.

"Are you nuts?" I hissed.

"Can't get food poisoning from chick peas," he said, as he bit into one.

"No. I mean eating *now*!"

He answered by shovelling the rest in. "Hear how it's coming in bursts? Next time there's a lull we run that way." He pointed.

"The lulls mean they're reloading?"

"Maybe. Warfare's got its own rhythm."

I couldn't see his expression, but his voice sounded almost peaceful.

We crouched together for a little longer, waiting for the ebb. When it came, Hamish was quarter of a block ahead of me before I'd broken cover.

"Shit!" I ran as hard as I could, crouched over, to catch up with him.

The shooting didn't start up again though, and my screaming, jumping nerves stretched a little further. We'll make it. *We will.*

Then I heard a strange, faint whistle in the air above us.

Hamish barrelled me backwards into the alcove of a shopfront doorway, and fell on top of me.

The explosion was so close that the doorstep vibrated under my head. The soft helmet activated gel inflations that protected my ears from the worst of the noise, but it couldn't do anything about the spewing wood and concrete that pelted us. I tried to squirm away, but Hamish held me firm.

I think I swore at him. I couldn't be sure. A bunch of thoughts flashed into my mind. *Where are you, Johnny?*

When Hamish finally let me move, my injured knee sent

a dagger of pain up my leg. My kneecap felt like it might just peel right off. *Shit.*

Hamish peered around the corner of the alcove and then almost immediately flattened back, motioning for me to look.

I leaned around him. A few car lengths down, right about where Corah's parlour was situated, was a smoking hole of black rubble. A few minutes later and we'd have been in there looking for... *Johnny*!

I fell back, shaking violently.

Hamish punched me hard in the shoulder and shook his fist at me, penetrating my shock. He signalled that we should go into the shop behind us and up to the roof.

I nodded, attempting to pull myself together, while he broke open the door lock.

Everything blurred for a while. Limping in and out of rooms, searching for manholes, tearing down the barricades erected against the back door to reach the fire escape.

I followed Hamish, did what he said, helped when he asked. A glimpse of feet under a bed in one of the rooms and the stink of body odour told me someone was hiding there. But we didn't stop and they kept out of our way.

The fire escape took us up three levels on the other side of the building, but it didn't make me feel less exposed. Hamish's pace up the stairs pushed me to my limits. I struggled to get enough breath and the Kevlar vest, though light, felt like it was weighted with bricks.

He stopped at the top, but instead of climbing in through a top floor window, he pulled a rappel claw from his kit bag and tossed it up onto the roof gutter.

I shook my head vehemently. I couldn't do that. No way.

He juggled the chords, got them arranged, and tried to clamp one around me. "Put it on."

"Nope." I pushed him away so hard that he nearly overbalanced and fell off the small landing.

He swore at me, but I didn't care. I wasn't going to hang in mid-air so I could climb onto the roof. I had a simple rule in life when it came to height. Always keep your feet on something that can bear your weight.

"I'll see you up top," I said.

"How?"

"I'll find a way."

I left him and went back down a flight of stairs to the window I'd seen ajar on the landing below. I tugged and heaved until the runners freed and the window slid up far enough for me to climb in.

Cartons filled the room: floor to ceiling with only narrow gaps in between – a storage space for one of the shops on the street. Turning sideways, I squeezed past the stacks until I located the door into the corridor.

I couldn't reach it. With a deep breath, I began lifting boxes, working as quickly as I could. One box was so heavy it sent me tumbling backwards into others. I lay trapped for a moment or two while I worked out which limb to move and how to extricate myself.

By the time I'd made enough space to get to the door, I was shaking with exhaustion and worried that Hamish had left me behind. I didn't really know what Hamish would do at any time, let alone when he was pissed with me.

I ran straight to the lift, fretting until it came. It took me to the top floor. I ran down the corridor looking for signs of an empty room with a manhole, but all the doors were firmly shut.

I banged on a couple. No one was answering.

A greyness began to cloud the edges of my vision. Panic

rising? Or anger? Or was I going to pass out from the pain in my knee?

I drew my pistol and banged a second time on a random door. "Open up or I'll blow the lock off. I need access to the roof."

A boy, about thirteen by the look of his gangly limbs and smooth face, opened the door. His lips were pursed in fear and his eyes shone with tears. He clenched his fists at his sides.

"Are you alone?" I asked.

He nodded.

I tried to reassure him. "Look, I'm not going to hurt you, but I really need to get to the roof. Do you know a way?"

He nodded again jerkily.

I holstered my pistol and attempted to appear calmer. "What's your name?"

"Ricardo," he managed to whisper.

"Ricardo, I'm Virgin. I need to get to the roof to try and stop the people who are setting off the bombs. Will you help me?"

A third nod. Then he stepped out of the door into the corridor. As he did, I heard a baby cry.

"You got a baby in there?"

"My seester," he said.

"Where are your parents?"

"Mamita works. She don't come home yet."

I thought of the bodies I'd seen on the street. "Listen, show me how to get to the roof then go back inside and lock the door again. No harm will come to you."

My words seemed to offer him little comfort. The fear in his eyes didn't diminish, and I couldn't blame him. I sounded crazy.

He pointed down to the far end of the corridor. "Go there."

I'd checked that door already. "It's just a cupboard."

"Inside cubord ees a cord. People make stairs up." He pointed to the roof.

"But it's locked. There's a keypad."

"Password ees *fire*."

That figured. "What's your mama's name?"

"Rosa."

"I'll come back and see you're all right. OK? See if your mama has come home."

His nod was uncertain, but the tightness in his face eased a little.

"You got food for the baby?"

He nodded.

"Be a good brother then. She needs you."

He went inside and, when I heard the lock click, I ran to the end of the corridor. The keypad accepted the code and the door opened. I felt around inside until I located the cord hanging from the ceiling and pulled. An improvised staircase made from plastic foam fillers fell down.

I climbed up into the dark roof space and waited for my eyes to grow accustomed. It stank, like all roof spaces, of ratshit and old dust, and decayed animal remains. After a few moments of straining my eyes, I spied a hatch that looked like the lid of a Solo rubbish bin. With relief, I prised it open and found my way out onto the flat roof top.

It was still daylight, but the shadows were lengthening. The smell of burning rubber choked my throat. I couldn't see Hamish, so I crouched by the open hatch, and pondered my next step. If Hamish had left me behind, I had to work out the quickest route to Juno's.

"I figure if we go to the south end of this building and jump across to that peak, the rest should be a straight line," said a voice in my ear.

I jumped, grabbing for my piece. "So help me Hamish," I said. "You do that again and I'll shoot…"

I stopped, realizing he'd pressed a pistol to my temple.

"You ever attempt to draw on me again and I'll put a bullet in you," he said softly.

I slowly – *so* slowly – turned my head until our eyes met. His were intense with concentration and yet empty of emotion.

"I'm going to let go of my gun now, Hamish. OK?"

He nodded.

Even more slowly, I took my fingers off the Smith.

He lowered his weapon, but kept it cocked.

It was the strangest experience, watching a more normal expression slowly return to his face. Like the lights brightening in the cinema at the end of a screening.

"You'd kill me?" I asked.

"Don't draw down on me and we'll never have a problem."

"Don't sneak up on me."

"You should be more observant."

If that was the extent of his apology, then I guess I just had to deal with it. There wasn't time to explore his psychoses, or my anger. I wished, briefly, that Sixkiller was here. Nate, at least, was predictable. And sane.

"I'll follow you," I said.

He nodded and crawled off to the edge of the roof.

The gap to the next building from that particular spot was only half a body length. With little effort, he jumped across, and I copied him.

Gunfire started up again close by as we crabwalked across loose tiles, using boarded up chimney stacks for cover. Hamish scared a possum out of its lair under an antennae hutch, and it scurried off and onto the power lines like a trapeze artist.

"See there," he pointed.

We were just above Juno's now. I recognised the way the roof peaked over the twin fireplaces and saw that the tiles had been reinforced.

"Let me go first," I said.

He was going to argue, but I cut him off. "They know me better, which means we're less likely to be shot on sight."

"They'll have guards on the roof entry."

"Sure," I said, instead of, *I'm not an idiot.*

I kept an eye out for boobytraps as I made my way across to the roof entrance above Juno's attic. When I got close to the hatch, I called out. "Papa Brise! It's Virgin Jackson. Per favor!"

No one replied.

A fresh burst of gunfire started up, sending me diving flat onto the tiles. "*Per favor*! Papa Brise! We need cover!"

The hatch wound upwards and the nozzle of an automatic protruded. "*Entrar!*"

I lifted my hand and beckoned Hamish then I shimmied closer. "Get your rifle out of my face," I called out to the guard.

The Uzi withdrew and a face peered up momentarily then disappeared again.

"*Es su!*" I heard a thickly accented voice say.

"Of fuckeen course it's her," said Papa Brise in reply. "What other fuckeen stupid bitch would be on the roof in the middle of the fuckeen holocaust?"

I took that as a cue to come in and began to lower myself down through the hatch.

Papa Brise had his own version of a holocaust going on – bloody smears on his face from scrapes and cuts, his hair matted with more blood, and the sweaty, greasy skin complexion of someone who hadn't slept in a while.

I looked around and saw that every table in Juno's

currently harboured weapons: rifles, small hand guns, knives, grenades, and ammunition. Atop the bar, screens flickered through images of Mystere from different vantage points.

"I thought the army had locked down the sat feeds?" I said.

"What the fuck are you doing here, Ranger?" asked Papa Brise in reply.

Two of his men had frisked Hamish and held him at Uzi-point against the wall, while another couple inspected the two rifles they'd taken from him. They had my Smith as well.

"Why do you still have feeds?"

The large man raised his eyebrows in a gesture of disbelief. "The world's gone to fuckeen hell and you come here to ask me about my comms? What kind of fuckeen crazy are you?"

I glanced at Hamish whose expression was all kinds of blandly dangerous. "Why do you still have feeds?" I repeated.

"Papa's got his ways." He bared his teeth at me. "Now for Chrissakes, Ranger, go fuckeen home."

TWENTY-ONE

"There's something you need to know."

Before I could go on, one of his men over near the front door began yelling in a Spanish-Indigene dialect I didn't understand.

Papa Brise barked back at him in the same language. He paced a little and then gestured to a crate in the far corner.

The men by the door went over and began pulling out hand grenades. As many as they could tuck in their jackets.

"What are you doing?" I cried.

"Shit is going down. Get the fuck out of here," he said, as he moved between tables, picking up and putting down cartridges.

Hamish twitched.

I had to do something before he took matters into his own hands.

"If you can get me a parlay with Kadee Matari, I can stop this," I said.

Papa Brise stopped his erratic loading. "How?"

"Tell me what started this."

"*What started this?* The fuckeen stoned witch killed my boy, Jorge. Fuckeen overdosed him, and left a fuckeen feather on his chest. *My boy!* So I take one of hers, gut them and eat their fuckeen eyeballs. Then she packs a car full of C-4 and rams it at me."

Jorge! Johnny had killed Jorge. I grabbed his arm. "It wasn't her, Papa Brise."

He jerked his head at me. "What you fuckeen saying?"

"The people I work for. They saw the Crow and Circle – the Korax – kill Jorge and leave the feathers so you'd think it was the Moonees."

His opened his bloodshot eyes wide enough for me to see the tributaries of burst veins.

"You fuckeen sure, Ranger?"

"*Fuckeen* positive," I said for emphasis.

He took a moment to rub his forehead and then pound it with the heel of his palm. "The stoned fuckeen witch didn't make a bid for my patch then?"

"No. But now she thinks you're making one for hers."

"What kind of a fuckeen fuckwit is she? Who wants to live in the Burning Grounds? Place stinks like fuckeen grilled dick and balls."

I tried to swallow that image down. I'd seen the Burning Grounds. Once was enough. "Help me get to her. Talk to her. So I can stop this now."

His gaze swept across to the screens. I saw what he saw. Wreckage. Bodies. Tears filled his eyes, and I knew they were for Jorge.

Then an explosion sent us diving under tables. All of the cantina's high windows blew out. The glass sprayed into the row of potted palms we sheltered behind. I found myself huddled close to Papa Brise.

He fell back from a crouch position and onto his haunches.
I smelt urine, and this time it wasn't mine.

"Go talk to that crazy fuckeen stoned witch," he said.

TWENTY-TWO

Last time I'd seen Kadee Matari she'd told me never to show my face again. She hadn't liked my questions, or my connection with the law. Assuming I could get to her alive, I had no clue how to convince her to stand down on this.

It'd seemed like a smart idea when I said it, but now, as Papa Brise sent one of his men ahead of Hamish and me into the street to send an audio device with a parlay message on it across to the Moonee gates, I wished myself anywhere but here.

The MY3s had already lost all that side of Gilgul to Kadee Matari and her spear-and-Molotov throwing bandits.

"You got one-fuckeen-hour to sort this out, Ranger. We go in hard and fuckeen heavy at sundown. Or she will. Either way it's fuckeen over tonight," Papa Brise said, as he gave us back our weapons. "Say, just so I know… you wanna be buried here with your man Hamish?"

Hamish made a low, growling noise, and the pair glared at each other.

"Come on," I said to them both. "Let's get this over with."

•••

Hamish and I crouched behind a courier van, waiting for some sign that the Moonees' explosive tipped spears might stop raining down on us. I closed my eyes and thought of riding my horse in the park. The shadows would be growing long out there. Benny loved to be out in the cooler hours.

"Focus, Virgin!" snarled Hamish.

I snapped them open again.

Behind me were the blown out windows of the army surplus store. I could see the boots on a dead body, protruding from under the counter. Was it Ron, the owner?

Across the street were a tribe of Moonee crazies, waiting to make their final push into this part of Gilgul as soon as it got dark.

"Focus on what?" I asked him.

"Seeing your brother again," he said.

"My murdering brother?"

"Family is family."

"You got any?"

He didn't answer.

I fidgeted a bit, checked my Smith was loaded and that the spare cartridge was still in my pocket. I kicked away an ant-ridden, half-eaten burger. Although the gunfire and spear-throwing had lulled, my muscles remained tense, ready to react. *Hurry up and wait* messages were frying my brain. The sun had begun to set.

"I don't get you," I said to Hamish. "You threatened to kill me just a little while ago, and now you're here, risking your life to help me."

"I don't like people pointing guns at me," he said.

"And I don't like being snuck up on," I countered.

Silence.

"I had some free time," he said.

"Right. Well, that explains it." Sarcasm somehow made me feel braver.

"This woman Kadee Matari we're meeting. You know her?" he asked.

"*I'm* meeting. Seen her once. It didn't go well."

"Of course it didn't."

"She's permanently high, but she's smart."

He nodded. "Practice increases tolerance."

He was full of trite platitudes. I suppose it sufficed for conversation.

"VIRGIN JACKSON!" blared out over a loudspeaker from across the street.

I gasped, feeling the familiar crush of my airways constricting in fear.

Hamish grabbed my chin and forced me to look him in the eyes. "Don't hesitate if you have to."

"What...?"

"What you need to do to stay alive."

I nodded. I wasn't planning on anything else.

He let go and ran his finger lightly, tenderly along my jawbone. It was the strangest moment so far in this ugly, ugly day.

Somehow though, it freed up my breath, and I raised my hand above the wheel of the car and waved. "HERE!" I bellowed back.

"COME ALONE TO THE KIOSK."

"I'M COMING NOW. DON'T FIRE!"

"They mean the ComTel kiosk. Diagonally across. Half a block down," said Hamish.

ComTel kiosks offered one-stop-communication. How poetic!

I stood up, half-expecting a bullet that didn't come. My

path to the kiosk looked safe – safe as it could be, littered with burning tyres and unexploded devices. And bodies. One of the bodies was only small. A girl. Her sneakers had come off, and her jeans had ripped above the knee. Who even brought a child to this place?

I picked my way through the debris, deliberately avoiding the dead. Halfway to the kiosk, the door of an upturned car groaned open. I hit the ground, expecting an explosion.

Nothing happened. No one came out. No Molotovs or explosive tipped spears thrown my way. Just the car springs giving way under the heat of the fire under the bonnet.

I got up and continued on, imagining I could hear Moonee sniggers. When I reached the ComTel kiosk, it was empty. I rattled the door for no good reason, and shouted out, "WHAT NOW?"

The pay-for-use screen inside it flashed up the head and shoulders of Rombo, the guy who ran the comms in Moonee. His wasn't a mug you usually saw outside Kadee Matari's territory. Looks like she was already staking her claim.

"Rombo?"

"She's waiting for you. Go with Jimmy Dharawal."

I glanced around and saw a man standing close. He had chains hanging from piercings on his face and a loaded spear in his hand. We'd met before.

"Jimmy Dharawal?"

He beckoned and stalked on ahead.

I followed him further along the street almost as far as the alley entrance to Moonee. Just before we got there, he ascended a set of stairs and stopped outside a room.

I knew the place as well. Sixkiller and I had been taken there by the MY3s not so long ago to talk to Papa Brise. He'd appeared on a screen in the room, not in person, and I'd been treated by his flaky medic.

Jimmy Dharawal frisked me twice before allowing me to enter. I'd left the Smith with Hamish, and Papa Brise still had my short-handled diamond blade, so he came up empty.

"She's waiting," he said.

Inside, Kadee Matari sat on one of the two couches. Her overalls were the same dirty white as the war paint on her face, and her eyes were distant behind smart-lenses. A hash pipe smoked on the cushion next to her.

"Sit down, Ranger," she said, while her eyes blinked and her fingers traced patterns in the air as she communicated with Rombo.

"Kadee Matari," I said. "Listen to me! *Please!*"

She stopped blinking, disengaged from her smart-lenses then she reached for her pipe.

I took the full force of her focused stare. Her left eye leaked moisture onto the burn marks on that side of her face. She could have had nanoplasty, but, for whatever reason, Kadee Matari had chosen to remain a scarred woman.

"You're using your final favour, Virgin," she said, sighing and shaking the feathers attached to her scalp in a gesture of impatience.

"I didn't know I had one. Last time I saw you, you told me never to come back."

"Life is fluid."

"Meaning?"

"One of the illegal immigrants you had arrested in your little park…"

"Yes?"

"Let's say it was convenient for me that you helped to lock them away. You gained a favour."

"Is that why you accepted my parlay?"

"In part. Now speak."

I didn't know how long she'd give me her attention, so I plunged in. "The Crow and Circle – the Korax – started this rift between you and Papa Brise."

She sat so still, I wasn't sure if she was breathing.

"They killed his boy, Jorge, and made it look like your people did it. They left a feather on his chest."

She ran her tongue around her lips. "Proof?"

"My word."

She gave a whip crack laugh that made me feel like an idiot. "You're asking me just to believe you?"

"I'm asking you to think. Papa Brise doesn't want this war. It's bad for business. Now the army are out there, just waiting for an excuse to gas you all and tear down the entire triangle. I came in through the old crane site. They're set up on all boundaries. The tourists left behind here are the only thing stopping them. But that's just a matter of time. Once they've worked out a plan, they'll move in." I was out of breath when I finished, and sweating from the effort of sounding convincing.

"Why would the Crow and Circle start a war between us? Did they not think we would learn the truth?"

She had a point. The Korax must have known that Papa Brise and Kadee Matari would eventually find out. Were they hoping it would be too late when they did? That the two gangs would have already wiped each other out? Or was there a reason I couldn't fathom? "I don't know. Honestly. But it's truth. If you stop now, withdraw, the army will as well. But you go on any longer, and Mystere and Moonee are done. *You* are done," I said.

I sank back into the couch and waited. The room was almost in darkness, the sun sliding away, and with it any chance that this would be over without more bloodshed. Where would I be exactly, when it all went to the bottom of hell? On this couch?

She continued to sit unnervingly still, intermittently bringing her pipe to her lips. When the shadows in the room had grown so long that I couldn't distinguish one from the other, she finally spoke. But not to me.

"Jimmy, call our people back. We go home. Make it happen quickly."

I stood up, my legs shaking with relief. "Thank you. For listening to me."

She lifted her glassy-green eyes. "Not you. Her."

I looked around. Aquila was perched on the back of my couch, her head cocked to the side as though she was waiting for me to notice her.

"You can see her?"

"You are lucky to have the eagle. She is rare."

I swallowed hard. Kadee Matari was one of us? Like Sixkiller, and Johnny, and me?

"Your eagle's presence tells me that you're one to be believed. There are greater things to fear than the fat man," she said.

"So I'm learning," I said.

She held up her lighter and ignited it so that the flame rose high. Then she held it to the bowl of the hash pipe and sucked it alight.

The fresh smoke that filled the room left me lightheaded. I wanted to leave, but her revelation made me hesitate. I went to open the door for air instead, but it allowed in the even stronger smell of burning rubber.

"Do you have a guide?" I asked.

"Once." Pain filled her green eyes. "I had to make a choice, smoke or beast." She held the pipe aloft as if to make a toast with it.

"I thought being stoned heightened spiritual awareness?"

She bared her teeth in a stricture of a smile, and I saw the turquoise stone fillings in her teeth. They almost matched the colour of her eyes. "A story told by fools and addicts. Purity begets true spirituality. But with it comes mania and obsession. Beware, Virgin. I see the signs in you."

"I'm not pure," I said.

She took another suck on her pipe then began blinking again. "You should go," she replied. "The army's coming."

TWENTY-THREE

I ran back in the direction of Juno's. Hamish intercepted me half a block down by grabbing my arm and pulling me across the road to shelter behind the transit van again.

"The army's here," he said.

"Kadee Matari's withdrawing, but I think it's too late," I said.

He pulled my combat hood from his kit bag. "Put it on and hope we don't get noticed."

"Hope?" I said, pulling it over my head.

"Sometimes it's all you've got. We go back to the jeep, quick, blend in as they come through then peel off at first chance."

The jeep was over a block away. It stood out as the only vehicle upright and not burning.

"Ready?" he asked.

I nodded and followed his lead, keeping pace with him all the way there. It felt good to be running flat out, burning off the residues of my adrenalin.

When we reached the jeep, Hamish flung himself in the driver's side, and I veered around to the passenger seat.

He pressed the starter and began to reverse. As we passed alongside a burning building, I yelled, "Stop!"

He hit the brakes. "What?"

I pointed to the apartment block close to the one that was burning. "That's the building we went in before, isn't it? The roof we climbed onto?"

"So?"

"There's a kid and a baby in there. Their mum is missing. I told them to stay there until she came for them. I need to get them out."

"Army's going to arrest everyone they can find. You included. Kid'll be all right now."

I thought of the boy's frightened face. "No," I said stubbornly. "The fire might spread before help arrives. I'm going to get them."

His eyes narrowed. "Then what? This is their home."

I hated his pragmatism, and the sprint to the jeep had left me exhausted. "Look, do what you want, Hamish. I'm going to get those kids."

He thumped the steering wheel in a rare display of emotion. "*Where* are they?"

"Fourth floor."

The army comms burst into life in my ears with a rapid exchange of directions and instructions. They were moving in on three sides: north, east and west. The south was bordered by the river and they'd cut off the bridge. Choppers were being deployed to put out the fires, and spot firefights.

"I have to go now!" I yanked off the hood and shoved it into the waist of my jeans. Then I jumped out and ran across to the foyer of Ricardo's building.

Inside was a mess of shattered glass and broken plaster board. There was a dent in the aluminium lift door from some kind of direct impact. Three bodies lay near the wall heater: two men and a woman. The men were spread out on their fronts and both had had the backs of their heads shot away. I didn't even try to look at their faces. The woman lay on her back, her shirt bloody. I touched her neck to check for a pulse, but found none. Her eyes were open and she looked worried. She wasn't much older than me.

Fuck.

I got up and hit the lift button. It pinged open right away despite the damaged door, and I jumped in. I needed a plan. I'd take the kids to Hamish's lockup. It would be safer than trying to get out of Mystere now. We'd lay low until morning when things would be clearer, safer. If their mother hadn't returned, then I'd call Sixkiller and get him to come and help me take them up to the city and find care for them.

I found the right apartment and knocked lightly. "Ricardo, it's Virgin."

After a long moment, the door cracked open.

"Is your mum back?" I asked.

He shook his head.

"I'm going to take you to a safer place. The fighting is over, but the building's about to catch fire and the army is coming in soon. Best you're out of here. They'll be coming through arresting people."

He trembled, so I lowered my voice. "I'll bring you back in the daylight and we'll find your mama. OK? But this is best for you and the baby."

He stared at me a bit longer, then nodded.

"Can I come in and help you collect some things? You got a bag?" I asked.

He stepped back, allowing me to enter. The apartment was cluttered with animal totems and smelled of dirty nappies.

The baby lay asleep on the floor wrapped in a blanket, sucking a comforter. Clothes were piled high on the couch and half-eaten microwave containers were stacked on the small kitchen table. A grease-streaked repro of a yacht race hung on the wall. I spied a bedroom through a door just past the kitchenette. On the sideboard, a chipped-chrome digital frame rotated through family photos. My stomach lurched as a smiling woman holding a baby flashed up: it was the woman in the lobby.

"Ricardo, is that your mama?"

He glanced at the frame and nodded. "Mamita."

I almost threw up and had to swallow rapidly against it. Should I tell him about his mother now, or wait?

"Virgin?" said a voice from the door.

Hamish was there, still wearing his hood and vest.

Ricardo cried out in fear, snatched up the baby and ran to hide behind the couch. The baby woke and started crying.

I motioned furiously to Hamish to remove his mask.

He tugged it off with an impatient gesture. "The army's three blocks away. They're shooting first, asking questions later. And the fire's spread to this building."

"I'm going to take Ricardo and the baby to your lockup."

"We'll go down the fire stairs and use the alleys."

"We?" I said, surprised.

"The chopper's located the jeep. We need to dump this gear soon. The vests have got trackers in them."

I began ripping the tabs open on mine and shrugging it off.

"What are you doing?" he barked at me. "Not yet."

"It's for Ricardo," I said, ducking down behind the couch where the boy cowered, holding the baby. "Ricardo, this man is my… friend. He'll help us get to somewhere safe."

"*Dónde nos vamos?*" Ricardo whispered.

"*Tiempo*," called out Hamish. "*Apúrate!*"

I got the gist of it and added, "Come quickly, Ricardo."

"Mamita?"

"Did she tell you to watch out for your baby... brother?"

"*Seester*," he said.

"Did she?"

Another nod.

"Then let's do that."

His eyes moistened, but he nodded.

"I'll carry your sister. And you stick right by my side. OK?" I told him gently.

"I carry Sasha," he said. "Only me."

"Fine. Only you. But we need some food for her. We'll be in the lockup until daylight."

He pointed to the fridge.

I went over and bundled milk tubes, left over pizza, sliced cheese, and some cans of soft drink into one of the plastic bags on the table.

Hamish was still in the doorway watching the corridor. "Fire's close," he said.

I held out my hand to Ricardo. "Stay near me."

The boy refused to take it, clutching the baby tighter.

"*Ven a mí*," barked Hamish in a hoarse voice.

Ricardo went straight to him, and took his hand. They stepped out into the corridor together.

I shrugged and went to follow, then ducked back to grab the photo frame from the sideboard. It might be the only reminder of his mother he'd get to keep.

The smoke was thicker in the alleyway, billowing blackly from the top level windows. I felt dampness in the warm air from the army choppers that were dumping water loads. Their wheeling spotlights incidentally lit our way as we hurried south, taking whichever alley got us furthest from the fire and the approaching troops.

"Tell me if you get tired. I'll carry her," I offered Ricardo. But he shook his head and kept up with us.

When we got far enough from the fire, I took the lead from Hamish. We stripped off the army vests, dumping them on the street, and then I circled us back around towards the lockup. Since the shooting had stopped, people were starting to appear at their windows and in doorways.

Army is coming, I called to them. *Stay off the streets. Stay off the streets.*

A few called out in return; others were too stoned, or scared, or suspicious to say anything. Maybe the fact that Hamish carried two semiautos had something to do with that.

I pushed our pace until we were on the far-east side of Gilgul on the street that harboured the funeral parlour and the lockup. Businesses here weren't technically part of the golden triangle of Mystere, but they were on the wrong side of bridge to be considered anything else. The solar-powered streetlights had come on, but most of the neons were out. It was enough to help us find the storage lockup.

Someone had let off a foam extinguisher near the doorstep.

"Careful," I said to Ricardo. "Don't slip."

I pulled the keycard from my pocket and tapped it on the lockpad. Nothing happened.

"What's wrong?" said Hamish. He suddenly pushed Ricardo, the baby and me up against the small doorway.

"What are you–?" I began.

Then I heard the choppy pulse of an engine. Within moments, a helicopter appeared above us. Spotlights wheeled up and down the street and sides of buildings. A loudspeaker boomed a message, demanding that everyone stay inside, that the army had now taken control of the area.

A lunatic hiding in a doorway opposite opened fire on the chopper. Rather than retreating, it descended, front machine guns engaged, spraying that side of the street with fire.

The hooded figure made a run for it, straight towards us, drawing the gunfire along.

Ricardo whimpered, and I slapped the key frantically against the lock.

"Try this one!" said Hamish, pushing his key into my hand. "Hurry!"

I dropped it. Picked it up. Tried it. And the door popped.

We surged into the foyer and Hamish slammed the door shut behind us just as the hooded runner reached the doorstep. He banged on the glass once and then careened off down the street.

We crouched, heads down to avoid the spotlight beaming in through the windows. The helicopter hung in front of the lockup, a booming, thunking, rattling predator. Its lights glanced over us as it sought the runner. Then the engine note changed, and it lifted to give chase.

Hamish was first to his feet, ushering Ricardo down to the cubicle he and I had been in just a day or so ago. Once inside, I steered Ricardo gently to the bunk bed and told him to lie down. The baby was crying and he cradled her against him, patting her back automatically.

"I'll get some food," I said. "She'll be able to settle now. And so will you. You want some pizza?"

He nodded.

"Right," I said. "Just give me a minute." I sorted through the plastic bag and brought out the picture frame, which I sat on the small table beside the bunk. Ricardo's eyes filled with tears when his mother's face appeared on the screen, but his breathing calmed.

"Gracias, Vir-gin." He said my name in two parts like it was broken.

I smiled and turned away, knowing that, in the morning, I'd probably be the one to tell him his mother was dead.

We snacked on cold pizza topped with extra cheeses slices, and I shared out the soft drinks. Hamish took his and knelt down in front of the lockup's built-in drawers. From the top one he produced a shortwave radio, some kind of signal jammer, and an electric razor. I wondered how many other stash points he had around the city.

"Where's the rabbit?" I asked, as I shook the baby's milk tube.

He held out the radio. "Call the Marshal. Let him know where you are."

"I don't know what frequency to use."

"You'll have a manual on your government phone."

"Oh."

I passed Ricardo the milk tube and he snuggled the baby in the crook of his arm. She sucked on the teat hungrily, her face full of concentration.

There was only one chair in the lockup. I set it against the door, out of Hamish's way, and took another slice of pizza. Sixkiller could wait until the gnawing hunger in my belly had subsided.

Hamish took some more food as well. We sat in silence until all of it was gone. By then the baby had drifted off to sleep, milk spilled on her chin, the teat half-fallen from her mouth. Her face was so small and pink and peaceful.

"What's her name again?" I asked Ricardo.

"Sasha," he said sleepily.

"Sweet," I said.

He blinked as though his eyelids were stinging from the effort of keeping them open.

"Go to sleep," I told him. "I'll wake you when it's time to leave."

He took the empty milk tube from Sasha's mouth, handed it to me and closed his eyes.

Gunfire rattled the lockup's windows throughout the night. Every explosion, every garbled loudspeaker instruction, every siren startled me from my restless dozing on the top bunk. It sounded like the army had come in hard and heavy. How many MY3s and Moonees had been detained? How many killed?

I woke properly at some stage, switched on my LiFo, and searched for the shortwave band emergency frequency in my files.

When I found it, I crawled off the top bunk and tapped Hamish on the shoulder. He was stretched out on the floor with his eyes closed.

He grabbed my wrist and jerked me close. "What?"

"Easy," I replied, peeling his fingers off my skin. "I think I should try the Marshal now."

He rolled away and then back, handing me the two-way.

No one responded to my call attempts, and after a while I climbed back onto the top bunk to nurse a growing stomach ache. How old had the pizza been?

Hamish stretched out on the floor again, and appeared to go straight to sleep while I squirmed and hugged my knees to deal with the cramps.

Just before dawn, I took the key and left to find the restroom. It was at the end of the corridor, lit by a dull emergency light, and I stayed in there until my stomach settled, and daylight seeped through the high, narrow windows. Feeling drained and low, I finally went back to the room and let myself in quietly.

Hamish was sitting on the chair staring straight ahead with an eerily blank expression.

"You left," he said mechanically.

"I was in the restroom," I replied. "Gut ache."

His face remained mask-like. "You've been gone for two hours."

"Like I said. I- I didn't feel well. Damn pizza."

"Don't do that?"

"What? Use the restroom?"

"You should have told me."

I glanced over at Ricardo and Sasha. They were both asleep still.

"Hamish, I appreciate you helping me," I said. "But I didn't ask you to. And I don't have to explain everything I do."

His stare peeled layers of my skin.

"Why *are* you helping me anyway?" I added, feeling too weary to be anything but direct.

He opened his mouth to answer, but the shortwave burst into life and we both jumped.

"*Jackson? Read?*"

I grabbed for the handset on the floor near Hamish, relieved to hear Sixkiller's voice. "Nate, I'm in a lockup at the back of Gilgul. Request immediate extraction for four people."

He repeated the coordinates to me and told me to hold.

Hamish was still watching me, though some of tension and strangeness had faded from his expression.

The shortwave crackled again. "A tip-jet'll collect yer in thirty minutes. Keep this frequency open. Stay inside until instructed," said Sixkiller.

A tip-jet? Only one person I knew travelled by tip-jet. Surely my mother wasn't back here and coming to get me? "I have a baby with me. We may require medical."

"Repeat that."

"A baby and a child."

"Extraction is for approved personnel only."

"Then don't come," I said. "I'll find my own way out."

I thought I heard him grunt, but it could have just been static.

"Hold," he said.

Hamish continued to study me while I waited. It was hard not to feel unnerved by his close attention.

Sixkiller came back. "Who is the remaining body?"

"Hamish Burns," I said.

"Hold."

Hamish started to pack away his electronic equipment. He collected the pizza crusts and empty cans and dumped them into the rubbish chute. Then he locked the drawers.

Sixkiller came back. "Confirming extraction for three personnel. Child, infant and you," he said.

"Forget it." I turned my back on Hamish and said quietly. "Like I said before, four or we make our own way. I'm not leaving him behind."

This time I really did hear the Marshal grunt with exasperation. "Negative," he said.

"Fine, then I'll–"

A clunk made me spin around.

Hamish and his rifles were gone.

I dropped the receiver and ran to the door just in time to catch a glimpse of the front security grill closing.

"Hamish!" I yelled uselessly. "Come back!"

He wouldn't. I knew.

Pressing my fingers into my pounding forehead, I went back to the handset. "Three for extraction confirmed."

For a moment Sixkiller didn't reply. I knew he'd be puzzling over my situation. Working out what was going on.

Finally he said, "Affirmative. Stand by."

TWENTY-FOUR

The tip-jet descended with the precision of a helicopter and a lot less fuss – aside from the aerial escort of guard-drones that floated around and above it. One moment the jet was in the air, amid its swarm of wasplike sentinels, the next it was on the bitumen in front of the lockup, taking up the width of the street.

I kept my hand on Ricardo's shoulder as the gangway lowered and an armed soldier ran out to meet us. He barely paused for the humming protection field to be disengaged before snatching up Ricardo and the baby.

The boy flailed his free arm and shouted for me.

"I'm coming," I shouted back, limping after them. As the gangway lifted us into the belly of the jet, I felt the blast of hot air from the rotating turbines. They weren't planning on hanging around.

The door hissed shut and the soldier set Ricardo back on his feet. The boy rocked Sasha to soothe her. His eyes were wide with fearful fascination. I doubted he'd ever been in the air before, let alone on a military grade transport.

The soldier peeled aside the faceplate of his soft hood and pointed to the front of the jet. "Commander Orlean will speak to you now, Ms Jackson. The child and the baby will be taken aft to be seen by the doctor."

The jet began to lift and Ricardo squatted down, giving a little yelp.

I kneeled beside him, touching him gently on the shoulders. "A doctor wants to see that Sasha is OK. Please let him do that, Ricardo. Then I'll join you."

"What ees doc-tor?" His voice had a shrill, cracking tone.

I racked my mind to think of the Spanish word and came up empty. "Er... *medica*... they take care of sick people," I explained.

He nodded, seeming to understand that. *"Mi hermanita...* ees not seeck."

"A baby can't tell you how she is. It's best if the... medica checks her. Mamita would want to know that Sasha is OK. Wouldn't she?"

He nodded.

"You're a good brother, Ricardo. Now go with..." I glanced up at the soldier to help me out with his name.

"Sergeant Orlean," he said.

I blinked. *Orlean?* What...?

The jet's nose lifted and a surge of acceleration and angle caused all of us to stagger.

"Step through to the forward cabin, please ma'am," he said.

I patted Ricardo on the shoulder again. "Go."

Commander Oceane Orlean sat ramrod straight in her ops chair, her hands weaving complex patterns in the air in the same way Kadee Matari had. I also saw the glint and slight discoloration of her smart lens as her eyes darted around.

That was where the resemblance ended.

The commander's blonde hair had loosened a little from her tight bun, and her suit showed signs of crumpling as if she'd slept in it. She was a bigger woman than I remembered from our first meeting, taking up the full width of the chair with her strong frame.

"Commander?" I said.

Another burst of upwards acceleration sent me diving into the seat opposite her, buckling up.

"Agent. What is the situation on the ground there?" Her eyes remained defocussed, as though she was multitasking.

"The MY3s and the Moonees have cooled their differences, but the army came in hot and heavy before things could settle. I don't know what the outcome will be."

"How accurate is your intel?"

"I spoke with Papa Brise and Kadee Matari. They both know now that the Korax triggered this situation by overdosing one of the MY3s."

"You spoke with them?"

"Yes."

"Well, the army need to finish it. We have a more critical issue to deal with."

Her words triggered a surge of exhaustion in me, and she blurred into a shadowy figure surrounded by a light halo. I was on my physical limit. My heart beat erratically in my chest.

"Virgin?" she said sharply.

"Water? Please?" My vision clouded over and I slumped back in the seat. All I could think of was Ricardo and Sasha. Ricardo would be terrified. I needed to get back to–

Fluid trickled into my mouth and I coughed.

"Swallow," said an insistent voice.

I gulped and found it was pleasantly flavoured.

"Keep drinking," said the voice.

I saw no reason to disagree, so I complied. The world began to come back and I saw the voice belonged to my mother who was bent over me, holding a tube, frowning.

I straightened in the seat and took it from her. "I'm sorry... I mean... I'm fine now... thank you."

She returned to her comm chair and belted herself back in. "The drink has electrolytes in it. They should revive you. My sergeant tells me that you brought a child and a baby aboard."

"Their mother was killed in the crossfire. The boy – Ricardo – was alone in the apartment with the baby. I couldn't leave them there. The building was set to burn."

"What do you propose happens to them now?"

Before I could answer her, a soldier brought in a plastic tray with a plate of chicken and rice, some protein bars, and a large container of juice on it. He spread a napkin across my legs then set the tray on my knee.

"Thank you," I said gratefully.

I ate quickly, inelegantly, my stomach overcome by the delicious smell of it. "The kids need food too," I said, in between bites.

"They are being attended to," she replied.

She watched in silence until I finished the plate, chewed through three bars, and guzzled down the juice. By the time I was done, the graininess had completely faded. I sighed with relief.

"We're only minutes away from landing, Virgin. And there are things you need to know."

Her tone was like a hand suddenly pressing down hard on my full stomach. "Yes?"

"While all our attention has been on Mystere another

incident has occurred. The Minister for Environment and Land Heritage and her entourage have disappeared in the park."

"What do you mean disappeared?" My heart fell into an all too familiar panicky rhythm. "What entourage?"

"They never returned from the meeting that you and Marshal Sixkiller attended."

"But how…"

"They called in to say their vehicle was having problems. Superintendent Hunt ordered a replacement vehicle to be sent out to pick them up, but when it reached the coordinates there was no trace of them."

"Where was that?"

She paused for a second. "The report says they were at a location called Los Tribos."

Los Tribos! "Who is *they*?"

"As you would know, the minister was being protected by the Federal Police."

"Was Special Agent Sam Williams one of them?" My voice sounded husky, as if I'd strained it.

She closed her eyes and accessed her smart lens. "Yes, his name is on the manifesto."

TWENTY-FIVE

The food I'd just consumed so enthusiastically threatened to dislodge.

"We're undertaking a parkwide search, but your knowledge of the southeastern sector is better than anyone else's. We need you out there," said Oceane.

"Of course," I said. "Where's the Marshal?"

"He's in the place you refer to as the Stables, coordinating the search."

I thought for a moment about the previous day. "The event near the Paloma station house, what did the analysis show?"

"The Marshal will brief you in more detail, but essentially there is no trace of the geyser and sinkhole that you saw."

"What do you mean 'essentially'?"

"It left a slight disturbance in the surface. No more or less than a dust storm or air traffic would cause. The sand below is as dense as anywhere else. There is no sign of slippage."

"Nothing? No traces of…"

"Of what? They are Mythos, Virgin. They leave no material forensics."

I released my seat belt, despite the flashing sign on the wall that told me to do just the opposite. "So they've been gone... what... sixteen hours?"

"Approximately. I'm sending an update to your LiFo. When we land, the Marshal will collect you. I don't need to emphasise how important it is that we find the minister alive. If anything should happen to her, Birrimun Park would be closed indefinitely. The anti-park lobby will gain the foothold they need."

"I didn't know you cared about the park."

She leaned back in her seat and I glimpsed deep fatigue beneath her composed expression. "It has become the focus of our investigations here. We don't wish it to be sold for redevelopment. It will be a lot harder for us to pursue an active investigation."

"I thought your authority extended everywhere?"

"The re-solidification of privacy laws and individual rights laws globally have made some of the enquiries we pursue problematic. Besides, we believe that the Korax have their tendrils deep into the anti-park lobby."

"You mean Joachim Spears?"

She looked surprised.

"I've conducted some of my own investigations," I allowed. "I don't like working blind."

I swore she almost smiled. "This would be with the help of your colleague Caroline Jorgenson?"

"What do you know about Caro?"

"We don't have the time to exchange personal case histories. But let's just say that your friend is very resourceful and has a deep communication network. We make it our business to keep an eye on people like her."

"You mean investigative journalists?"

"That's one name for them."

I didn't like what I she was implying. "I need to go and check on the children," I said, suddenly wanting to get away from her.

"Very well, Agent Jackson. But you should know that I'll be staying in the country until the minister is located. You and the Marshal will both report directly to me."

"You're running the investigation personally?"

"I choose my own priorities. That's a concept you should be familiar with."

I searched for a sign of sarcasm in her expression but didn't find it. She seemed perfectly serious.

"Thanks for coming for me then," I said stiffly, and got up to leave her cabin.

"Virgin?"

I hesitated. Waited.

"I believe your father holds the key to this."

She spoke as if he was still alive. I stared at her. "How?"

"I know you have his journals, despite the fact that you pretend not to. He was a very astute man; in some ways, he was a visionary."

"*You* searched my apartment? I thought it was the Feds."

"I didn't say that. But be aware that we're on the brink of an event that will change everything. The Mythos are appearing more and more to regular humans. Soon we won't be able to contain the bleed. They want our world."

"Why?"

"*Why* isn't even really relevant. Colonization is never in the best interests of those being colonized. Our own history shows us that. And believe me, *we are being colonized*."

"Then I'll do everything I can to help you, but in return you must find someone decent to care for Ricardo and his baby sister."

She pursed her lips and then relaxed them. "Agreed."

"Goodbye, Commander."

"Goodbye, Agent."

Sixkiller was waiting for me on the roof of the Cloisters.

He caught me up on his side of events, looking for the minister and Sam, as we walked down the fire stairs to the lift.

"I need a shower," I said to him, "and some time to think."

"Yer've got three hours. I gotta investigate a Mythos sightin', then we'll go out to the spot where they disappeared."

"Where is that?"

"Los Tribos," he said.

I sucked in a breath. "Figures. I'll see you at the stables mid-afternoon."

He pressed the lift button for my floor. "Don't be late. Ohitika's been with me since yer left me in the park. Longest time I can remember."

"Oh," I said, knowing what that meant.

"Yer can tell me about Mystere and Hamish on the ride out," he said.

"Right."

I scooted quickly out of the lift and straight into my apartment, hoping Esther didn't see me. When I shut the door on the world, I wanted to collapse with relief. But a hot shower beckoned first. I calculated out my time. Fifteen minutes to shower, an hour and a bit to sleep, and the rest in transit.

I stripped off and hit the hot water, turning the pressure and the heat to high. Maybe scalding water would sterilize away last night's memories? Or dilute them? Oceane had promised to help Ricardo and Sasha. Soon as I'd grabbed a little sleep, I could concentrate on finding Sam.

I wrapped myself in a towel and rolled into bed. I should ring Caro as well but...

A noise jerked me out of a dead sleep a short while later, Aquila screeching at me from my bedside table.

"What?" I said groggily, sitting up. Only a few hours had passed according to my clock.

She flew onto my basket of clean washing, and continued to screech.

I rubbed my face and blinked the bleariness from my eyes. "You want me to get dressed?"

She made some clicking noises that I associated with approval, and suddenly disappeared through the wall, only to return a few seconds later. She repeated her agitated antics until I got up and pulled some fresh clothes on.

My body ache was fierce as if I'd been poisoned, or afflicted by a tropical fever. And my kneecap felt like a hot poker had been shoved up underneath it. My eyeballs scratched against my eyelids for good measure. I went into the kitchen and located a glu-caffeine blister pack in a container that I usually kept for microwave noodles. They were high performance grade and I always had a bad comedown when they wore off, but right now I needed the fix.

I swallowed a couple and stuffed the rest of the pack in my jeans pocket.

That got me onto the downtown bus. Aquila stayed with me every step of the way. She insisted on sitting on the bus driver's head; and I took the hint and sat at the front of the bus.

When it stopped at Nicole Avenue in downtown, she flew straight out through the queue of incoming passengers.

I stumbled off the bus after her, knocking into someone.

My disincarnate was already halfway along the street,

while I was still apologizing. I cut it short and trotted as best as I could after her, my heart beating at a hyper-caffeinated rate that bordered on heart attack.

She finally flew onto a sandwich board outside a shop front with pink signage. Faux sequin lights flashed around the shop's window edges. It would have been unapologetically garish if the chrome trimmings inside hadn't gleamed with such intensity and the floors hadn't been tiled gleaming black and sparkling white. Somehow the overall effect was glitzy.

A Rivera Salon?

I peered in the window and immediately caught sight of the girl that the Aswang had tried to attack.

She saw me staring and smiled.

I had to smile back.

Now what?

She drifted over to the door and opened it. "You want to have your nails done, ma'am?"

I glanced down at my hands. My fingernails were chipped; one of them was split, almost to the quick, and starting to fall off.

"Sure," I said. "If you can fit me in now."

"You got good timing. Been quiet today with all the riots and stuff down south," she said. "Come inside."

Aquila entered the salon before me, flying right over to the far beauty station and landing on the top of the lamp.

"Sit over there," said the girl, pointing to the same place.

I eased into the chair and put my hands out for her to examine, trying not to stare at Aquila who was just a few millimetres away from my face.

What do you want? Why here and now?

The girl placed a large bowl of warm water in front of me. "Hands in," she said.

I did as she asked, and the warm water might have been soothing to me if it hadn't been for the TV screen on the wall showing images of burning cars and bodies being bagged.

"Goddam bad business that," she said, noticing the direction of my gaze. "Army shoulda stayed right out of it. Let 'em all do each other in. Then we wouldn't have to worry no more."

I breathed deeply against the naiveté of her comment. Aquila had led me here. Specifically. I had to work out why and get back to the stables in time to meet Sixkiller.

She lifted one of my hands from the water, dried it off and set to work on it.

"You got real bad cuticles," she said. "And what's with all these cuts? You been in a fight or something?"

I nodded. "Something."

She began to rub cream into my skin and the sensation lulled me. I felt my eyes closing, and I had to force them open.

"You worked here long?" I asked her.

"Since I left school," she chirped. "Family business."

A tiny surge of adrenalin trickled into my limbs. "You're Joe Rivera's daughter?"

She glanced up sharply. "Sure. Say, you look familiar. We met before?"

"Not that I can remember. But I think your dad knows a good friend of mine."

"Who'd that be?" She stopped rubbing and began filing my broken thumbnail.

"He owns a diner in the quarter. Chef Dabrowski."

She shrugged. "Don't live in my papa's pocket, you know."

"What about a psychic named Madame Corah?"

Her hand trembled and the nail file slipped, grazing my skin. I pulled my hand back instinctively, but specks of blood appeared.

"Jeez, sorry," she said. "Lemme go out back and get a dressing and a cool pack to put on that."

"It's nothing," I said. "Just start on the other hand."

She hesitated and I saw real embarrassment in her expression.

"It's OK, really," I reassured her. On the scale of injuries and hurts I'd sustained since Marshal Sixkiller had come into my life, this didn't rate. Nor did the finger pain in any way usurp the way my entire body hurt me right now.

What concerned me more was her reaction to Corah's name. I lifted my uninjured soggy hand from the bowl and thrust it at her.

Reluctantly, she took it and towelled it off. I sat quietly, letting her get back into a rhythm before I struck up the conversation again. She was well into buffing, before I judged it the right time.

"So do you know Madame Corah as well?"

She stiffened. "Don't think so," she said. "Why?"

"I was at the reopening of a diner restaurant in the quarter. My friend's place. And, well, I saw her – Corah – talking to Joe Rivera. Mean, everyone knows your dad. He's kinda famous. And I know Corah."

She went back to buffing. "Papa gets a lot of invitations to things, you know. That diner is one of his favourites though. He's been going there a long time."

"Me too. They do the best sauerkraut. And the imported vodka will knock your socks down. Your dad like the vodka?"

"Probably. Mainly though, he likes the way the owner's real good with celebrities."

"How do you mean?"

"Dad says they respect your privacy and shit. Doesn't let the paparazzi in."

Aquila, who'd been preening happily, hopped across to the girl's shoulder, and began grooming the hair above her ear.

I felt my mouth drop open in surprise and quickly stared at the floor to hide it. What had the girl just said?

Respect your privacy and shit. Dad had always said the same thing about Dabrowski's.

And there it was... the thing I'd been overlooking. The most obvious answer in the world. *The diner.* Anything precious Dad needed to keep safe would be there. It's where I'd find the recordings from Los Tribos – if there were any to find.

I pulled my other hand out of the water and flashed my One Card at her.

"Nice chatting," I said and ran.

Greta was at the counter tonging cupcakes onto a plate when I banged on the door. She unlocked and let me in.

"You know we close between lunch and dinner?"

"Where's Chef?" I asked her. Sixkiller would be waiting for me at the stables in little over half an hour.

"In his office doing accounts. I'll buzz you through," she said, sensing my urgency.

I ran to the stairs and pushed open the security gates that Chef had installed after the diner reopening.

Greta must have called him as well because he was waiting at the door to greet me.

"Virgin?"

"Chef, did Dad ever ask you to hide something for him?"

He frowned and shut the door behind me. "You look like old pastrami. What is the problem?"

"I don't have time to explain it, Chef. But I need to know if *at any stage* he left *anything* with you?"

He shook his head. "I would have told you this when your dear papa died."

I ran my fingers through my hair, trying to think. I'd been so sure… "Maybe he hid something here without you knowing?"

He made an expansive gesture with his hands. "But why…?"

"It would be small like a data stick. Please think, Chef."

The big man walked to his window and looked down. "Your papa did not speak personal business much. He did not ask me to hide things for him."

"This is really important, Chef. The most important thing that I'll ever ask from you. When he came here without me, did he come to your office much? Or did he have a regular spot?"

He swivelled, eyes alight with an idea. "Come!"

I followed him downstairs and over to the counter. "Without you, your papa would sit here. Lucky I keep these stools when we redecorate. In my country we are sentimental."

The stool he pointed to was the farthest from the beer taps, around the corner of the bar on its own.

I ran over to it. It was solid chrome except for the vinyl seat. No place to hide a data stick. "Greta, how do you clean these?"

"Just spray and wipe over," she said, leaning on the bar with curiosity. "Why?"

"Do the vinyl seats detach?"

"Sure." She straightened and came around from the other side of the counter. "They screw right off. We glued them in recently though. Stop the kids messing with them."

I began frantically rotating the seat. It spun easily at first, getting tighter as it got to the end of the thread.

"Watch out," said Chef, pushing me away.

With his huge forearms and big hands, he wrenched hard and broke the glue seal. The seat popped off its strut.

I took it from him and felt inside the tube. My fingers encountered a small rectangular contour. I tugged on it and a memory stick fell out into my hand.

Adrenalin began pumping through me. "Where can I look at this?"

"Office," said Chef, waving his hands. "Go!"

I had the stick inserted into his desk screen before he'd even reached the top of the stairs.

"Chef, I need to look at these alone," I said, as he entered.

He stopped and frowned.

"Please," I added. "*Please*."

He nodded, not happy, but willing to let me be. "You will tell me what Chef can do to help? You say this is important…"

"Many lives important, Chef."

He shrugged and stepped outside, closing the door behind him.

Taking a deep, quivering breath, I clicked open one of five video files.

TWENTY-SIX

The first three were timestamped, time-lapse videos of Los Tribos, revealing nothing but windblown sand and some wildlife passing through. In the last few frames of each, though, was a curious distortion, like a thumbprint on the lens, which seemed to materialize from the base of the tallest of the Los Tribos fingers. I couldn't decide if it was dirt on the camera or a glitch in the data file.

In the fourth, there was a timestamp, but the location changed to a ultraviolet recording of an unidentified section of the park wall. There were no coordinates or a label to identify where it was.

Almost immediately the distortion appeared on the video again – a much stronger image this time, that appeared to boil up from the sand at the base of the wall in frightening spurts of energy.

Where is this? I had to know.

I opened the fifth and final file, hands sweating. It wasn't raw footage, as I expected, but a crudely edited video that overlaid the Los Tribos footage with the Wall footage. When the mild distortion occurred on the Lost Tribos video, the same burst of emissions occurred in the ultraviolet range at the base of the Wall in the fourth video. The timestamps synced as well.

Somehow, Dad had worked out that the two locations were connected.

The distortions weren't recognizable shapes, but even with the distance imposed by the recording and the passing of time, there was no mistaking their turbulent unpredictability.

Was this the Mythos in their true form? Or could it be some kind of precursor to them appearing? An energy wave of some kind, perhaps, as the material of our world tore open?

I rewatched the final two files again and again; enhancing sections of them, straining to pick where, along the thousands of miles of park wall, the fourth video was situated. On the umpteenth time through, I isolated a section at the top of the wall and saw the faint evidence of graffiti. *Branch Holy.*

My LiFo rang and I answered it in a daze.

"Virgin, where are yer?" Sixkiller demanded.

"I think I know where they might be, Nate."

"Who? The minister?"

"The minister. Sam. Everyone who disappeared."

"Speak," he said.

"I found some time lapse footage that my dad took in the park a few years ago."

"Why didn't yer tell me?"

"I wasn't sure it existed. Today Aquila helped me work out where it might be. Dad had hidden it at the diner. And... without showing it to you, you need to know that Los Tribos and Branch Holy, and probably La Paloma, are all connected to the Mythos."

"What do you mean?"

"Honestly, I don't know how to explain it, but I've seen it. You said you don't know how they arrive in our world. Well, the tapes show it, I think."

"Do you know what you're saying?"

"Are more of your people here yet?"

"No. They arrive tomorrow."

"Tomorrow will be too late. Or maybe it's too late already. Can you come straight to the parkside section of the wall opposite Branch Holy?"

"Virgin–"

"Please, Nate! Bring Benny, and Billjee, and any Mythos weapons you've got." I touched my backpack on the seat next to me. The box was safely in there still. And the baton. "Call me when get there. Watch out for sinkholes."

"For Chrissakes, tell me what you think's going to happen!"

"I don't know. But it's happening now. The Mythos are causing trouble in Mystere as a distraction, I'm sure. With the army taking control there, all the attention will be on the south section of the city."

"How do you know?"

"You said they need conflict to thin whatever separates their world from ours. Ohitika, Aquila, Johnny's fox, and the sinkholes are all signs... please just come!"

He was silent for a few breaths. "It'll take an hour or more on horseback. Quicker by hova."

I weighed the delay against the noise of a machine. If Sixkiller rode there, he'd arrive dangerously close to dusk. Everything got harder, less certain in the dark. But then again surprise was our only real weapon. "Horseback," I said.

"Will that be soon enough?"

"I hope so."

"By the way, Pascal Cabria has vanished. And we got the

facial recognition back on the girl on the bus. She's one of the Rivera children."

"I know," I said. "About the Rivera thing at least. And Corah's the connection between Dusan and Joe Rivera."

"What connection?"

"I'll explain, I promise. But if anything... unexpected happens tonight, speak to Caro. She'll tell you."

"Vir–"

I cut him off and pressed speed dial for Caro on my cell phone.

"Ginny? I was just about to ring you. I found out who owns the private security company that was protecting the Minister and the anti-park lobbyists at your meeting."

"Who?"

"Short answer is Joachim Spears. Long answer is that he went to a lot of trouble to hide his connection to the company. It's taken me a while to track it."

"So he's the money behind the anti-park lobby?"

"I'd say almost definitely."

"Thanks Caro. You're a marvel."

"I know," she said. "Now why were you calling?"

"I've had to tell the Marshall you've been helping me. If he comes to you, tell him *everything* we know."

"Why, where are you?"

I hesitated. "You know how much I love the park, don't you?"

"Of course I do, but–"

"The park and you, Caro. Same deal."

"Ginny, what's going on?" she said sharply.

"I'm texting you some information I learned today about Joe Rivera. Add it to our flow sheet. Listen, I gotta go. Get some rest now."

"Ginny!"

I hung up and called Rav Namaditje. He answered on the fifth ring.

"Virgin?"

"Hi, Rav. Bad time?"

"Not at all. I'm just finishing a shift."

"You said the hospital wanted to use my blood to test on some inflammatory conditions?"

"Yeah. That's correct."

"Would that include a disease like multiple sclerosis?"

"I haven't seen the study profile, but I feel confident in saying that it would. In fact, I'm certain it would."

"I'm going to send you a text in a minute confirming that I agree for the hospital to use my stored blood for any research into a cure for MS. Will that be legal?"

"Do you have an authenticated signature you can attach? Like you might use on legal documents?"

"Yes."

"Then I expect so." He was silent for a moment. "What changed your mind?"

"I haven't got time to go into it right now."

"Why don't we have coffee tomorrow? You can tell me then," he said.

I smiled at the thought. But I didn't get to have a normal type of relationship. Not now. Not likely ever. "Sure. I'll call you."

"Bye, Virgin."

"G'bye, Rav."

I typed the message, attached my approved signature and sent it.

"Take the EMV lanes," I told Vic Milano as we hit the Ringway.

"You paying the fines then?"

"There'll be no fines, Vic."

"On account of you being in the s- service?" His sibilant emphasis on the last word could have been sarcasm, or reverence. From the little I knew of him, I figured it was the former.

"Somethin' like that," I said glumly.

He closed the partition and left me alone. Another thing I liked about him. He didn't need small talk.

I chewed on some biltong we picked up at the gas station, relishing the saltiness, and chased it down with an entire tube of water, followed by an extra-large takeaway coffee.

Energy slowly trickled back into my muscles. The world became a tad less grey. I fished the blister pack of glu-caffeine from my pocket. Soon as we reached Branch, I'd swallow the rest of them.

Aquila was riding on the bonnet of the car, talons hooked into the windscreen wipers, her feathers seemingly unruffled by the wind. She'd been with me again since Chef's office, appearing on the top of the computer screen as soon as I pulled the data stick out and jammed it into the coin pocket of my jeans.

Only a few weeks ago her presence had triggered intense anxiety in me. But now, as I'd become attuned to reading her posture, the tones of her screeches, and the expressions in her bright yellow eyes, it was oddly comforting.

From where I sat in the back seat, through glass and plastic, she looked alert. Expectant. It made me feel less insane for having ordered Sixkiller to the park wall. Less crazy for believing something significant was happening today.

I leaned back into my seat, thinking about the last few weeks. Sixkiller's revelations, Caro's illness, Sam's betrayal, learning that my mother was who she was, and now, Johnny murdering Jorge – the weight of it all was dangerously close to crushing me.

Kadee Matari's remark about spiritual receptivity and madness suddenly didn't seem ridiculous. Reason, belief, trust had pretty much deserted me. I only had one thing left.

The park...

"Hey, you want me to keep the meter running while you sleep?" said a voice in my dreams.

I jerked awake and saw that Vic had pulled into the bus bay outside Beauvoirs. He had the partition open and his arm hung through.

I licked my dry lips. "Thanks for waking me."

"You really know how to push limits, don't you?"

"We all do that."

"Not like you. Not that I've seen."

"I'm just stubborn," I said, thinking about Birrimun. Then added, "Really stubborn."

"So what now?"

"Now, I pay you, and you go back to your regular work for the evening."

"Last time I dropped you somewhere and you told me to do that, a little bit of hell busted through. Don't know if I trust you to be left alone." He said it lightly, jokingly, but I heard an undertone of sincerity.

"You've got better things to do than worry about me and hell, Vic," I said. "Like feeding your family."

He lifted his chin to that and turned away. "Just feeding myself these days, Virgin. Kids went back to Africa with their mum."

"Oh," I said. This wasn't the time to share private lives, so I let it drop.

"Might be that I just hang around tonight. Looks like a

good place to catch a bite to eat," he said.

I remembered Aquila's reaction when I'd been in Beauvoirs before. She'd been frantic, seemingly unable to enter.

"I'd recommend the drive-thru burgers back up University Road. This place has got tickets on itself."

"You trying to get rid of me?"

"No, Vic. Fact is, I'd be glad if you stayed around, but I'd feel a whole lot better if you went and had burgers for dinner."

He nodded. "Got it. You watch out for wild dogs then."

"You too," I said, beeping my charge code at him.

I got out, and he waved, spinning the wheels back in the direction we'd just come. His kind of offhand concern wasn't something I was used to, but I didn't hate it.

Sunset was still about half an hour away, so I decided it was best to quickly walk the perimeter of Beauvoirs again before I went in. Nothing had changed since my last visit, other than the weather. Thick clouds rolled in from the east, and the humidity was a damp hand on my skin. The wind came in gusts, bringing the scent of rain, sending the creepers quivering.

I watched the buildup for a few minutes, aware of the light slowly leaching from the sky. Summer storms saturated the air, but never really cooled anything. I wished that I was parkside of the wall, enjoying the moment, not lurking here waiting for something unknown to reveal itself.

How stupid was I going to feel when Sixkiller arrived, and nothing had happened?

With a sigh, I headed down the side of the building past the tennis courts. Just as I turned the corner to the front of the building, a car pulled into the driveway, and Professor Dusan exited the back seat. I jumped back to avoid being seen, but he hurried inside without looking around.

As soon as the car had left, I ran to the front window and looked in. I couldn't see him in either of the front bars, which meant he'd likely gone downstairs. Should I follow him? Sixkiller was still a while away, but Beauvoirs was full of customers.

Aquila fluttered to the ground beside me, her beak open ready to protest.

"I have to see what he's doing," I whispered to her.

She gave a desolate squawk. I wanted to reach out and stroke her feathers, explain that it would be fine. But to anyone watching, it would look more than a little strange.

Instead, I took the glu-caffeine blisters from my pocket and popped them in my mouth. Then I went inside before I could change my mind.

TWENTY-SEVEN

Getting to the basement bar unnoticed wasn't easy. Waiters ferried meals past with unrelenting frequency and a bouncer drifted amongst the tables casting regular glances at the staircase.

I took a table close to the cordoned-off stairs and the sign that said *Closed* and waited for an opportunity.

It finally came by way of a woman who knocked her wineglass over. The sound drew everyone's attention, including the bouncer. Immediately, I jumped over the cordon and took the stairs three at a time, relieved to let my glu-caffeined muscles off the leash.

The parlour was empty; the door to the bar shut. I pressed my ear to it and heard Dusan's voice. The scent of rum and cloves lingered heavily in the air down here, as though someone had washed the walls with it. Maybe it was designed to mask another smell?

A loud clunk was followed by silence. I waited for a while, but couldn't hear anything more. Finally, slowly, I opened the door.

Inside, the room was dark and empty and all the chairs sat stacked on tables except for one. Dusan's throne lay on its side.

I approached carefully, using the torch on my LiFo. As I got closer, I saw that beneath the base of the chair was a hole. The basement had a cellar beneath it!

I retrieved the baton from inside my backpack, held it in front of me then began to descend the narrow stairs.

It took minutes, and some steep turns to reach the bottom. Every step, I imagined coming face to face with Dusan. Eventually, though, the staircase ended in a flat, dark, narrow passage that angled downwards in a single direction. My senses told me it was heading towards the back of the building and the park wall.

I crept along, feeling my way with the outstretched baton, not daring to put the torch on again. The temperature was cooler here, the walls made of smooth slabs of rock. Who had dug out these caves? Or had they always been here?

I tried to keep track of the distance I'd come, counting my footsteps on my cell phone. After what I believed was a few hundred metres in, the passage began to widen and I heard voices again.

I edged up to the next bend and peered around. The passage ended in a small, irregular-shaped cave where a group of people lay in a circle. The area was dimly lit by pinpricks of sunlight from the roof, revealing that they were bound together in sacrificial poses. I recognised Joelle Anders on this side of the circle.

Dusan stood in the middle of the group, staring at the roof. Joelle Anders tried to sit up and speak to him. Her tone was pleading, but I couldn't make out her words. Dusan touched her and a moment later Joelle collapsed back onto the cave floor.

I found a foothold in the rock wall and used it to gain a slightly higher vantage point. From here I could see Sam lying behind Joelle, unmoving.

My heart hammered louder and harder in my ears. I eased back down, and got my LiFo out of my pocket.

"Virgin," said Sixkiller, after two rings.

"I'm in a cave underneath Beauvoirs," I said. "I've found them."

"The minister?"

"Yes. They're alive, but barely."

"Dusan?"

"He has them tied up."

"What about Cyndia?"

"No sign of her."

"Don't go near him, Virgin. Is Aquila with you?"

"No. She couldn't seem to come inside."

"We're almost here. Ohitika's frantic. You were right. I think something's about to happen."

"Wait," I said.

I climbed up and peeked around the rock edge again. The soft ceiling lights had dimmed further with the approaching sunset. Dusan held a heavy slab of oval-shaped rock in both hands, which he appeared to have lifted from a dark cavity filled with water in the middle of their circle. It looked just like the gnamma hole at the foot of the eastern butte.

The water began to boil up and hiss. Steam rose, evaporating quickly, until I could no longer see any water left in the hole at all. A noxious sulphuric smell drifted out instead, drying my mouth, making my eyes sting. My ears blocked and I felt pressure in my skull. The air crackled and sizzled as though charged.

"Virgin! Are you there? Virgin?" Sixkiller's voice seemed so thin and far away.

I started to lift the LiFo to my ear to reply, but something erupted from the waterhole, startling me, and I dropped it.

I froze as the noise echoed around the chamber.

But Dusan didn't appear to notice. He began to limp round and round the gnamma hole, chanting softly. Dark distortions began to seep up from it. As they changed shape, so his body started to bubble and shift. It sent the distortions into a writhing frenzy. They twirled up to the ceiling, fell, and rose and, among them, before my eyes, Dusan became Cyndia.

Shapeshifter!

The distortions began to spill out into the wider cave, roiling over Sam and the others. Cyndia fell to her knees, still holding the slab, her head thrown back in a kind of ecstasy, as they gradually filled the cave and started to buffet the roof, trying to burst through.

I climbed down again, and felt around for my LiFo. I had to warn Sixkiller. But just as my fingertips reached it, I heard a shout. I strained past the edge of the rock to see Sam grappling with Cyndia.

He's alive!

Cyndia swung the slab at him and missed. Tried again and connected. They both fell.

Sam! I found the LiFo and jammed it to my ear as I fumbled for the black box in my pack. "Nate!"

"Virgin! What's happening?"

"Dusan is Cyndia. I mean... she'd taken his shape. It's not him. And the Mythos are coming up through an old gnamma hole in the cave floor. I think they're going to burst through the base of the wall where you are. There're thousands of them, Nate. *Thousands!* I'm going to try and stop them."

"What? You're not making sense. How can you–"

"I took the black box from the safe house. The disruptor–"

"No, Virgin," he said. "It could kill all of you!"

Cyndia was on top of Sam now, holding him down. The distortions wrapped Sam's body up, and wound around his neck, choking him. He plucked at them, but his fingers came up empty.

"Nate, take care of Caro and Benny," I said. Then I dropped my LiFo and ran at Cyndia, knocking her off Sam.

I felt the zing of the distortions brushing my skin, their energy, and the dread, and the suffocation. My throat closed over too, but I lashed out with the baton, bludgeoning some space free around our bodies.

"Virgin!" Sam gasped.

I didn't look at him, in case I hesitated. Instead, I stood up and pressed the heat sensor on the disruptor. I felt the device warming in my hands.

Cyndia was on her feet again, so I stepped quickly across to the far edge of the gnamma hole.

"Sam," I said hoarsely. "When I'm in there, put the slab back on top!"

"Virgin, no!"

"DO IT, SAM!" I yelled.

Cyndia ripped off her skirt and I saw her brass leg clearly. The other was covered with fur. With an agility that belied her strange lower body, she sprang at me.

I braced against the impact, and stayed on my feet, clutching the box. When I was sure she had a strong grip on me, I thrust off with all the power left in my legs... and toppled us both into the hole.

OPERATION KORAX

Report submitted to Commander Orlean by Marshal Nate Sixkiller on secondment to GJIC from the US Marshal Service.

Excerpt accessed 0600, 11/12/2052.

Conclusion:

...In summary, I believe that the Mythos have been using the ancient Australian outback gnamma hole system to "break through" into our world. The actions of agent Virgin Jackson, including her investigations assisted by journalist Caroline Jorgenson, have enabled us to collect enough data to draw this conclusion.

While her use of the experimental ionic disruptor seems to have been effective in stemming the breach, no trace of Agent Jackson has been found. Minister for the Environment Joelle Anders, special agent Sam Williams and the rest of the minister's security detail were, however, recovered alive. The full list of personnel is attached. I should note that, after extensive debrief, we are confident that Professor Dusan was impelled by an Empusa to act as a gateway guardian for the Mythos. Since the breach has been sealed, the professor appears to have been entirely rehabilitated. We will, however, keep him under observation.

I formally recommend that we study the gnamma hole system to identify its connection with the sinkholes at the Paloma station house, and to prepare for the next push. History teaches us that the Mythos are nothing if not assiduous in their attempts to colonise.

Report ends>>

On a more personal note, Commander, I'd like to say that although it has been concluded that Agent Jackson was annihilated by the ionic disruptor, I hold – perhaps, stubbornly – to the hope that she is still alive. I seek permission to focus my efforts on her rescue. Special Agent Williams from the terrorism unit of the Federal Police has asked to be read in on this mission. I also have reason to believe that a private sector retrieval team is being set up independently by a former counter terrorism operative. It might be in our best interests to co-ordinate with them.

Would you like this request in writing?
Nate.

ABOUT THE AUTHOR

Marianne de Pierres is the author of the acclaimed Parrish Plessis and award-winning Sentients of Orion science fiction series. The Parrish Plessis series has been translated into eight languages and adapted into a roleplaying game. She's also the author of a bestselling teen dark fantasy series entitled *Night Creatures*, and writes award-winning crime under the pseudonym Marianne Delacourt. She lives in Brisbane, Australia.

mariannedepierres.com • *twitter.com/mdepierres*

"Time twisting action-adventure as only Wesley Chu could imagine it. I enjoyed it a lot. Read this book!"
ANN LECKIE, author of the Hugo and Nebula Award-winning *Ancillary Justice*

"Smart, fast, and fun."
BRENT WEEKS, New York Times bestselling author of the Lightbringer series

"Exciting, interesting, and never forgetting the fun of ideas, this is brilliant new stuff."
PAUL CORNELL, author of *London Falling*

"A powerful and compelling search of the past for redemption in the present, by turns thrilling and sweet and gut-wrenching."
KEVIN HEARNE, New York Times best selling author of *Iron Druid*

"A gripping, taut space opera about keeping hope in hopeless circumstances. Immensely enjoyable."
ROBERT JACKSON BENNETT, author of *City of Stairs*

"Chu has taken a simple, brilliant premise and built upon it an epic universe full of thrills and wonder."
JASON M HOUGH, New York Times bestselling author of *The Darwin Elevator*

*"More than a compelling, innovative take on the perks and pitfalls of time travel – **Time Salvager** is a sharp study of how human nature might prove mankind's salvation, or eventually doom us all. This is world-building that will make you fear for the future. In a good way."*
CHERIE PRIEST, author of *Maplecroft*

"A clever, cautionary sf tale with cool gadgets, characterization that surprised me in the best possible way, and multiple cunning twists."
KATE ELLIOTT, author of the Crown of Stars series

"With time travel, force-field kung fu, and a huge helping of wit, Wesley Chu transmogrifies a bleak long-whimper apocalypse into vicious, high-octane fun."
MAX GLADSTONE, author of the Craft Sequence

WESLEY CHU

TIME SALVAGER

"A time-twisting action adventure as only Wesley Chu could imagine it. Read this book!"
Ann Leckie, author of the Hugo and Nebula Award-winning **Ancillary Justice**

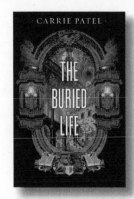

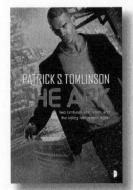
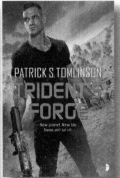
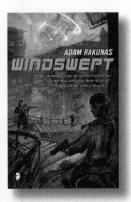

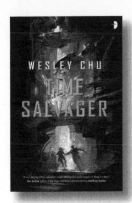
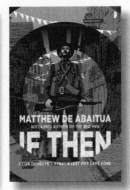

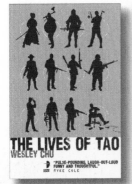

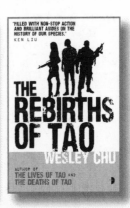

Introducing Virgin Jackson and Nate Sixkiller...

PEACEMAKER

MARIANNE DE PIERRES